Broken Promises

A Dangerous Love Affair

Kachet'

Acknowledgements

I want to thank God for giving me creativity and the opportunity to share it with the world. I'm nothing without you.

I want to thank my family and friends for their continued support through the process. I love you all!

I want to give a special thanks to Antonio(Tone) Adams for staying on my head and keeping me motivated day after day. I love you friend! I want to also give a shout out to Jamila Anderson for your expertise.

Chapter One

~

Hazel Parks

"Mommy, no. I'll do better. I pro-" My words trailed off as my head was submerged into the cold, filthy water. My stomach turned into knots as the stench from the sewage, contaminated water sunk into my pores and into my scalp.

This was my life whenever I didn't live up to her standards. Because I didn't get a perfect 4.0 because I had one A minus, she was torturing me, a feeling I knew all too well. Unfortunately.

"Hazel, you make me do this to you. Why must you keep being insubordinate?" She asked, not giving me a chance to explain because my head sunk into the water again. This time longer than the last. I could feel my life drifting from my body.

"Nooo!" I screamed as my eyes fluttered open. I felt a cool breeze up my spine as I tried to shake off the "nightmare" I just had. Except this wasn't a nightmare but a flashback. That was my reality, years ago.

"Baby, you okay?" Ethan asked me, coming into our bedroom with his jacket and shoes still on, obviously just getting in. I didn't realize I was crying until he used his fingers to gently wipe away my tears that were streaming down my face. My body cringed at his touch, he hadn't touched me in weeks. I glanced at the clock that read 4:32 a.m. and then back at him. I chose to ignore him because I didn't have shit nice to say to him. That was an argument waiting to happen.

Ethan wasn't in the streets, so him coming home in the wee hours of the morning was disrespectful as hell and unacceptable. He usually finished with his last client at or around midnight so for him to stroll in here close to five, only meant one thing, he was at one of his many hoes house giving them something that was supposed to be just for me.

I walked past him to go into the bathroom that we shared. I stepped into the shower, letting my body relax as the hot, steamy water cascaded down my body. My mind drifted from Ethan's cheating ass to Violet, my foster mom. It's crazy how she still wandered in my mind, bringing back memories I couldn't forget if someone paid me to. I needed something better for my life but with the path I was taking, I didn't see that happening. I got out of the shower with my mind in overdrive. I needed to release all the built-up anger that never goes away. Right when I think I'm in the clear of bullshit, some more shit pops up. I'm tired of it all.

I sent my best friend Syan a quick text asking if she could meet me at Planet Fitness. What better way to let off some steam than at the gym? I put on my Nike athletic gear and pulled my curly hair into a bun at the top of my head. I stepped back into my room to see that Ethan was no longer there. I sucked my teeth as I thought of what had taken place earlier. Ethan had promised me that he would do better and stop cheating only for him to do the shit in the same day. Who the fuck does shit like that? All he ever did was feed me *broken promises*.

I grabbed my purse from the nightstand before I exited the bedroom. I grabbed a bottled water from the fridge and that's when I noticed Ethan sitting at the dining room table, eating the plate I left for him. I looked at his pathetic ass once more before I grabbed my keys from the hook, where we held our keys. Syan had already texted me back saying she would be there in fifteen. I knew that she would be up because she always had a crazy work schedule with her being a nurse.

Syan and I met in high school, our sophomore year. She was an exchange student from India. When she first came to the states, she barely knew how to speak correct English but could cuss like a sailor. Hearing her soft, angelic voice that held such a strong accent use that type of language was the funniest shit ever. That was my first impression of her.

Growing up in foster care with my foster mom and dad, their three children, and five other foster kids like myself put me in difficult situations. We lived in a five-bedroom home where Violet and her husband Steve shared a room. Their twins Ashton and Ava shared a room and their oldest daughter Morgan had her own room. That left the six of us foster children to share two rooms. I was the oldest and had to share a room with Destiny and Nadia who were five and seven at the time. They both pissed the bed faithfully every night leaving me to suffer the aftermath.

One day, I fell asleep in the bed with my uniform still on. My back had been hurting severely from sleeping on the hard floor on many nights. All I wanted was a couple hours of sleep in a somewhat comfortable bed. We had a full-sized bed that constantly squeaked even after a sneeze so imagine how it sounded after a series of coughing when having an asthma attack. I hated the noise it made more than the asthma.

Violet had taken the younger kids to the park and to see a movie. See, Violet wasn't mean all the time, well at least not to the younger kids. What was supposed to be a nap that only lasted a couple hours, turned into me going to sleep until it was time to go to school. When I woke up from my slumber, my clothes reeked of piss as if a grown ass man stood over me letting out all the liquids he consumed in his lifetime.

The little clothes that I did own were still in the washing machine like they had been for five days since wash day. I knew for a fact they had to smell like mildew because I was familiar with things like this. Morgan, who oversaw laundry, never put my clothes in the dryer for whatever reason. She had it out for me since I was fostered into that home. Because I wasn't allowed to touch any appliances, I was left no choice but to go to school in the exact clothing I went to bed in. I even contemplated if I should ask if I could stay home. That wasn't even worth the ass beating I would've received had I asked that "silly question", as Violet calls it.

I tried to use my wash rag to go over my clothes as much as I could to hide the smell, hoping that they would dry on the twenty-minute walk that it took for me to get to school. I was lucky enough to have my clothes dry but no luck at all with the smell. The stench that my clothes held, made me want to crawl inside a hole and die.

Being bullied was something I didn't wish on anyone. Although, I was never physically bullied, their words hurt more than any punch could hurt, maybe even ten times worse. I knew my situation wasn't the best and I didn't need it to be broadcasted throughout my high school. I will never forget Eva Richardson. She didn't care what came of out her mouth and once she got started, it came out like word vomit. She kept coming with the jokes that lowered my self-esteem more and more.

"Damn girl, did you bathe in piss?" Eva said, causing my dark skin to turn purple. To say that I was embarrassed would be an understatement.

"No." I said shyly, while quickly grabbing my lunch tray, so I could move as far away as the crowded lunchroom would allow me.

"Don't move too fast, the whole lunchroom is going to smell like piss, you black monkey!" she yelled. It was as if on cue, the entire lunchroom housed laughter. Everyone was laughing and pointing at me. It was that moment, that made me question suicide. Humiliation was written all over my face.

"What the fuck did you just say to her?" I heard someone say, a voice that wasn't familiar. I looked up to see a beautiful girl who's race I was unsure of. Her hair was long and jet black. She had the prettiest green eyes.

"Who the fuck are you, bitch?" Eva asked, not backing down to this mysterious girl, I guess no one knew.

"The bitch who will beat your ass if you don't apologize to her right damn now." She stated, calmly. Everyone kept looking from her to Eva, anticipating what was to come next.

"That will never happen. Do you know who the fuck I am?" Eva challenged her. I guess because she was the assistant principal's daughter, that was supposed to count for something.

That wasn't the response the mystery girl was looking for. Without warning, she gave Eva a right hook that caused her to fall to the floor. The fight lasted only a few minutes, until security was able to pull her from atop of Eva. She yelled obscenities the entire time the three security guards pulled on her little but strong body.

"Thanks for taking up for me. You didn't have to." I finally said, giving a weak smile. "I'm fine, really." I added once she gave me that 'bitch please' look.

"Girl, don't worry about that. I'm Syan and you are?"

"Hazel." Just as the words left my mouth, security escorted her and a limping Eva to what I knew would be the principal's office.

A light knock on my door, caused me to snap back into reality. I didn't even know how long I had been sitting in the car that was now parked inside the Planet Fitness parking lot. I turned off my engine and exited my car.

"Hey boo. Thanks for meeting me." I said, giving my best friend a hug.

"Hey. Girl, you know I need to be in the gym every free moment I get." She said, pointing to her stomach that didn't even look bad. You couldn't tell she had just birthed an eleven-pound baby boy only three months ago.

"Whatever. You look fine to me. I know bro ain't complaining." I said sporting a smirk, referring to Hector, her husband who kissed the ground she walked on.

She waved me off, not trying to hear what I was saying. "I'm trying to get thick like you ,best friend. You are my inspiration." She said, making my dark skin blush.

My body was one that people would reference to the old Coca Cola glass bottle. I was stacked in all the right places standing at 5'5. I wore my size ten proudly and very well, might I add. My stomach stayed toned due to my many visits to the gym. I was bad as hell, I just hate it took so many years for me to really understand that.

Syan Gonzàlez

~

After working out with Hazel for two whole damn hours, my body was beat. Tired wasn't even the word. All I wanted was to soak my body into my massive tub in my master bedroom. I just hoped that Jr. was still asleep in his own room. I may be safe to get forty-five minutes to myself ,if I'm lucky. I never knew with the bipolar ass son I had. At just three months, he was already a piece of work. I shouldn't have expected anything less because of who his father was, Hector Gonzàlez. He's crazy as hell but I love him with every fiber in my body.

I met Hector when I was a senior in high school. His parents moved next door to my aunt, who I was staying with at the time. My parents along with majority of my family were still back home in India. I moved to the states with my aunt when I was fifteen years old. My parents were very strict. They followed everything in our culture to a T. I had enough of my father and his traditional tactics when he told me that he arranged for me to be married on my 18th birthday. Not only was I arranged, but he chose a man that was well over twice my age. What do I look like being eighteen and married to a forty-two-year-old grown ass man? He was out of his rabbit ass mind and I told him that exact thing right before I boarded my plane. That was the last time I seen or heard from my father. That was thirteen years ago. Here I am twenty-eight, and married with a beautiful, healthy baby boy who I wouldn't trade for anything in this fucked up world, we live in.

I washed over my body quickly for the last time, as I heard Lil Hector's small voice over the baby monitor that was installed in every room of our six-bedroom estate. I tied my robe around my small frame and went to get my baby boy. When I picked him up out of his crib, his face matched mine as we smiled at each other. The love that I had for him was one that's hard to put into words. He had me wrapped around his tiny finger and didn't even know it yet.

"You ready to eat, huh?" I asked him, kissing his fat, little cheeks that were soft as butter.

I pulled out my engorged breast, hoping that it wouldn't take long for him to latch on. To my surprise, he latched on in record time. It usually took him a minute to get it. I loved breastfeeding because not only was it better for the baby, but for my body too. My stomach had gone down tremendously before I even started the gym.

Once he was asleep, I put him in the bassinet that we kept in our bedroom. I dialed my husband, hoping that he would be done with his meeting so I could take this nap God was about to bless me with. After I got no answer after calling twice, I put my ringer on silent and let this beautiful thing called sleep consume me.

***

I had only been sleeping for an hour, but when I glanced at my phone to look at the time, I had over forty missed calls, all from my husband, no exaggeration. Just as I was about to return his call, I heard his heavy ass footsteps coming towards our bedroom.

"Bae, what's going on?" I asked him as soon as his foot neared the door entrance.

"You called me while I was still giving the meeting, I called you back and you never answered, so I figured something was wrong." He said, looking at me then our baby. That's what I loved most about him, before he does anything he made sure me and Jr. were good.

"Bae, I just wanted to hear your sexy ass voice before I napped. That's all." I said, looking into his sexy gray eyes.

I admired him and his toned body that looked so well in his tailored Brioni suit. Hector's skin was an olive complexion. His skin tone almost matched mine except my skin was a little darker. His long, silky hair was brushed to the back in a neat ponytail. His full goatee was freshly cut. The way his eyes slanted, making the wrinkles in his forehead appear, could only mean two things. He wanted to fuck or he was about to say some crazy shit.

"Syan, you already know the line of work I'm in so when I call, I expect an answer." The tone in his voice let me know just how serious he was. I didn't know if I should've been pissed or turned on. "How long little man been sleep?" He continued, softening his tone.

"A little bit over an hour." I said, trying to remember exactly how long we had been sleep.

"Alright, I'm about to set the alarm. Meet me in the guest bedroom downstairs and be naked." He said nonchalantly, sending a tingling sensation to my center that had my juices flowing ever so freely down my legs.

I sashayed down the stairs with a goofy ass grin plastered on my face, knowing how good my husband was about to make my pussy feel. In the words of Kevin Hart, "It's about to go down!" We only had about thirty minutes, depending on if our son started cock blocking or not. With the way my body was already reacting, it wouldn't be long before I got mine.

"Damn mamí, why you gotta be so fucking fine?" He asked, not really expecting an answer. He ran his thick tongue across his lips while he continued to stare at my body with hunger. Just the sexual tension, had my pussy purring.

He walked up to me as I continued into the room, we met in the middle. My lips connected with his as soon as we were in close reach. My juices were flowing non-stop as my tongue explored the inside of his mouth. I could taste the mint that lingered on his breath from the Extra Spearmint gum he loved so much. He gave my ass a firm squeeze. My mouth watered at the thought of pleasing my man in the way that he loved. I couldn't wait any longer. I dropped to my knees and my hands toyed with his belt buckle as I tried to free the monster in his pants.

Once I was face to face with the beast, I licked the tip as I used my right hand to massage his balls. When his dick grew to its full peak, I worked him into my mouth as I used both hands to twist inward on his shaft just before I took all eleven inches in my mouth, using no hands. Yes, my man was very blessed in that department and I knew exactly how to please my husband. I continued deep throatin' him until he pulled me away. I knew my man which meant I knew he didn't want to cum so early.

He grabbed my little ass up and threw me on the bed. He knew when to make love and he knew when to fuck. Right now, we both just wanted to fuck. I loved his rough side and all the kinky shit we did when we were in that mode. He used his index finger as he played in my wet, awaiting pussy. Right when I thought I had enough, he used his tongue and ran that long muthafucka from the beginning of my pussy to the end of my ass crack. He then fucked my clit with his tongue in a very fast pace that had me cumming hard as hell.

"Fuck baby! Damn!" I shouted, loud enough that our next-door neighbors could have heard me. I didn't mean for it to be so loud, but I couldn't help it. Hector was showing his ass. I grinded my pussy against his lips as he made it his mission to suck up all my sweet nectar.

"Let me hit it from the back, Mamí." He said in his deep Spanish accent. That was my personal favorite position and plus it had us both cumming fast, so that was the go to position when we were pressed for time, like on today.

I did as I was told and happily got on all fours, putting the perfect arch in my back, something I've learned to perfect over the many years I've been fucking Hector.

"Fuck." He grunted as he eased all eleven inches of thick, meaty dick inside of me. I bit my lip as he continued giving me those deep strokes I craved so much. With every stroke I matched his, throwing my ass back, making it clap in the process. We were going at it like we were in some sort of competition, trying to win that gold medal. I could feel another orgasm building up as he quickened his pace even more.

"Shit, baby. I'm about to cum." I said, barely above a whisper. My brain was too focused on the euphoric pleasure I was enduring, not on my vocals. Seconds later, we were both cumming harder than ever. My chest heaved up and down as I tried calming myself down from that intense fuck session. Not even a full minute later, our son's loud cries filled the guest room. For him to be so young, his lungs worked like a grown ass man. Y'all see what I mean now? He's making sure he doesn't have any siblings in the future. Cock blocking ass.

Chapter Two

~

Harmony Woods

"Hello, thank you for calling Robinson's Advanced Dental Clinic. This is Harmony speaking, how may I help you?" I spoke into the phone for what seemed like the millionth time today.

I didn't know what it was, but the phone had been constantly ringing nonstop, getting on my damn nerves. This was my job everyday as a receptionist, so I was used to the phone ringing off the hook. Maybe it was the fact that it was three hours past my lunch hour and we were short staffed, so no one could cover for me. Not only that, but I didn't have time to stop for breakfast on my way to work like I normally did, because my raggedy, undependable ass car decided to clunk out on me. I didn't have time to even see what the problem was this time, because I was already running late so calling an Uber was the next best option.

"Harmony go ahead and go to lunch. I'll cover your break." Mr. Robinson said, interrupting my thoughts. Mr. Robinson was the owner of the clinic and he dropped in occasionally, showing his face. He wasn't bad looking at all. He was dressed in a business suit, looking like he had just stepped off the shoot for the GQ magazine. My eyes darted to his long dreads that stopped at his waist then his freshly cut beard with specks of gray throughout all his facial hair. His deep brown eyes that seemed to be looking through my soul, sent a shiver up my spine. Something about this man wasn't right. I didn't know what it was, but I decided to shake it off.

"Okay, thank you Mr. Robinson." I said, quickly standing to my feet so I could hurry and get some food into my yearning stomach.

"Harmony, please call me Timothy." He said, his dark skin now blushing. I nodded my head and nervously smoothed out the imaginary wrinkles in my skirt, just before walking away. I knew that he would probably look at my ass, creepy muthafucka. Today I was wearing a navy blue pencil skirt with a white peplum top that sat my 34DD's up. On my feet were nude colored Jimmy Choo pointy toe pumps.

I gave myself credit when it was due and it was clear that I was a bad bitch. I was thick as hell, wearing a size twelve with a waist smaller than Nicki Minaj. I had a deep chocolate complexion with not a blemish in sight. My slanted brown eyes gave me an exotic look. With the way I took care of my body and appearance, you would think I had a man to brag about but sadly that wasn't even the case. I had been single for nearly five years. I had my days when I would be sad and lonely, but I also had days when my motto was "Fuck these niggas". I frowned up my face as I thought about these dirty dogs we call men.

My last relationship was with Kendrick and that nigga was the definition of a fuck boy. We met in Southwest Detroit. He was 'that nigga' from the number streets. He was deep in the fast life, lacing me with more money than I'd ever see coming from being a receptionist. Don't get me wrong, I was paid a decent amount with the exception that I had a degree under my belt. The only thing he did do right was throw me sexy ass Benjamins and give me dope dick. Damn, I missed what he could do for my body. I hated that nigga though. Let me fill y'all in on how Kendrick deserved his title, fuck boy.

I remember that day like it was yesterday. I had just given my speech for my Social Welfare class, which also happened to be my final. I knew I did a good job because the class erupted in applause the moment I closed my speech, which took the pressure off my back. I was another step closer to getting my bachelor's degree in social work.

At the end of class, the professor asked if I could stay after class. I was skeptical because her ass barely uttered a word to me since I'd been busting my ass in her class the entire semester. It wasn't until I couldn't read her facial expression that I felt even more wary about her asking me to stay. I reluctantly stayed, waiting for the room to clear out, so I could see what it was that she wanted from me.

"Ms. Woods, there's something I would like for you to see." She said, handing over her phone. With my brows furrowed in confusion, I took the phone and pressed play on what I assumed was a video.

My mouth hung open as I saw who was supposed to be my man. My boyfriend of two years, fucking the shit out of my professor. My blood began to boil as I continued to watch the five-minute clip of their fuck session. Not only was he giving away my dick, he was fucking her better than he'd ever fucked me. Pleasure was written on both their faces as her ancient ass rode him like a pro. I was pissed.

"You have two options. Keep fucking my man and I'll fail you or stop fucking him and I'll let you pass my class with an A, the grade you deserve. Pick wisely, but I think you should choose the latter." She said with a smirk on her face. I weighed my options as I thought about punching that smirk right off her face.

I let out a frustrated breath of air, calming myself in seconds. Something I'd learned to do, to stop myself from getting into bullshit that was always thrown my way. "He's all yours, Mrs. Jenkins." I said with a smile on my face, putting emphasis on Mrs. I wasn't giving that bitch the satisfaction of seeing me sweat. Especially not over a nigga that didn't care enough about me to not fuck my fucking professor. Like seriously, out of all the bitches in Detroit, he chose my professor. That white bitch should have been off limits, period. I hated his trifling ass for even putting me in that predicament. People better stop playing with Karma 'cause I bet he'd die with a sick dick.

The day that I walked across the stage, accepting my diploma was also the day I spent the night in jail, for beating Mrs. Jenkins' ass. She dropped the charges once I explained to her that I would inform her lovely husband of her infidelity. I couldn't believe she tried to fuck me over about my nigga when she had a whole ass husband to come home to every night. The nerve of bitches, I tell you.

"Can you add more mayo please?" I asked the guy who was making my sandwich at Subway. Nigga was being skimpy as hell on the condiments. I was going to have cotton mouth eating that dry ass sandwich he was making me.

"You can have whatever you want baby girl." He had the nerve to say, sporting a smile with his tooth missing in the front. Niggas was getting bolder by the second. I gave him a faint smile so he could give me my food and I could get the hell on quick, fast, and in a hurry.

After I ate, I felt so much better. If my stomach could, it would thank me. The hours seemed to be flowing by so fast, that it was time for me to punch that clock again, just for me to do it all over again in the morning. I grabbed all my belongings quickly because my Uber driver was already waiting.

The entire ride home, I thought about my car situation, hoping there wasn't anything major wrong with it. This Uber shit wasn't going to work for long. I had money saved, but not that damn much. My account would be completely wiped out by next month. My stress levels were through the roof. As soon as I step foot into my apartment, I was going to be in desperate need of a tall glass of wine and my best friend to vent to.

Ivory

~

"Bae, Harmony calling again." My man said, annoying the hell out of me. He wasn't what was getting on my nerves, but the fact that Harmony kept calling me was. I could bet my last dollar that she wanted to vent to me about some shit I didn't want to hear about.

"Hey boo. What's up?" I answered into the phone, rolling my eyes in the process, irritated that I was even about to entertain this conversation.

"Hey girl. What you doing?" She asked, irritating me even more.

"Girl, nothing. Just chillin' with my man." I beamed, sporting a smirk. Luckily, we weren't on a FaceTime call, because it wouldn't have gone unnoticed.

"And when will I meet this dude? I'm starting to think yo' ass is lying." She questioned.

"Soon. You'll meet him soon. How was work?" I asked, changing the subject. I wanted the conversation to be focused on her life, not mine.

"Girl, I was late as hell going to work because my dumb ass car broke down again." She practically yelled, filling me in on how fucked up her day was. She had more bad days than good and I hated hearing about that shit. Nobody's life was that damn bad. More bullshit happened to her in one week than the whole season of Love and Hip-Hop Atlanta.

"Damn, what's wrong with it now?" I let the words fly from my mouth harsher than I intended. I regretted it the moment I realized the tone that my voice held.

"Don't say it like that, shit. I don't even know 'cause I haven't had time to get it checked out. I was thinking about getting off early tomorrow, then again, I might just wait until Saturday when I'm off. I need to collect as much money as I can." Harmony was saving to open her own center to help troubled youth. Her car going out, only prolonged her of opening the center.

I sat on the phone with my best friend for a couple of hours trying to put her mind at ease of all the problems in her life. I loved my best friend without question but it's just something about her that irks all the nerves that I do have left.

I had enough problems with my Mama. That bitch was delusional. She was mad at me now because I took her side nigga off her hands. I didn't even know why she stepped out on my daddy, 'cause she knew the nigga was crazy. That's another story that I'm not even about to get into. She just better hope he never finds out about her cheating ass. If word ever gets to him, she'd be floating in the Detroit River in the blink of an eye.

"You about to go back to work?" I asked my man since he was grabbing up all his shit from off the floor. The moment he stepped foot into my bedroom we were on each other like white on rice. After the sex we just had, my head was in the clouds and I ain't even had a blunt yet.

"Naw, I'm about to go see Tatiana." He said, wiping the smile right off my face.

Tatiana was his three-week-old daughter. I was the girlfriend who couldn't stand my man's baby mama. Ashley was ghetto as fuck and just messy. He could have gotten anybody in the hood pregnant, but he had to choose that scum bucket hoe. That was a definite no no. Yes, this nigga had a baby on me and I still claimed his ass. I needed to stop though, because my ratchet ass cousin, Rayneka, told me word around the street was my nigga ain't claiming nobody. Every time he in the hood, he screams, he's single as fuck. I was gonna check his ass about it, but we've been doing good, so for now that shit was on the back burner.

"You coming back later?" I asked, in a cheerful voice. I wanted a repeat of what we did a couple of hours ago.

"Probably not. I'll hit you up tomorrow." He said, irritating the fuck out of me. This was when I started listening to the shit Rayneka told me, when he did stupid shit like this. That's fine if he didn't wanna come back over until tomorrow but damn, I had to wait until tomorrow to talk to my nigga and it was only seven. He acted like he had a curfew.

"Bye Kendrick. You know the way out." I spat as I went into the bathroom inside of my room. I made sure to slam the door once my body was completely inside. Last time I called myself having an attitude, I slammed the door right on my foot. I was so heated, I didn't even notice my foot was in the way. I slammed it so hard I broke my baby toe. I rolled my eyes as I replayed our last conversation. He better get on the bandwagon before I lose my self control and fuck his homeboy. I've been eyeing that nigga since I got with Kendrick, two years ago.

Chapter Three

~

Xå Black

"What's up little sis." I said jokingly to my big sister Brigail. Her ass was tiny as hell. She didn't even make the cut for being at least 5'0.

"Boy be quiet and figure out what you want from the menu." She fussed, rolling her eyes.

Today was Sunday which was family day. Me, my sisters, and Mom always spent Sundays together. We started that up seven years ago back when my Pops was killed. Moms usually cooked a big dinner at the house, but occasionally we went out to eat. We were at Lelli's Inn, an upscale restaurant out in Auburn Hills, MI. Leave it up to Brigail to choose some sadity ass restaurant.

"Pipe down girl. He was only joking with your stuck-up ass." My younger sister Brielle just had to add her two cents. Her ass lived for drama and was always ready to jump down somebody's throat over me.

Anytime they were both in the same room, you could expect them to be at each other's throats. Brielle lived to have a smart comment after everything Brigail said. That's just how they were and had been since they were younger.

"Y'all not about to start this shit today." My mom said giving them that look, daring them to say something back. Her voice was so soft, but her facial expression told it all. My mama, Brenda Black, didn't play that shit. Growing up, what she said was law and if you challenged it, you would pay with your ass.

My mama was my world. She was most definitely a piece of work and a force to be reckoned with. She was the prettiest woman I had ever seen, besides my sisters. She didn't look a day over thirty-five. When all of us were together, you couldn't tell who the mom was. She had the prettiest vanilla skin with not a wrinkle in sight. She had pretty brown eyes with thin lips. She kept her body in shape because her ass lived in Zumba and Yoga classes. Her body was better than half the women I've been with.

Brielle talked more shit then a little bit but when mama told her ass to shut up, that's exactly what she did. That's the only time she listened to somebody. If your name wasn't Brenda Black, you couldn't tell her shit. I kept telling her she was gone' come across the right one and meet her match. Little sis was good with her hands and people often called her Muhammed Ali's daughter but she gotta keep in mind everybody not gonna fight fair. People these days love running to guns instead of using their hands.

"Ain't nobody thinkin about her." Brielle said, mugging Brigail like she did some foul shit to her.

"So, brother, how's work been?" Brigail asked, turning the attention on me. I knew her well enough to know that she was just trying to change the subject.

"Business is good. I have two more therapists on the team and they both bring over fifty more clients a piece. Your boy doing his thang." I boasted proudly. I was that nigga fasho.

I'm Xå (pronounced Zay) Black. I'm just a nigga from Detroit that made it out of the hood. I graduated from Wayne State University with a master's degree in business and a PHD in psychology. I have my own office where I have thirty therapists, ten psychologists, and twenty psychiatrists. We dealt with adults and children with mental needs such as anxiety, bipolar, schizophrenia, autism, etc. I was making bread the legal way but eating just the same.

"That's good little brother. At least one of my siblings got them self together." Brigail said, shooting shots at Brielle. My little sis was twenty-five years old and had been in school on and off since she was seventeen, because she still hadn't chosen her career path. She had finished all her general education courses, but her problem was she was very indecisive. If she let it, that shit gonna be her downfall. You have to know what you want for your life then go for it with all you got. I probably had a lot to do with it because I spoiled her ass rotten. Everything she owns was paid with my black card. Her and Mama had me wrapped tightly around their pretty, manicured fingers.

"You always act like you're better than somebody. Excuse my language mommy but I'm not about to take this shit from her. I guess since she's the pastor's wife, her first lady title done got to her big ass head. You still that ghetto chick from Joy and Linwood. Don't let that religion shit gas up your head." Disgust could be seen on her face by the way she scrunched up her face as she spoke.

"Bri, calm that shit down man. This is not the time nor the place." I said, getting in the middle of their bullshit like I always found myself doing more times than not.

"What the hell is wrong with y'all, disrespecting me? Cussing and carrying on like I'm not sitting right here. I didn't raise you like that so don't act like I did, damn it. Got me up in here acting like this in front of all these good folks. Do you need a moment to get yourself in check Brielle Nicole Black?" Mama had a mean, stern look on her face, challenging any one of us to say anything out of line. Like I said before, she didn't play that shit.

I was listening to my mama but in the corner of my eye, I seen the silhouette of the baddest broad I'd seen in a while. The closer she got, the more I was able to make out her physical features. She was light skinned with naturally curly, long hair. You could tell that the hair on her head wasn't bought from the local beauty supply or any bundle distributor. She wasn't thick like I preferred but she had a straight body. She had to be a size seven. Her waist was almost invisible making her hips wider and ass poke out more. She had small breasts but nothing I can't work with. She was wearing the hell out of the white jeans with the rips all over that looked like they were painted on. She had on an off the shoulder white top with red pumps on her feet. I ran my tongue across my lips as I thought of different positions I could have her in.

She must have caught me undressing her with my eyes because her eyes were trained on mine. She gave me a smile and a wave letting me know she had indeed caught me. Her eyes roamed my body and I could see in her eyes that she liked what she saw. I didn't go around bragging about my looks, but I can guarantee you I wasn't lacking in that department, not even a little bit. I had smooth, caramel skin with deep brown eyes. I had a head full of waves that I kept cut low. My jet black silky hair would put you in the mind of that yellow nigga Christian Keyes that every female fantasized about. I kept a long beard that stayed trimmed perfectly.

I followed her gaze with my eyes as she stared at the tattoos that filled my arms. She could only see up to my elbow because I wore a short-sleeved Gucci t-shirt with Balmain jeans. I was dressed casual today and outside of my norm because any other time you wouldn't catch me in anything but a suit or work out gear. I spent all my time at work or in the gym that was inside of my expensive ass apartment building.

"I don't know about Brielle, but I need to excuse myself for a minute." I said, breaking the silence between the four of us. I excused myself from the table, walking in the direction of that fine ass redbone.

"What's your name pretty lady?" Her cheeks turned beet red as her face searched mine.

"Ivory." Her voice and appearance for some reason fit her name. Hmm, I like the way Ivory rolled off her tongue.

"I'm Xà." I extended my hand out to hers and when she put her hand out, I grabbed her tiny hand and brought it up to my lips. She allowed her face to form a smile as I kissed her soft skin.

"Can I have your number?" I asked, shooting my shot. I wanted it to be known that I was pursuing her in every way.

She rattled off her number to me as I keyed it into my iPhone 7. I glanced at her one more time as I walked away. Something about her told me she would be trouble but nothing I shouldn't be able to handle. One thing about me, Xả Black, I was a determined ass nigga.

"You gone mess around and catch something fooling around with these thots." My Mama shot as I sat back into my seat. Her smart remark caught me by surprise.

"Ma, you don't even know what a thot is.' Brielle said, cracking up.

"Girl, I know everything you know plus some. I watch VH1 every night for all my TV shows. Joseline say that in every damn episode." She said, shocking the hell out of me. Her ass swears she's young. You can't tell her that though because she like to get violent and shit when she's mad.

"Maybe you better stop listening to Joseline before she get you in trouble." I shot back, taking in the hard glare she was giving me. It was times like this that I cherished the most. Spending time with my three favorite ladies was just what I needed.

Brigail Jordan

~

I sat at the dinner table with the stank face the remainder of dinner. I couldn't be around Brielle for a prolonged period of time without wanting to smack her. If I wasn't the saved woman I am today, I would have been put my hands on her. Her problem was she didn't know when or how to shut up.

After my brother paid the tab, we all departed and went our separate ways. As I walked to my car, this guy called himself tryna holla' at me by continuously blowing his horn as I bypassed his car. I politely flashed him my wedding ring that probably cost more than the car he was driving and where he laid his head combined. Everybody swore I was stuck up and forgot where I came from but it's not even like that. I'm well aware of where I came from as well as where I am today in my life. I hopped into my husband's 2017 Mercedes S-Class Maybach and headed in the direction of our home. It didn't take long because I only stayed fifteen minutes from the restaurant.

"Hey honey." I called out to him, making my way to my husband to peck his lips. Before I got close enough, he waved me off basically telling me not right now. He was on the phone as usual.

Being the pastor's wife had its challenges but being married to a well-known pastor had even more. When Jordan and I first got together, he had a small church with about twenty members but only half really showed up to church every Sunday. Now that we had a mega church with well over a thousand active members, I barely saw my husband. He was always working. Working on how to reach more youth or his powerful sermon that he preached every Sunday. Sometimes I hate that he was well known because I missed my husband and most importantly my best friend.

"Hey," He called out to me, finally paying me some attention. Showing me that smile I loved so much. I missed my husband so much and it pained me to look into his eyes lovingly when I had too many skeletons in my closet. I think that's why I disliked my sister. It was like she could see right through me. Deep down inside, I knew just like she did that I'm still that ghetto bitch from the hood living in a facade. I pushed all negative thoughts to the side and kissed his luscious, pink lips passionately.

My husband was sexy in every sense of the word. Jordan Jenkins was the sexiest man in my eyes, He has a deep chocolate skin tone with slanted, brown eyes. He stands at 6'0 towering over my small 4'11 frame. He has a small build with a little muscle. Although he is a pastor, he stayed with the latest fashion and wore clothes outside of suits. Right now, he's wearing dark jeans with the rips at the knees, a short-sleeved button up shirt with the Air Jordan 13's he had pre ordered long ago.

As I stared into his eyes, my kitty thumped with need. I was long overdue to feel my husband's touch. My body yearned for it. We weren't like normal married couples who had sex multiple times a day or even once a day. I was lucky to get it once a week, if that. It's almost been three weeks since he's touched me. I gave him an intense stare, using my eyes to communicate what I needed. I wanted him in the worst way.

"Baby, let's go to the bedroom." I cooed, breaking the silence because he hadn't responded to my plea. We could've had sex right here on the kitchen floor, but he was the boring, traditional type. You know the type that only likes it in missionary. Me, I wanted to be adventurous and spontaneous. Get me right from the front, back, side and on the floor, bed, counter. I was down for whatever.

"Honey, now is not a good time. I have to be at a meeting in thirty minutes."

"Well, we can get this done within five." I pleaded, damn near begging for what was entitled to me in the first place.

"I'll take care of that when I get back." He spoke in a firm tone meaning I should just leave it alone.

He grabbed his things and left out the front door, leaving me alone with my thoughts. That wasn't the best idea for me, to have ample time to think. Thinking leads to actions and my actions lead to consequences I would much like to avoid all together. That's why I'm in this situation now!

Brielle Black

~

I rolled my eyes for the thousandth time as I listened to the many reasons Miguel thought I should be with him. Don't get me wrong, everything he said was true. He had a valid point but failed to mention what the real problem was. This fine, big, cocky nigga wasn't packing shit. His dick was smaller than my pinky finger. I really felt bad for the nigga. He had so many great qualities but that's some shit that cannot be overlooked and swept under the rug. I needed something I can feel in my stomach.

When I have a nigga, I turn into a real freak. I would refer to myself as a nympho. Every thought of mine had something to do with sex. I eat, breathe, and live sex. I learned that early on. Once I got a dose of some dick, it was over. Sex was my addiction and that's how I became a teen mom. I got pregnant with my son at the age of fifteen and my mom and dad almost killed my ass when they found that positive pregnancy test in my room. Once I started showing and my belly started protruding, Xả swore he was somebody damn daddy and tried to beat my ass.

"Miguel, just stop. You missing the point." I finally mustered, annoyed that this nigga isn't getting it.

"Well, tell me what's up baby. We can fix whatever it is." His voice was laced with so much hope. If only it was that simple.

"Unless you plan on getting your dick enlarged, it ain't shit that can be fixed." I'd snapped, letting out my true emotions. He needed to know what was up and I was tired of sugar coating shit for him. He's a grown ass man. His ass was older than me.

He looked at me intensely as a lone tear slid down his face. I know men have pride issues when it came to their manhood, but shit he gotta know he ain't got shit. He washed and looked at that motherfucka every day.

"So, that's how you really feel?" He questioned, looking off to the side, trying to avoid eye contact with me.

"Yeah and that's something I'm not willing to compromise with."

"Alright Bri, I'm glad you finally being honest. I guess that's why you always mysteriously got sleepy after you got head, leaving a nigga with blue balls." He said, making me chuckle. His balls were much bigger than his dick so him getting blue balls was probably magnified by ten.

He ran his thick tongue across his lips as he stared at me waiting for me to respond. I envisioned him using his thick, long tongue against my clit giving it a lashing. That's one thing he knew how to do right. His head game was too strong. Let me tell y'all, this one time he ate my pussy so good even after he stopped, I was still cumming. That shit lasted at least twenty minutes. I thought something was wrong with me but naw that nigga tongue was just lethal. I pushed those thoughts to the side before I do something I'll regret later. I'd happily want to sit on his face for old times' sake.

***

"Come on Jaden, let's go." I was currently at his grandmother's house to pick him up. He had spent the weekend with his dad and he had school in the morning. I was tired as hell and I hated being around this bitter bitch for more than two seconds. Respecting my elders didn't apply to her because she rubbed me completely the wrong way and I'm not the one for bullshit. I could smell it a mile away. E know I hated when he did that shit. We usually met somewhere, but apparently something came up, so he had to drop our son off with her. I refused to let him know where I laid my head so him bringing Jaden to me was out of the question.

"Ma, I'm ready." He said walking up to me. I was already ready and waiting at the door.

"Kiss your grandma goodbye." I told him, nudging him in her direction. I didn't like the bitch but that didn't mean he couldn't have a relationship with her. I wasn't that type of mother. I didn't do anything that could potentially damage him in the future.

After he did what he was told, we hopped into my freshly washed 2017 Range, heading in the direction of our home. We stayed in Rosedale Park in Detroit. It's a nice little area and I didn't want to leave the city. Xả bought me a nice four-bedroom brick home with a big yard in the back that had a mini basketball court, large pool, and trampoline. It was nice as hell inside too. My brother had it laced in all types of expensive gadgets. One thing about my brother was he wasn't gone half do nothing.

"Go ahead and get in the shower." I told my son as I kicked off the Steve Madden pumps that were on my feet. All I wanted was to take a bath and get into my bed, but a mother's work was never done. I have to tackle Jaden's head. He had thick long hair that went down his back. I faithfully re-braid his hair every week because I refuse to have him looking any kind of way. You better believe I always had my shit together, so he will too. I hate when I see a mother and her child and she fresh to death while the baby looks dirty and homeless. That shit really messed with my mental.

It didn't take too long to braid his hair. I braided small braids and put those braids into two french braids. His dad had taken him to get a line up over the weekend, so my baby was looking good. Jaden didn't have a choice but to have light skin because both his parents were bright as hell. He had thick eyebrows like his daddy and charming eyes and lashes that matched mine. He had deep dimples too on both his cheeks. My baby was very handsome and the perfect combination of me and E.

I felt my body relax as the jets in my tub let out hot water on all my pressure points. I loved my bathtub and I loved my brother even more for getting me hip to all the shit I had in my house. I let my eyes close as my body sunk further into the tub. I washed over my body a few times before I stepped out the tub. Without putting on anything, I jumped into my bed and allowed sleep to take over my body.

Chapter Four

~

Hazel Parks

My legs bounced up and down as I listened to everything the doctor told me about the condition I was in. Pissed was an understatement, I was fucking furious. I mean anybody who was just diagnosed with chlamydia would be. I sat on the bed in the doctor's office with tears in my eyes. I knew deep down that this wouldn't even be my walking papers. I'm going to stay because Ethan is who I'm accustomed to. He takes care of me financially and I know he loves me after ten years of being together.

"Hazel, you really need to take care of yourself. I've had to treat you for gonorrhea before. You passed that just to come down a similar path? Will I be treating you for aids next?" My doctor looked into my eyes with concern in her eyes. I knew where she was coming from but, she couldn't understand. No one does. Violet had it embedded in my head that nobody wouldn't want nobody who's never had shit or won't ever be shit. I stayed because I felt that's what I had to do. I might not have another chance at love.

"No ma'am, could you please just write out the prescription that I need?" I have to go to work." I pleaded with my eyes that she would leave well enough alone. Ethan had always been a touchy subject for me.

Without speaking, she got up from the stool she was sitting on and left out of the room. She came back moments later with my prescription as well as pamphlets about sexual diseases, domestic violence, and some other stuff. I get that she was concerned but this was my life and I had to figure it out for myself.

***

I paced the floor as I waited for this nigga to show his face. I already heard his car pull into the garage so he should be coming in any minute now. I don't know why I stayed as long as I have but I couldn't leave him. Like a moth to a flame, I was stuck to him. Addicted to him and all the bullshit that came with him.

"Baby, what you doing up? Another nightmare?" Ethan asked, coming into our bedroom walkin swift as hell like shit was sweet.

Now wasn't the time for him to play his role like he cared. He clearly showed that strolling in this bitch well past 5 a.m. The disrespect got worse and worse as the time went on. I was almost fed up.

"Let's start with how I got chlamydia nigga and then go into why the fuck you coming into our home at 5:38 a.m? Are you fucking stupid nigga?" I screamed at him, tired of his bullshit. I let his ass slide too many times and he continued to shit on me. When would it all stop?

"Whatever nigga you fucking gave you that shit and I pay everything in this house, so I come in when I fucking please." His words came out like venom followed by a slap to the face. He grabbed me by my neck and squoze tightly, closing my airway. "Don't ever talk to me like you don't have no fucking sense with yo ungrateful ass. If it wasn't for me being captain save a hoe, yo ass would be in somebody's homeless shelter." His voice trailed off as I felt my body going in and out of consciousness. Just as I felt I was slipping away, he removed the tight grip he had around my neck and my body slid down the wall as I gasped for air.

I don't know what happened to Ethan and how he became the disrespectful ass monster he is today but he wasn't always this way. I will never understand why he treats me like shit when I bend over backwards to make sure he's happy and satisfied. I treated him like a king and in return he treated me like the black sheep. I was treated like that enough growing up in my adolescent years. I'll be damned if I repeat that cycle and I'm grown as hell. I wiped away the tears that slid down my face, deciding that will be the last time I cry for somebody that doesn't deserve me.

***

Three weeks later

My eyes fluttered open as the sound of the alarm boomed throughout the bedroom. I wanted to call off for work so bad but I needed the money. I started off just volunteering at Safe Haven Nursing Home but over the last couple of weeks, I'd been working full time. My life needed change and that had to start with me. I was tired of needing people's help.

I slowly got out of bed moving in slow motion. I was dreading this sixteen hour shift I had signed up for. I stepped into the shower, enjoying the pressure from the water. My body was tense and my brain was stressed. What I needed was a break and vacation. I scrubbed my body a few more times before I stepped out of the shower. I quickly put on my uniform which was pink scrubs that had stars all over. I wanted to leave in enough time where I could stop and get breakfast. I haven't had the desire to cook anymore especially because I wasn't in my own place. I didn't want to feel like I was stepping on anybody's toes.

"Good morning." I said to Syan as I passed her in the kitchen. She was cooking her husband breakfast like she did everyday. I loved and admired their relationship.

"Good morning boo." She moved around the kitchen with a smile on her face. I knew the reason behind her smile because I heard it in the wee hours of the morning.

I had been staying with Syan and Hector for a few weeks trying to get myself together. I was saving to get my own place. Seeing them together was a constant slap in the face that I didn't have that in my life. I often wondered if I would ever be good enough to be someone's wife.

"I'm doing a double today so I'll see you sometime tomorrow." I gave her a hug and walked out the house to my 2017 Alfa Romeo Giulia, a birthday present from Ethan. I loved my car because too many people weren't riding around in one, especially not in Detroit. I thought about giving it back because I didn't want him holding anything over my head but that thought left my mind as quickly as it came as I thought about all the bullshit I've been through because of him. I was keeping this car plus some.

"Good morning Ms.Evans." I greeted my newest patient. She was just too sweet and a beautiful person inside and out. She had the prettiest vanilla complexion with high cheekbones. Her eyes were almond shape and light brown and she had pretty pink, plump lips. She had to only be in her forties but she had three strokes and she had diabetes. She couldn't care for herself anymore. Poor thing didn't have any children or family, considering she never had any visitors but she was in good hands because I had her.

"Good morning baby. How are you doing on this fine Wednesday?" She beamed, sporting that million dollar smile I've grown to love over the time she's been under my wing. She had such a warm and calm spirit.

"I'm doing okay. At least its hump day. How are you? Did you take your meds yet?" I asked with my brows raised, I knew how my coworkers could be.

"No, they said you would be the one to give them to me." She sighed with a slight frown. A lot of the workers here tried to avoid working as much as possible leaving it to me. I hated that shit.

"Okay, let me do a walk through and check on the other patients then I can give you your meds, then get you ready for your appointment."

By the time I checked on my other patients and got them everything they needed, it was time for Ms.Evans to get ready for her appointment. She had therapy every week on Wednesdays and I took her every time. After she was situated we got into the company's car which was a Dodge Journey and handicap accessible for the patients who were confined to a wheelchair. It was sad to see so many elders with no one to help them. I hope if I was to ever get old and needed help that I had children to take care of me because I had no family to call on. It was sad but that was life. I didn't have everything I wanted. Hell, I didn't have everything I needed, but I had to make the best of the little things I did have. I heard the saying once, when life gives you lemons, make lemonade. That was a quote I lived by daily.

After Ms.Evans was called to go upstairs to her appointment, I sat in the lobby like I did every Wednesday, lost in my thoughts. I let my mind drift to all the memories I had good and bad. I was destined to be broken from the beginning.

"Lights out everyone." Violet screamed in her bullhorn from the hallway. Like clockwork, every light in the house went out. I hated when that time came. Every night I ended it, crying myself to sleep.

I closed my eyes, praying for a better life when I heard the door creak open followed by heavy footsteps and a rough pair of hands tugging at my shirt. "Come on, you know the drill." He scoffed, pulling me up to my feet.

I walked down the long hallway that lead to the steps to the basement. Ricky, Emanuel, and Jonah were already waiting for me at the bottom of the steps like I already knew they would be. I hated my foster brothers just as much as I hated Violet and Steve. I bent down, resting my hands on the couch as they all took turns putting their nasty dicks in and out of my innocence. I wasn't granted the pleasure to willingly give my virginity to a boy of my choice. It was taken from me at the tender age of eleven by Steve. I hated him with everything in me. I prayed to God that he at least spared Nadia and Destiny, something he didn't do for me.

I hated when Violet went out for Bingo night because this is what happened every time she went twice a week. My tears didn't mean shit and my cries went on deaf ears as I cried until I couldn't cry anymore. I was hurt beyond words. I always screamed to the top of my lungs when it got to Steve's turn because he always plunged into me forcefully, causing my young vagina to bleed.

"Baby, I'm ready." Ms.Evans said, causing me to snap back to reality. Her voice was so soulful. She had the kind of tone that soothed you.

I gave her a small smile and we walked out of that establishment. I had never seen so many black certified doctors. It was a good sight to see and to know that a black man owned it made it that much better. "You're such a sweet person Ms.Evans. I love your personality. I feel like I've known you my whole life."

"Child, I feel the same way about you." She replied, smiling ear to ear. I meant everything I said and I wanted to let her know if no one else cared about her, I did. I knew first hand about feeling alone in this cold world. I hated feeling that way and I wouldn't wish that on anybody.

Syan Gonzàlez

~

"Enjoy the rest of your night Mrs. Gonzàlez." My assistant Kelly said as I was preparing to leave. She seemed over the top sweet at times and I never trusted bitches like that. You could never be too sure.

"Thank you. You do the same." I told her as I looked over my shoulder, getting onto the elevator. I was tired as hell after doing that twelve hour shift. I was already sleepy when I came in after staying up with Jr. all night. He was sick and running a fever so he was very fussy. I hated when he was sick because his little ass was mean as fuck. I was going to call off work but after I thought about his cranky ass attitude, I left his ass with his daddy. He can deal with that whining ass little boy.

I sped all the way home, taking advantage of the speed I had with my 2017 SRT Hellcat Challenger. When it came to cars and driving, I was like a man. I was in love with cars and especially sports cars. I had a need for speed. Hector hated when I drove this car because I was a dare devil on the road. He was gonna worry his ass to death but he had nothing to worry about. I was a great driver and knew how to drive for myself, as well as the crazy ass non-driving muthafuckas on the road.

I walked into the house, setting the alarm. We lived in a private gated community in a six bedroom mini mansion with four and a half bathrooms. Our house was nice as hell and if we were celebrities. Cribs, the TV show, would love to showcase our beautiful home. My husband worked his ass off to get everything we had the pleasure of owning. He sold guns to all the big time kingpins across the world. Yes, my baby was worldwide in the game, not just national. I worked because I wanted to, not because I had to. I was never the one to just sit on my ass all damn day. That wasn't me, not in the least bit.

I did a walk through throughout the house like I did every time I came home from work. I checked Lil Hector's room first as always to see that he wasn't in his crib. When I got to the master bedroom, there were my two favorite guys sleeping peacefully in the middle of our king size bed. I gave them both multiple kisses all over their faces. They were in such a deep sleep, they didn't even stir when I rained kisses on them. I stripped out of my work scrubs and headed straight for the shower. I was washing myself for the second time when the glass door to the shower slid open, revealing my sexy ass husband. Seeing Hector standing before me with nothing on had my pussy throbbing and juices flowing.

"Hey daddy." I cooed, grabbing his hand to lead him closer to me. He grabbed my ass, giving me a long passionate kiss, making my knees feel weak. I opened up my mouth a little, just enough for him to slip his tongue into my mouth. I could taste the weed that lingered on his breath.

His hands roamed my body and I could feel the heat radiating from my center. He slipped his hand between my legs and his fingers toyed with my clit. I let out a small moan as I enjoyed the pleasure he was giving me using his fingers. I loved the way my husband could make my body feel. Only he could pull that shit off.

"Lift up baby." He said, tilting his head to the bar we had installed in our shower for times like this.

I lifted my small body up with no problem putting my pussy in his face. The moment his tongue connected with my pussy, butterflies filled my stomach. He licked my lips and french kissed both sides before he parted them with his hand, giving himself room to latch onto my clit with his mouth. He rotated his tongue in circles then bit it lightly.

"Fuck, baby! Damn...I'm about to cum!" I shouted, feeling my nut build up. I felt my hands slipping from the rod. The pleasure I was feeling was too much, I was about to fall. Right when I felt my body about to slip, he used both hands to hold me up by my ass and he spread them apart. He ran his thick tongue from the beginning of my pussy up to my ass crack. That gesture always sent a chill up my spine. He munched on my clit some more doing tricks with his tongue I couldn't even begin to explain.

"Shit. I'm cumming." I moaned in a low tone, as my sweet nectar dripped into his mouth. He slurped up all my juices before letting me down. I leaned against the door because my legs felt like noodles, there was no way in hell I could stand on my own. I kissed his soft lips, inserting my tongue tasting my own juices that tasted like the pineapple smoothie I made sure I drunk everyday.

"You ready for this dick?" His deep tone whispered against my ear.

I nodded my head and I guided him to the bench we had inside of our shower. He sat down and I happily glided down his big, juicy meat. I bounced up and down in a steady but fast pace as he sucked on my nipples. I was about to be on my second nut and I needed this to be my last. I was already ready to tap out.

"Bend over." He ordered, tapping me on my thigh. I bent over touching my toes, waiting to feel him inside of me again. He plunged his thick dick into my sopping wet pussy causing me to let out a high pitched whimper. He fucked me nice and slow giving me deep, long strokes. As my pussy got wetter and wetter, he sped up his pace and I tightened up my pussy muscles every time he was pulling out, putting a tight hold on his dick.

"Damn girl. Fuuck." He groaned, moving in and out even faster now.

"Daddy, I'm cumming again." I whimpered, feeling a jubilant warmth throughout my entire body. I was in awe.

"FUCCCCK." He groaned yet again. This time, shooting all of his soldiers inside of me.

I sat down on the bench unable to stand as he washed over my body being super gentle when he washed my sensitive pulsating vagina. After he washed my body completely, he did the same for himself then he carried me to our bed that Jr. wasn't in anymore. I checked the baby monitor and saw that he was sound asleep in his crib.

The moment my body hit those egyptian cotton sheets, my body immediately relaxed. My husband kissed my forehead, cheek, and then my lips before he pulled the covers over my body. He got in the bed and I snuggled close to him, laying my head on his chiseled chest. I felt my heartbeat slowing down so I closed my eyes, letting sleep consume me.

I woke up from my peaceful sleep to a million international missed calls. It had to be someone I knew from back home. I had the same number for as long as I could remember so it could be anyone. I let out a frustrated breath of air as I dialed the number back, wondering who it could be and the reason for their call.

"Hello." I spoke into the phone when the phone stopped ringing. I could hear whoever held the phone breathing but not saying a word.

"Surabhi." My dad called me by my Hindu name which meant beauty. It was crazy hearing his voice for the first time in thirteen years. His accent sounding even stronger now.

"Yes, daddy? To what do I owe the pleasure of this call? It's been a while." I uttered in a very sarcastic tone.

"Your mother is sick. I'm afraid she's in her last days." He announced, his voice cracking. The last time I spoke to my mom was five years ago when I told her I was getting married. She called periodically up until that point, but when I broke that news to her, the calls stopped completely. I didn't know how to feel as I listened to my dad tell me how she was diagnosed with ovarian cancer two years ago and she's in stage four now. The cancer had spread all over her body and chemotherapy had stopped working months ago.

"So why wait now to tell me? That's my mother! I had the right to know sooner!" I screamed, I could feel my heartbeat accelerating as I listened to the bullshit that came out of his mouth. Quite frankly, I wanted to slap the dog shit outta him. He was so lucky he wasn't in my face.

I didn't realize I was crying until my husband wiped the tears from my face. I couldn't describe the emotions that were going through my body. I didn't have to talk to her everyday to love her. She was my mother, hell she was the reason I was brought into this world. I hated it came to this for me to hear my dad's voice again.

"I'll be there in a couple days." I roared into the phone right before I hung up on his selfish ass.

"Baby, I already booked the fight. We leave in the morning." Hector said, making me smile. I loved how attentive he was. I knew if I didn't have nobody in this world, I had my husband.

***

My heart raced as we drove to the hospital. My hometown looked so different from what I remembered. It could have been the new businesses that were on every corner or the newly built mansions spread throughout the city. I came from money. My family supplied oil all across the world, raking in billions.

Once we got our visitor's pass we took the elevator to the third floor. The door to her room was slightly ajar. I knocked lightly before pushing the door completely open. My dad sat at her side, holding her frail hand. My father looked much older than the last time I saw his face but he still looked the same nonetheless. He had a head full of gray hair. He had a few wrinkles in his forehead. He still had those piercing green eyes that matched mine. I took in all his features before my eyes landed on my mommy.

She looked like she was in a peaceful sleep. Her body was tiny and frail. She wore a bald head, most likely from the chemo. One look at her and you could tell she was sick and on her last leg. My heart broke as I really took in her features comparing how she looked now from the last time I saw her beautiful face.

"Hey mommy, it's your baby girl Surahbi." My voice cracked as I took her hand in mine. Her eyes fluttered open at the sound of my voice.

"She doesn't talk anymore, but she listens. She can understand everything you say." My dad finally spoke. The tears flowed as the words came out his mouth. My mom just laid there disintegrating before my eyes. I excused myself from the room to recuperate. I felt so many emotions at once.

When I walked back into the room, my dad and Hector looked like they were in a heated conversation. Jr. was in my husband's arms, peeking around the room. He was so alert to be that young. I glanced at my mom and she was staring into space. I wish I knew what she was thinking. Really, I just wanted to hear her voice again. I didn't realize how much I missed my family until now, my dad included. Life is so precious and it can be snatched away from you in an instant.

My husband and son spent a couple hours with me at the hospital before they went back to the house we were staying at for the time being. I stayed at the hospital overnight filling my mommy in on everything she missed out on in my life. As I talked to her, I saw her shed a few tears. It broke my heart to see my mom in this light. After talking to her for hours, I felt my eyes getting heavy. I had a long day and was tired as hell. I shifted myself in a somewhat comfortable position as I sat back in the recliner chair in her room. Sleep came almost immediately.

"What's going on?" I cried, asking the doctors for answers. I woke up to all the machines going off. It had more sounds going off than win you win free spins at the Casinos slot machines.

"Ma'am calm down. We're trying t-." His words were cut off because the defibrillator went off, showing that my mom's heart rate was non existent. She was gone.

I managed to look in her direction and she looked like she was in a deep sleep. I felt helpless and hopeless as I stared at my mom's lifeless body. I at least wanted to spend a few days with her. I never expected this. I walked into the hallway, unable to take in the sight before me any longer. My dad rushed past me with tears trickling down his face to go into my mom's room. The wail that he let out made my knees give out as I fell to the ground sobbing for the years I've gone without seeing or talking to my mommy. I never would have expected my experience coming back home would be this way. If someone would have told me a few weeks ago this would be my life, I would have shot their ass.

Chapter Five

~

Harmony Woods

"Girl, why you got your face balled up like that?" Ivory asked, causing me to soften up. I'd been walking around with the stank face for the past few weeks now for whatever reason. Honestly, I think I just need some dick.

"Girl, it's nothing. Just life." I partially lied. She had practically dragged me out the house to get a tattoo with her by some nigga who was supposed to be the best in the city. "Do you know what you're getting yet?" I quizzed, changing the subject.

"Yeah, look," She handed me her phone, showing me these roses that had hella color. It was dope as hell, just not for me. I doubt any color would show anyway on my dark mocha skin.

"That's nice." I complimented, still browsing the photo book with some of his work, along with a few sketches here and there, I guess he had drawn. They were all nice as hell.

"Ivory, he's ready for you now." Who I assumed was the receptionist, gestured for her to go to the back. She had a pretty caramel complexion, nice size, and she wore a Fantasia cut that brought out her pretty features. I could tell she loved art by the way she was tatted up. She had a sleeve on both arms and some tats on her neck. And those were the ones visible to me, who knows what else she had under her work attire.

She wasn't back there too long, maybe a half hour. She walked back, smiling ear to ear with a devious grin on her face. I didn't know what she was up to but her sneaky ass had something up her sleeve.

"He's ready for you." She wore a sly grin as she spoke.

I walked to the back, palms sweating because it had dawned on me that I was really getting a tattoo. This was my first one and I was beyond nervous. I chose to get a woman with a crown. Not just any woman but she was a black queen, a goddess, with the big hair and all. I envisioned it like she was walking and right under her feet, I wanted it to say 2 Corinthians 5:7. That was the scripture that said, walk by faith not by sight. I always knew if I ever was to get ink permanently on my body, it would have to mean something to me and that meant everything.

"Hi." I said shyly standing before the sexiest light skin nigga I had ever seen. He had smooth vanilla skin with a head full of curly hair that was braided into two braids, stopping in the middle of his back. His hair was freshly lined up and his braids were neatly done.

"Wassup beautiful." He flashed me a smile revealing his perfect pearly white teeth.

I flashed him a smile described to him how I wanted it and where I wanted it. While I was talking, he looked like he was focused, envisioning what I was explaining to him. He grabbed his sketchbook and drew up my tattoo not missing a beat in less than ten minutes. Damn, he was good as hell. What he drew was beyond my expectations and looked better than I had imagined.

After he got the drawing copied to my skin, he opened up a pack of new needles then cut the tattoo machine on and that sound alone had my heart beating faster and my palms start to sweat again.

"It's Harmony, right?" He quizzed, wearing a smirk.

"How do you know?" Brows raised as I looked back and forth between him and the needle going into my thigh.

"The girl that just left my chair. I think her name was Icing," He paused, looking at my thigh then back to me. "Or something like that."

"Ivory." I chuckled lightly, not wanting to move. I didn't want anything to go left so I stayed still as possible. That's why she was grinning, trying to play matchmaker and shit. Sneaky ass.

"Close enough." He was so focused at the job at hand, he didn't notice me stealing glances here and there. He was simply dressed in navy blue sweats and a white t shirt with some white Huaraches on his feet but he was sexy as hell.

We made small talk as he finished up with my tattoo. The pain wasn't that bad but I damn sure wasn't in a rush to go to anyone's tattoo shop anytime soon.

I admired my new tattoo in the full length mirror, it was dope as hell. "Thank you..." I paused realizing I didn't even know his name. "You know my name but I have yet to know yours." I continued with a small pout on my lips.

"It's Ethan." He replied, sporting that million dollar smile that could get any bitch panties wet, mines included.

When I walked back out to the lobby, Ivory was seated on the bench with a smirk on her face as I walked towards her.

"Bitch, you ain't shit." I joked as we walked out of the tattoo shop.

"Girl whatever, we both know you need some dick in your life and he seems like the perfect candidate." She giggled, making me laugh along with her. Lord knew she was right. It was no longer a want but a definite need.

"Excuse me, ma." Someone said, trying to get one of our attention as we walked to Ivory's car. We both turned around and Ethan jogged our way to catch up to us.

"Wassup Ethan." I said, knowing he was talking to me.

"I got everything except your number, ma."

"Well, that's because you didn't ask." He licked his perfect, pink lips that I imagined licking my soul out. "A closed mouth don't get fed." I cooed.

I read off my number as he keyed it into his iPhone before he pocketed it and jogged back to his shop. I put an extra pep in my step as I continued to Ivory's Range Rover. I was feeling myself, knowing that I could pull niggas even on a chill day.

After we left the tattoo shop, Ivory dropped me off at home. Today which is Saturday, I volunteered at Vista Maria, an agency that helped children and young women to better themselves. I did the girl's' hair to help boost their confidence and self-esteem. I loved helping the girls and giving them something to look forward to. They were a piece of work, don't get me wrong but just knowing I'm empowering young women and doing a good deed, melts my heart. I didn't have anyone to look out for me while I was growing up.

"Wassup Mayweather." I joked with Merci, one of the young girls I worked with at Vista Maria. She was seventeen years old and could fight like no other. She did what she had to do. Because of her size, other girls liked to try her.

"Hey sister." She giggled, rolling her eyes playfully. I loved her like she was my sister and I tried my best to lead by example.

"I missed you the last time I came. You lost your privileges again, huh?" I asked, searching her eyes for any nonsense. I was investing time, energy, and sleep in her. I couldn't count how many times I stayed up until five in the morning knowing I had to start getting ready for work at six, researching different organizations and centers that would benefit her greatly. She would be released soon and I didn't want her to get out with the same mindset she had when she came into the agency.

"Harmony, you don't understand how these girls pick on me for obvious reasons. I can't and won't allow someone to cause harm to me. I've been mistreated my whole life, I can't keep getting stepped on. I swear I try to stay to myself and diffuse the situation but that never works. You know just like I know how these girls can get." I felt my eyes tearing up as I listened to Merci. I was her before. I was picked on almost my whole life and I knew what it felt like to get fed up and sick of being sick and tired.

"I understand more than you know." I simply replied, taking her hair out of the bun it was in. Her soft, smooth hair combed straight through as I parted and braided her long tresses.

Merci was the prettiest girl to me. Her skin was the color of white chocolate but tanned in a way. She had gray eyes that changed colors often. Her slim frame and short stature, standing at 4'9 is what made girls come for her. Her sweet spirit matched her physical appearance. She was truly beautiful inside and out.

"Thanks sis, I love it." She had the big kool-aid smile as she admired her hair in the mirror. I had braided her hair to the side in small cornrows. I even swooped her baby hairs in the front. She no longer looked like a tomboy but a beautiful princess.

"You're getting out soon. How you feel" I asked, waiting to hear how she genuinely felt about it. She had this look on her face as if she was in deep thought. I stole glances at her as she thought of the right thing to say, while I gathered the things I needed for the next girl's hair.

"I'm happy that I've done my time and I'm able to get out now, but I'm sad because I'm getting out but there's no one on the other side looking forward to that. I don't have family to go *home* to. It's just me." Her voice cracked at the end and tears flowed freely down her face. I couldn't hold it in anymore. I gave her a tight hug and we cried together. I couldn't understand how people gave their precious creations to the system. No one wanted to be brought into this world just to end up as another statistic.

"You have me, Merci. I'm looking forward to spending time with you. If no one else loves you, just know that I do." I meant every word as I said it aloud, staring into her eyes for reassurance.

It wasn't easy feeling unloved as a child. I grew up in a house with my family that I didn't, and still don't feel like they loved me. That was even worse in my opinion. Everyone needed love. Without it, you wouldn't feel whole, complete. Everyone in my household had fair skin so I had no choice but to believe my dark skin was why they treated me that way. They say all black is beautiful, but is it really? We lived in a world where people believe the lighter the skin, the better. When I was a child, every year on my birthday, my wish was that I could be lighter and look like the rest of my family. I felt and looked like an outsider. I didn't realize my black was beautiful until I got older and wiser.

"I love you too." She wiped her eyes and went to get the other girls.

I finished the girls hair a little after five and I planned on lounging at the house, relaxing and sipping on something light. When I got home, I whipped up some jambalaya, turned my TV to 'Lifetime Movie Network' with my wine bottle in hand. I was halfway through with the first movie when my phone dinged with a text.

313-555-0000: Hey beautiful

Me: Hi, who's this?

I chose to act like I had no clue who was texting me although I had an idea. Feeling a little too bubbly, I sat my wine bottle down on the coffee table, not wanting to take it too far. I was buzzing so I left it at that.

313-555-0000: It's Ethan but I gotta feeling you already knew that.

Me: Lol, I wasn't 100% sure so I had to ask. Is that a problem?

I made sure to attach the thinking emoji to the text. I swear they had an emoji for every emotion. I was one of those people who had to use at least one in every text. I didn't feel like my message was complete without it.

Ethan: You busy? Can I call?

Butterflies filled my stomach as I re-read the message over and over and thought of how I should respond. As I typed a response, my phone started ringing mid text. It was him.

"Hello." I spoke in a low voice into the phone. I was nervous and rusty as hell with this dating shit.

"Wassup ma. What you doing?"

"Watching a movie. Being a homebody as usual." I sighed, realizing I was lame as hell and needed to get out more to enjoy life.

"Would you rather be eating at a good restaurant with me, blessing me with your presence?" His deep, sexy voice had my panties wet the moment I heard his voice on the other side of the line. My mind drifted back to his manly, fresh scent that he had on earlier today. I loved a man that smelled good.

"As lovely as that sounds, I'm going to have to decline, because I just ate." I said, putting emphasis on just.

"Well it's other things we can do. I just want to be in your presence. Is that okay with you?"

I chuckled lightly, "Sure. What about the movies?" I suggested, I can't remember the last time I saw a movie at the theatre.

"Text me your address and I'll be there at ten if that's not too late. You don't have a curfew do you?" He joked, prompting me to laugh. He was fine, persistent and funny. That was fine by me.

"I see you go jokes but ten is fine. See you then." I let the line go dead and ran into my closet, in search of something to wear. I liked to take my time getting ready and that was for any occasion. You couldn't rush perfection.

Ethan

~

I finished with my last client around eight, so that gave me time to run to my crib to take a quick shower and change. When I got home, Hazel's scent still roamed throughout the house. I missed her but I wasn't checking for that bitch right now. I was on to the next and Harmony might just be the broad to get that spot.

After I got out the shower, I threw on my outfit which was some light wash, distressed jeans, a Gucci button up with the matching belt and loafers. My hair was freshly braided thanks to this thick ass Jamaican hoe I fuck around with from time to time. I made sure I had my bread with me then grabbed my keys and phone and headed to my baby, my brand new black on black Corvette.

I made good chicken at the tattoo shop that I owned, Legit Ink. Not only was I living off that, but I still had money left over from the trust that my grandparents set up for me. That's how I was able to open up my shop with not one problem.

"I'm outside." I spoke into the phone after Harmony picked up on the third ring.

"Okay, I'll be out in a minute." Her sweet voice filled my ears making me smile. Yeah, she might be that one. Not the one to marry or no shit like that, but the one Ima kick it with regularly until I get bored and find something better.

She came out the house looking good enough to eat. She had on a royal blue bodysuit that clung to her body like a latex glove, that showed every curve she had which was damn near too many to count. I jumped out the whip and jogged around to the passenger side so I could open the door for her. I can be a gentleman, knowing I'm going to get what I want at the end. She didn't seem like the type to let me sample the pussy on the first date but I'll bet my last dollar it won't take more than three dates for me to get in them guts.

"Thank you." She smiled, showing her perfect set of teeth. Shorty was a solid ten fasho.

"No problem." I winked, before jogging back to the driver side.

We made small talk on the way to our destination. The music playing in the background filled in where we didn't. Since we weren't too far from the east, I headed to the AMC Theatre in Madison Heights. That's really the only theatre I frequented. It was nice as hell and those comfortable ass reclining seats were a bonus. Had a nigga damn near falling asleep on the movie every time.

We decided to see The Purge: Election Year because that's what she wanted to see. We got some expensive ass snacks from the concession stand, slightly changing my mood. Every time I bought snacks from the movies, I always thought how that shit was highway robbery. Everything they had was taxed like a muthafucka.

After we left the movies, we stopped at Friday's to grab a little appetizer and some drinks. I wanted to see how she was with a little liquor in her system. Most importantly, was she willing to bust it open for a real nigga.

"How old are you?' She asked, her beautiful brown eyes sparkling as they looked into mine.

"I'm twenty-eight, ma. I'll be twenty nine in a few months. Do you go to school or work?"

She took a sip from her drink before responding. "I am in school for my masters but I have my bachelors in social work and I work as a receptionist." She replied in one breath.

Shorty took me by surprise saying she was in school, had a degree, and a job. She seemed like the type to sit on her ass all day or pimped niggas for a living. I wasn't used to a girl of her caliber. I was diggin' her for sure but if she was looking for marriage, kids, and the big, white picket fence, I wasn't that nigga. Why you think I stayed with Hazel for over ten years and still hadn't popped that question? Maybe a little later down the line but right now, I was chilling.

***

"What's up son? " I said, dapping my little nigga up. It was my weekend to get Jaden and since Hazel wasn't at the crib right now, I was going to take him to that house and not the one we usually stayed at in Dearborn Heights.

Keeping Jaden from Hazel wasn't too hard because I stayed out however long I wanted to anyway. I got his mama pregnant a couple months after me and Hazel made it official over a decade ago. Hazel was something, she wasn't naive because she was hip to the shit I did to her, but she acted like it was okay. She was weak and I helped with making her that way. I knew she was always gonna come back running to me. She belongs to me and only me. She wasn't going no damn where.

"Hey dad." My son said cheesing hard as hell with his deep ass dimples he inherited from his mama, poking out. My little nigga was my pride and joy and I was proud to be his daddy.

"Wassup baby mama." I smirked, looking Bri in her eyes. She was sexy as hell wearing those tight ass jeans with rips in them with a crop top showing her toned abs. She had on some sandals, showing her pretty ass feet.

"Nigga, bye." She said flicking me off. She usually left my mama crib before I got there to pick up my son, but I pulled up when they were walking to the porch.

I was glad to see Brielle. She was looking good and doing good by the looks of the new whip she was driving.

"What's with the hostility?" I retorted, stepping into my Escalade without waiting for her answer.

I drove to the house with my mind on Hazel and Harmony. They were alike in so many ways. I had to pursue Harmony but also keep Hazel close because I didn't need her getting comfortable without me.

"Dad, where we going?" My son asked, recognizing we weren't going in the direction of my house.

"Remember I told you my secret about having two houses," He nodded his head, yes, so I continued. "We're going to stay at that house." Confusion was written on his face as he nodded and said, "Okay."

We pulled up to the crib about fifteen minutes later. My son immediately gravitated to the eighty inch flat screen that was mounted on the wall, and connected to the Xbox One. We played the game until it was time to call it a night.

Brielle Black

~

After I dropped Jaden off with his trifling ass daddy, I headed to the mall for a little retail therapy. Ethan and I were never a couple but while we were dealing with each other, we made a baby in the process. During my pregnancy with Jaden, I found out about Ethan's girl Hazel and so many other chicks he fucked around with. I never met the chick or even saw her for that matter but from what the streets say, they have history together. I just found it strange how nobody had ever seen the mystery bitch.

I checked my account on my Huntington app, nodding in approval of the hefty amount my brother had transferred to my account. I loved my brother for always looking out for me but I also knew he wouldn't be able to support me and my son forever. I wanted my mom to talk proudly of me just like she did Xà and Brigail.

I stopped into Forever 21 first, finding a couple of cute outfits for me. After I shopped around in a few more stores for myself, I stopped into Foot Locker to grab a few pairs of matching gym shoes for me and my son. I also stopped at Macy's and Nordstrom to grab some outfits for him as well. I spent a couple of hours in the mall before loading my car up with all the shopping bags I accumulated from today.

I found myself pulling into Ruth's Chris treating myself to lunch. I was hungry as hell and I knew steak and shrimp would easily solve that for me.

"Table for one?" The hostess asked, sporting a friendly smile.

"Yes please." I said, matching her smile.

"Would you like a booth?" I trailed behind her as she continued further into the restaurant.

"You know what, umm..."

"It's Mercedes." She giggled, looking over her shoulder. "I'm sorry, I forgot to introduce myself. Today's my first day."

"You're fine. Mercedes, I'll just take a seat at the bar if that's okay."

"Of course." She led me to the bar that was semi-packed. I observed my surroundings, glancing at the patrons that were in my view.

I glanced at the menu to see if anything new was added, even though I was already sure of what I wanted. The only thing that was different was the new margaritas and a few other alcoholic beverages that I would be sure to try out.

"Are you ready to order?" The waiter at the bar asked. I could tell by his personality and cheerful voice he was cool as hell and knew how to party. I bet he knew every gay, hype club there was in the whole state of Michigan.

"I most certainly am." I smiled, trying my best to match his award-winning tone. I continued with my order and gave him the menu before he walked away.

"Do you mind if I sit here?" I heard some guy asking me.

Without even looking up from my phone, I replied "This is a free country, sit wherever you please."

"This country is far from being free, but I'll take that as you don't mind." He said, making me chuckle lightly.

I felt his presence as he slid unto the bar stool next to me and his manly cologne invaded my nostrils. His scent so intoxicating. I looked up from my phone, checking my surroundings again and to match the face to that godly scent. I looked to my right to see the sexiest chocolate man I'd ever seen in my entire twenty-five years of living. Damn, he was beyond fine as hell. His hair was neatly lined up and the waves in his head damn near made a bitch seasick. I could see his muscular build through the polo shirt he was wearing.

I quickly looked away when he caught me undressing him with my eyes. He was eye candy for sure and I couldn't say that I didn't like what I saw.

"You can look as long as you want. I don't mind." He smirked. Damn, his fine ass had caught me. I was glad he couldn't read minds too, because I would be in trouble with all the nasty thoughts I had circling through my nervous system.

"I'm sure you don't." I joked. It was no need in lying, I was already caught.

"Christian." His deep, raspy voice sent a chill through my body as he gave me a firm handshake.

"Brielle." I said, smiling way too damn hard. I could feel my cheeks getting hot and I knew my high yellow ass was beet red.

When the server brought my food over to me, I dug in with no hesitation as if Christian wasn't even sitting there. I wasn't that girl who was afraid to eat in front of guys. I was in love with food too much. The garlicky shrimp was in sync with my taste buds as I devoured the shrimp scampi.

"I love a woman that can eat," He stated calmly. "Can I take you out to eat sometime?" His smile so contagious.

"Of course. As you can see, I love to eat." I smiled. Is it possible to be in love already? I never was the one to believe in love at first sight, but damn, can you blame me? It was either that or my infatuation with him was extreme.

"Can I have the bill please?" I asked, catching Brandon before he disappeared again.

"Brandon, add whatever she had to my bill." Christian interjected.

"Okay, not a problem." Brandon stated before turning towards me giving me a knowing look followed by a wink. He was a mess, but I loved it.

"Thank you, but you didn't have to."

"I know but I wanted to. Here, put your number in my phone." He said, handing me his Galaxy S8 Edge. As much as I hated Androids, this was halfway decent and that was a huge compliment coming from me; a die hard Apple lover. I dialed my number from his phone so I could store his number as well.

"It was a pleasure meeting you, Brielle." He took my hand in his, planting a delicate kiss. I don't know how but he already had some brownie points and we hadn't been on one date.

Chapter Six

~

Hazel Parks

"Hey boo, how you feeling today?" I asked Syan, shifting the phone between my ear and shoulder as I got into my car, leaving from work.

"I'm feeling blah, but I get better each day. Between you and Hector's ass, I'll be back as normal as I can be in no time." She joked, making us both laugh. It was good to hear my best friend laughing. Ever since her mom passed, she wasn't the same and that's totally understandable.

"What's my baby doing?" I asked, referring to Jr., my handsome god baby.

"Girrrrl, you can come get your baby. He's on his play mat trying to scoot around. I swear his ass been here on this earth before." She laughed. I knew bringing him up would put a smile on her face. He was her greatest accomplishment and if I ever got the chance to be a mother, I hoped to be a fraction of how she was as a mother.

"He can come over as much as you want when I get my place." I smiled, pulling up to the house that I had an appointment with through Turner's Realty. I had an appointment to see a few houses. I heard so many great things about the company and after googling them, I saw their success rate was 95%, I would've been a fool not to make an appointment.

"Yeah, you say that now. You're gonna be begging me to get him after a couple hours."

"Whatever girl, you know he loves his god mommy, but I'm walking into my appointment so I'll call you back later."

"Okay boo. Love you and good luck."

"Thanks, love you too." I dropped my phone into my purse when the line disconnected and I stepped out the car. We were meeting at a beautiful three bedroom, one and a half bath brick home in Rosedale Park, off Grand River Ave. There was a Jaguar parked in the driveway that I assumed belonged to the realtor who had to be inside. I continued the walkway and knocked three times when I approached the door.

"Hello. Hazel." I extended my hand out to her while giving a friendly smile.

"Malaya. Nice to meet you. Come on in." She motioned for me to follow her. The tour went by quickly as she explained everything about the house including some facts about the neighborhood. She was on her shit, so I saw firsthand how the black owned business was doing so well.

"Did you want to look at the other homes or were you set on this one?"

"I'll take a look at the others and I'll choose the one that speaks to me the most." I giggled, following her out the house.

We drove around to see four more houses and they were in close proximity to each other. I ended up choosing the third house, that was also in Rosedale Park. The spacious walk in closet in the master bedroom and the patio that oversaw the huge backyard was the deal breaker for me. After the background check, and she was able to verify the check I wrote her for 15,000, I had my keys in hand with a huge smile on my face.

I was happy to have saved enough money for my beautiful home. Ethan was known for dropping a couple stacks on me whenever he fucked up, so I had saved enough money to where I could buy the house and furnish it completely, and still be able to live a comfortable life.

I couldn't stop smiling even if someone paid me to as I drove to Art Van Furniture in Dearborn. I saw so many different living room sets that caught my eye. I wish I could have bought them all so I could switch out whenever I wanted. After looking over and over the same sets, I finally chose a cocaine white set that had diamonds studded in the cushions and the tables. I was in love with the set and I knew it would go along with the walls I planned on painting a soft lavender. The dining set I chose had a rich oak finish with a three seater bench along with four chairs. I loved it because it was rustic and not like everyone else's. It was very nice quality with a different style.

After I paid for my items, I got the delivery date for Monday and it was Wednesday so that gave me time to get the house painted like I wanted. It felt so good to have my own. I was always dependent on someone else and I finally was able to break that cycle and do for myself. Yeah, most of the money came from Ethan, but it rightfully belonged to me after all the bullshit I had gone through because of him.

"I'm a homeowner." I sung into the phone almost in tears. This was by far the biggest accomplishment of my life.

"Congratulations sis." She shouted, matching the excitement I had.

"Thanks sis. You gotta come by sometime next week, when I get everything together." I sat my things down and laid on the floor, taking in this beautiful moment.

I checked out the cart I had on Amazon for the things I saw that I wanted for my house, whenever I got one. It was a long time coming and definitely overdue.

It had my bedroom set along with pictures to hang on the walls and things for the bathroom and kitchen.

I went to bed more peaceful than ever. I was the happiest woman in the world, even though I slept on the bare floor in an empty house. Having my own was more than enough. Finally. Something was going right.

Syan Gonzàlez

~

(One Month Later)

Ever since my mom passed, I kept in contact with my family in India, including my dad. Life was too precious to live selfishly. I hate it took for us to have a loss to reunite as a family again. They even agreed to visit me and my family and I was looking forward to making more memories with my family.

"Baby, dinner is ready." I called out to Hector who was in the living room playing that damn game.

I peeked around the corner and I had to grab my phone so I could snap a picture of the beautiful sight before me. Hector was sitting in the recliner with his muscular body on display, remote in hand, watching the game intensively without a care in the world. Jr. sat beside him in his swing, holding a remote identical to his dad's, staring at the TV like he knew what was going on.

"Here we come bae." He responded late as hell. He played the game for a couple more seconds before he got up and picked our son up, who was drooling uncontrollably. He was in his teething phase.

"Give him here babe. So you can eat." My arms were stretched out, reaching for my son.

"I got him baby. You enjoy your food. I'm sure I can manage."

Without uttering another word, I smiled and dug into the Chicken Tikkla Masala; a dish my mom taught me how to make when I was ten years old. That was my favorite Indian dish and had been since I was younger. It's just chunks of chicken marinated in an orange, curry sauce usually served over rice. It was so good and had the perfect amount of spice.

I finished up with my food and took the baby out of Hector's arms, so I could give him his bath and put him to sleep. After he had his bath and I fed him, he was sound asleep. Since I already had my pajamas on, I got into my bed and fell asleep sooner than I expected.

"Where you going?" I whispered with my eyes still closed, feeling Hector get out of bed.

"To get Gabriella. Lisa's been blowing my phone up talking about her mom can't get her today."

I rolled my eyes at the thought of Lisa's scandalous ass. I didn't hate anyone because I never let nobody have that much power over me but if I did, that bitch would be the first on the list. Lisa is Hector's baby mama, the mother of six year old Gabriella. We both made mistakes in our relationship, not saying his daughter was a mistake but him cheating damn sure was. But I get the fact that we were young taking on adult responsibilities. That we weren't fully ready for commitment. That wasn't a priority on our list at that age, hence his daughter. And I had a slip up too.

That's what I loved about our relationship. We were realistic and the bond we shared was like no other. Hell yeah, I got in his ass about cheating and I got my revenge by fucking one of his workers but at twenty-two and three, our brains weren't even fully developed. We moved past it. However, I don't like the bitch, not because of the infidelity, but the fact that she had to poke holes in the condom to get pregnant with Gabriella. She was a manipulative, sneaky bitch and that's what I don't like. I don't trust bitches and that's why the only friend I had was Hazel.

"Well at least the bitch got a job now." I murmured, still feeling sleepy. It was six in the morning and I hadn't got my full beautyrest, plus I was off work and planned to sleep past eight if Jr. let me.

Lisa thought getting pregnant with Hector was her meal ticket, but she was sadly mistaken. At first, every time he dropped five stacks in her account for Gabriella monthly, she would take herself on shopping sprees at Saks Fifth while her baby was wearing five dollar outfits from Walmart. The bitch was just trifling. I'm not saying there's anything wrong with shopping at Walmart but don't have ya seed looking cheap as hell and you have on red bottoms. Prioritize bitch, that's all I'm saying. She learned her lesson though, hopefully.

"Go to bed." He chuckled, before exiting our room.

***

Today was my first day back on the job and it was chaotic as usual. I had five more hours and five had already passed. I was ready to get off and enjoy the rest of my night at home in my bed.

"Hey girl, I made lunch for everyone. It's in the breakroom." Kelly said coming up to me as I examined my patient. I was a nurse on the intensive care unit, and this particular patient had been shot ten times and survived. We had put him in a medically induced coma, but for the most part he was breathing on his own, surprisingly.

"Okay, I'll grab a little." I stated while putting some more pain medication in my patient's IV. I gave Kelly a faint smile, maybe she was just genuinely nice.

By the time my last break came, I was hungry as hell. I saw the dish Kelly was talking about and it was some type of steak stir fry and there was rice and dinner rolls as well. I knew damn well I wasn't supposed to be eating like this at this time of night, but I dug in anyway.

The first bite was so good, I had to close my eyes because it was seasoned so well. She almost gave me a run for my money in the kitchen. By the third bite, my body started feeling off. My head was pounding and I could feel my throat closing up. My airway was almost invisible.

"Syan, you okay? Can you hear me?" I saw Jessica, my coworker's mouth moving but I couldn't respond. I felt myself crossing to the other side.

"I-I-I.." I tried to speak but I couldn't. Colors started to get blurry as I tried to get up and get my Epi pen. Everything started to get blurry and the colors that were all merging together after a while just faded to black.

I woke up to my body hooked up to a few machines and an IV in my arm. My husband was at the side of the hospital bed. I knew I had to have an allergic reaction, but to what? I was only allergic to shrimp and I didn't see any in the stir fry, plus everyone I worked with knew I was highly allergic anyway.

"Baby, are you okay?" Hector rushed to my side when he'd seen me looking around, checking my surroundings. I was still dizzy and everything was fuzzy.

I nodded my head, indicating I was okay. I still couldn't talk because my throat still felt tight. I nodded my head to the notepad and pen so I could tell him I needed water. Once I got some water, my throat started to feel better and my vocal chords started to work.

"Baby, I don't even know what happened." I pondered, trying to come up with anything logical that made sense as to why I had an allergic reaction. Nothing.

"What did you eat?' He questioned with a serious expression on his face. I could tell he was irritated by the way the muscles in his temple flexed.

"I ate some steak stir fry. That's why I'm confused."

"Where did you get it from?"

"This girl I work with, Kelly. She made it." I said it slowly and my brain processed what I had said. My mind started racing a mile a minute. Was this bitch really coming for me? I knew I couldn't trust that bitch.

Hector stormed out of the room and I knew he was about to cause a scene. "Aye, where's Kelly at? The one that works with my wife?" He questioned. I don't know who. I knew it was about to be some shit.

I don't even know how far he thought he was about to go when no one on this floor probably knew Kelly, or me for that matter. We didn't work on this floor and this hospital was so big. I saw new faces everyday. I couldn't hear my husband's voice anymore and that was odd, because if he was still on this floor, I would be able to hear him causing mayhem, no doubt. That thought came and left as I saw Hector damn near dragging Kelly into my hospital room.

"Bae, what are you doing?" I asked, already knowing the answer. I knew my husband.

"What the fuck did you put in that stir fry?" He barked, all up in the girl's face.

"Umm steak, garlic, on–" She paused when Hector pushed her against the wall.

"Do you think this shit a game? Do I look like I'm fucking playing to you?"

"I-I-I might have made a mistake and put sh–shrimp flavor instead of beef." She cried, looking shook. I knew my husband looked crazy and his demeanor was already intimidating, but I couldn't feel bad for a bitch that tried to kill my ass. I don't even know that bitch for real and Syan didn't beef with nobody. Period.

"Bitch, you knew what the fuck you was doing." He yelled so loud that I jumped right along with her scary ass. If you cherished your life my suggestion to anybody would be to not fuck with me, our son, or anyone close to us.

Hector González

~

I don't know why people insisted on fucking with me knowing I had a few loose screws and everything wasn't all there. I looked at this bitch with murder in my eyes. Anybody who fucked with Syan González or Hector González Jr. must've had a fucking death wish.

"Give me one good reason why I shouldn't kill your ass right now?" I threatened through clenched teeth.

"I-I-I have a son. I'm so sorry." She cried, looking like a kid with snot and shit running down her face.

"She do too." I said, pointing to my wife. This bitch must have thought I was a joke.

"Sir, we're going to have to ask you to leave." Some rent-a-cop looking ass nigga approached me coming too close for my liking,

I loosened the grip I had on ole girl and she darted off like her life depended on it, and in this case, it did. "Don't ever get that close to me again. Now back the fuck up before your moms have to plan your funeral." I barked, staring into his eyes. I had his ass scared. They needed to hire people like me for security if they wanted to intimidate people. Clown ass niggas.

"Baby, I'll be back to get you. They have to observe you for a couple more hours, I got some shit to handle." I kissed her lips before exiting the room and bumping his soft ass on the way out.

Ole girl looked familiar and I found myself pulling up to Lisa's, only to see if my suspicions were accurate. What should have been a twenty minute ride was cut in half.

I banged on her door like the damn police. "Who the fuck banging on my damn door like that?" She snapped, swinging the door open, damn near breaking it off the hinges. She was wearing what looked like something that came out of my daughter's closet, with the way her ass and titties were spilling out the too-little-tank top and shorts.

"Where your sister work?"

"She work at Beaumont. Why?"

"What's her name?" I questioned, hoping she wouldn't say what I thought. She wasn't that damn crazy.

"K-K-Kelly." She stuttered avoiding contact as I towered over her.

That was enough to send me to the edge. I grabbed her by the neck and pushed her against the wall.

"Bitch, are you tryna die?" I gritted through clenched teeth. "That stunt you pulled almost cost my wife her life. Since you tried to take hers it's only right if I successfully take yours." Her eyes bucked open wide, almost popping out of her head.

"No no no no no!" She sobbed. "I was just trying to send a message. That's all."

"You sound stupid as fuck. What message?" I scolded, fed up with the bullshit.

"That I'm coming back for you. I was the mother of your child first," She whined sounding like a little ass kid. We were too damn old to be playing childish games.

"Man get out of here with that bullshit. She's my wife not some little girlfriend. She's here to stay. Permanently. By the grace of Gabriella, I'm sparing yo life. You might not get lucky if you try some shit like this again.

You'll be taking a dirt nap and Gabi will be calling Syan, mommy. Fuck with me if you want to."

I got in my whip and sparked up some cookie to help release some of the demons on my back. I had enough stress already in my line of work. I didn't need baby mama drama too. I heard enough about that from my boys. I sat in Lisa's driveway smoking like this was my shit. I was the one who footed the bills in this muthafucka anyway.

"What's up baby?" I answered my ringing phone.

"Hector come get me before I blow this bitch up." My wife yelled and I quickly put my car in reverse heading back to the hospital.

"Whats going on?" I asked with my brows raised. I hope I didn't go to jail today.

"They talking about they're suspending me because they don't tolerate violence." She said angrily and I knew she was rolling those pretty ass eyes. She ain't gone get enough until they get stuck.

"Fuck that. You don't need that job anyway. Quit!" I barked, getting irritated again. I didn't want her ass working in the first place .

I pulled up to the front and my wife was already waiting outside with a mean mug on her pretty face. She was sexy as hell when she was mad. She got into the car after I opened the door for her and she plopped down onto the leather seats with her arms folded. My wife was a real life brat when she didn't get her way and I had myself to blame for that.

"Give me a kiss." I stated cooly. She gave me a peck on the lips and I gave her that look, "try again," and she climbed up in my lap and tongued me down with my car parked in front of the hospital entrance. I wanted to fuck her right then and there. She had my dick brick hard, dying to release.

"Alright that's enough." I tapped her to get up. "Be ready to ride this dick as soon as we step foot into the house." I chuckled, already knowing how our night was about to end.

Chapter Seven

~

Xá Black

"Wassup ma." I spoke, stepping into Ivory's apartment. It was nice. I looked around, thankful it was clean and in good standing. You wouldn't believe how many times a chick invited me to her place and didn't even attempt to clean or hide the filth. That was unattractive and trifling as hell.

"Hey Xá." She said sexily, switching hard as hell making her little ass jiggle in the dress she was wearing.

"So what's on the menu?" I questioned. I hope she could cook, cause I was hungry as hell.

"I made meatloaf with gravy, cabbage, macaroni and cheese, and cornbread."

I nodded my head in approval. It smelled good. I hoped it tasted as good as it smelled.

"You can put on a movie if you want." She tilted her head to the TV. "I'm going to fix our plates, then join you." She winked.

She came in a couple minutes later, holding two plates in her hands. She sat them down on the glass coffee table before disappearing then returning, holding two wine glasses along with a bottle of wine. I dug into my food and it was good. It smelled better than it tasted, but it would do the job until I got something else.

As soon as I started to get into Central Intelligence someone started banging on the door. My hand automatically went to my gun that stayed on me at all times. Psychologist or not, I stayed strapped cause niggas are crazy.

"Give me a sec." She got up and stepped outside the door.

"Why haven't you answered any of my calls?" Some nigga yelled.

"Nigga, cause I've been busy." She snapped.

"So you been so busy you can't even hit up your nigga to at least check in?" I shook my head in disbelief. I don't know why I have such bad luck in my choice of women but that shit is getting old. I got up and threw the rest of my food in the trash and put my dishes in the sink. One thing for certain Xá Black won't be any bitches' side nigga. I grabbed up my stuff and left out the door and Ivory stood next to some nigga in a heated conversation.

She looked at me as I walked past her without saying a word. Dude looked pissed and I wasn't with stepping on the next man's toes. I'm just glad I found out what type of chick she was before I invested time into her.

I found myself going in the direction of ma dukes house. I missed her and her cooking. Mama cooked pretty much every day, unless we had plans to eat out. I parked my car in the circular driveway behind Brielle's car. I used my key to let myself in and smiled when I heard my nephew, Jaden's voice. I loved little man like he was mine and I did for him like he was my seed.

"What's up, Unc." He dapped me up and I had to laugh cause his ass swear he was grown.

"What's up J. How's sc–"

"Hey brother." Brielle sung, interrupting me while running towards me to give me a hug. This is what she did every time she saw me, acting like she ain't seen my ass in years.

"What's up sis." I said, hugging her back. Me and her were the closest between my mom's three kids.

"Ma, we were talking. That's rude." Jaden's smart mouthed ass stated.

"Boy, that's *MY* brother." Bri joked, making all three of us laugh. I loved Bri's relationship with my nephew. They were the best of friends, but he knew where the line was drawn and how much shit he could say or do before she's upside his damn head. My sister was a great mom and you wouldn't think she had him at the tender age of fifteen.

"Where's mama?" I asked.

"Now you know her ass is in the kitchen." She sassed, giving me that look, cause that's where mama always was.

"What's up old girl." I joked with my OG.

"Boy, I done told you about calling me that shit. You not old unless you look it, you hear me?" She asked with her brows raised and the most serious expression on her face.

"Yes ma'am. What you in here cooking?" I quizzed, opening one of the lids to the pots that were on the stove.

She smacked my hand away so quick, even I was surprised. "Don't you touch anything in my kitchen and you ain't washed yo' damn hands boy."

Mama would get in my ass whenever she felt I needed it, grown or not. I went to the closest bathroom to wash my hands. When I went back into the kitchen she had my plate sitting at the bar. Brielle and Jaden's greedy asses were already smashing. On my plate was some honey barbecue wings, cheesy potatoes, collard greens, and cornbread with a tall glass of tropical punch kool-aid on the side. Brenda Black could cook her ass off. Everyone loved her cooking and people often offered her money for a dish or a plate in return.

I joined my sister and nephew and put the smash on my food, although I had eaten less than forty five minutes ago, but Ivory's non seasoning ass wasn't hitting on shit. I hated eating bland food. If you don't know how to season food and make that flavor pop, your black card must be revoked. At this point, you're making us look bad as a whole.

I chopped it up with ma dukes, Bri, and nephew before it was time for me to go. I had to be at work at seven which meant I had to get up at five to get my morning workout in. When I got to the crib, I set the alarm, hopped in the shower, and took my tired ass to bed.

I got to work earlier than usual and so did Hunter, my nigga from the college days. That nigga was my best friend, my right hand mans.

"What's up nigga." I dapped Hunter up and gave him a brotherly hug.

"You got it. Tell me something good." He replied referring to X&H Recreation Center, the center we were opening for the youth in the Detroit community. Our mission was to help build Detroit back up and that started with the youth. We were going to help them find jobs and apartments. I was tired of seeing the black youth on the streets, especially the young men involved in gangs and other dumb shit. Most of all, I was tired of seeing them in jail or in news stories about how they were shot up.

"Sasha is still designing it and you know how she is." I gave him a knowing look. Sasha was a perfectionist. She wasn't gonna give me the green light until everything was exactly how she envisioned it in her mind. That's why she was great at what she did, and one of the best interior designers across the U.S.

"The day of the grand opening is when it's really going to hit me. Thanks man, for going into business with me." He smiled. I knew he was genuinely happy. Just like me, he was a nigga from the hood with big dreams tryna make it.

He came up to me with the idea of opening a center about a year ago and with the right connects we had a space and employees lined up. Our grand opening should be no more than two months away. Maybe less depending on Sasha's perfectionist ass.

"No problem man. You my nigga. We gone eat together."

We talked a little bit longer until we both had to depart to our own offices to see our first clients. Mine happened to be my favorite, Ms.Evans. You couldn't tell by looking at her that she had gone through so much. Shit that no one should have to experience.

Hunter Williams

I had a short day at work today because I only had a few clients. I've been working at Xá's since he got this place up and running straight out of college, seven years ago.

Let me introduce myself. I'm Hunter Williams. I'm a therapist and I really focus on the children, so majority of my clientele were the youth. I'm thirty-one years old with awards and certificates that doctors with twice my experience haven't gotten.

"Alright man, I'm gone for the day." I peeked into Xá's office letting him know I was leaving.

"Alright Bro. Hit me up with the details for your birthday too."

"Fasho." I nodded, exiting the office, then the building completely.

A nigga was turning thirty-two next week and I was having a little something at the club my boy owned, Toxic Temptation. I was never the partying type but life was too short and I wanted to at least have one party in my lifetime.

"What's good old man." I laughed into the phone, talking to my pops. He hated when I called him that shit.

"Nigga, ain't shit old over here. Ask Roxanne." He joked, talking about his girlfriend. His ass was too damn old to have a girlfriend but I was just happy that he could finally move on after my mom passed two years ago.

"Yeah, okay. What you up to?" I asked pulling into my condo Downtown.

"I'm about to take my lady out, but I was just checking on you son."

"Be safe out here and don't do nothing I won't do." I chuckled, already waiting for his smart ass response.

"Well that leaves no limits. Talk to you later son." We ended the call as I stepped into my house.

Memories of my mom flooded my thoughts as I looked at the many pictures of us on my wall. I'm the only child so it was just me, my mom, and dad. I missed her so much and I often questioned God, because I couldn't wrap my mind around the reason for him taking away my queen, my heart, my everything. I was a mama's boy for sure and anyone who had her as a mom would've been too. She was a great mom and the closest person I knew to being perfect.

I grabbed my favorite picture off the fireplace. It was a picture of my mom and dad. They were standing so close together, almost one, as they stared deeply into one another's eyes. I was in the background watching them with an expression I can't read. I had to be about six or seven. The relationship my parents had was like no other. To this day, I've never seen a genuine and passionate love as strong as theirs. I would give away everything in exchange to feel the love that my mom had for my dad.

I sat the picture back in its place. I felt my eyes producing tears I didn't want to fall. I hadn't cried since the day of my mom's funeral, when I called her a thousand times hoping and praying to hear her voice just one more time. My life would never be completely the same, because without her, I wasn't my whole self.

I started the shower up before getting in and relaxing my mind and my body. I stayed in the shower for a good fifteen minutes before getting out and drying my body off. I smiled as I looked at my reflection in the mirror. I was the replica of my Mary Ann Williams. I had a caramel complexion and the same features on my face as my mom. Thick eyebrows, low slanted eyes, full lips, and a pointy broad nose with a slight curve to it.

I kept my hair in a low fade with a full beard. Tats adorned my chest and arms. I stood at 6'4 with a muscular build. I was about two hundred and forty pounds. I knew I was that nigga, I just needed a lady that knew that as well.

I put on some joggers, a compression shirt, and a pair of KD's to go on my afternoon jog downtown. I had to jog with the way I ate. I would look like a tall sumo wrestler if I didn't exercise daily.

The breeze felt nice and the sun kept creeping behind the clouds. I had on my headphones as J. Cole played my background. He was my favorite rapper hands down. I liked his style and the way he moved. He didn't rap bullshit like a lot of these wack ass, so called rappers.

I glanced down at my phone to put 'False Prophets' on repeat. That was my favorite track. He was speaking real shit. In those few seconds I was looking down at my phone, I bumped into the most beautiful woman ever. She had an even dark skin tone. She had light makeup on and her dark brown eyes sparkled even in the shade.

"Sorry, miss." I apologized, even with that mean mug on her face, she was fine as hell.

"If you'd stay off that damn phone, you would've seen me walking." She snapped. Damn, shorty's attitude made me chuckle cause she was mad at the wrong one. Typical female, taking their frustrations on whoever's around.

"You right. Having a bad day?" I questioned. I felt the need to make conversation with her cause she looked like she needed it.

"Yeah and you not paying attention ain't making it no better." She fussed, rolling those pretty ass eyes in the process.

She walked off and I watched her stop at the bus station. Her whole body language screamed attitude. You could see it in her body language, and most definitely on her face. I jogged up to her cause I felt the need to be her knight in shining armor.

"A woman like yourself shouldn't be riding this bus." I countered.

She looked at me, rolling those eyes again while she shifted her weight from her left side to her right side. "A man like you shouldn't be all in my business."

"I'm not here to be in your business. I just want to offer you a ride. I know all about this bus and I know it's not for you. Plus, I can see that you're already having a bad day and getting on the Woodward bus, at this time with those crazy folks, is just going to make it worse."

The look on her face seemed like she was thinking about it. I knew it was hard to trust niggas in this day and age, but I was a stand up guy with good intentions. I wasn't with the phony shit.

Harmony Woods

~

Today had to be 'Fuck With Harmony Day'. I had finally got my car out of the shop for the engine to blow on my way to work. All the money I had in my savings went to a new transmission. That and paying for the labor, had my pockets and bank account on e.

When I got to work, there was no one to help me at the front desk, I wasn't able to take my lunch break, and the clinic was packed to capacity with bad ass kids getting their check ups before school started back up. When I got off work, I called for an Uber to get me and not even five minutes into the ride, he had to drop me off on Woodward, because my card had declined.

Now here I was, standing at the bus stop talking with this Caramel God about giving me a ride home. He was fine as hell and didn't look like a serial killer, but should I risk my life and safety? So many negative thoughts clouded my mind but reality set in and I didn't even know if I had enough change at the bottom of my purse to even get on the bus. I wasn't even sure how much bus fare was.

"I guess that would make my day less shitty." I smiled, taking in his fine ass. He had specks of sweat on his forehead. His toned body might as well had been out because the tight ass workout shirt he had on showed it all. I looked away not wanting to stare too long.

"Cool, well I'm Hunter. At least now I'm not a complete stranger." He joked, making me laugh. I could have used that laugh hours ago when all I wanted to do was crawl in my bed in the fetal position and cry.

"Harmony." I said, shaking his hand.

"I jogged down here from my place but we can get on the People Mover to get my car from the crib."

"Okay, lead the way Mr.Hunter." I liked the sound of his name rolling off my tongue.

The ride on the People Mover wasn't long at all. The train didn't move slow, as old as it was. We had to walk for about two minutes to get to his condo that was so beautiful and off the water. Expensive too, might I add, I knew because I was going to apply, but the rent was too much for me to handle. I didn't need an eviction too.

I waited in front of the building, while he pulled his car to the front. He had the new BMW M6 Convertible I dreamt about having. You know a nigga got money when he riding around in a 2017 and it's still summer 2016. My body melted as I sunk into the buttery leather seats. He had the top down and I enjoyed the night's air as my beautiful curls danced in the wind. This was a beautiful moment and I welcomed the feeling with open arms. It was short lived because before I knew it, we were pulling up to my apartments in Highland Park.

"Thanks for the ride Hunter." I said while closing the door, then I walked into my not so luxurious domain. It was a lot different from the scenery at Hunter's but this was my world, I was far from his.

I warmed up yesterday's dinner, spaghetti, and turned on Lifetime Movie Network, my routine whenever I was in my feelings. For some reason I loved to watch movies that matched my emotional state. Sometimes it put me deeper in depression and other times it helped me get over whatever sour lemons life threw my way.

I wish I had my mom to go to when all I wanted to do was break down and cry. I'm twenty eight with my life no where I planned. My life had taken so many turns and detours. My mama turned against me when her nigga started paying more attention to me than her. She blamed everything on me. Telling me how I'm trying so hard to steal her man.

She did the ultimate betrayal when she chose her nigga over her flesh and blood, her daughter. I was never checking for him. What fucked me up the most is the fact that they're not even together no more after he fucked her best friend. I know deep down she knows how wrong she is for saying and doing the shit she's done but she's too damn stubborn to see it and acknowledge her fuck ups. If you claimed to be a grown ass woman, I expected you to act accordingly and own your shit.

I felt alone in this world. I didn't have any siblings or cousins to talk to because everyone disowned me. It was just me, and I didn't want to keep bothering Ivory with my problems. My circle was so small, trusting bitches wasn't my thing.

I let out a deep sigh before turning the TV off and going into the kitchen to wash the few dishes that were in the sink. One thing I learned from my mama was to never go to sleep with a dirty kitchen. As a child, I washed the dishes and cleaned the kitchen every night, from the time I was seven years old to seventeen when I got kicked out.

After I finished the five dishes that were in the sink, I went to my bedroom and stripped out of my work attire and took a quick shower. When I washed my body enough to my comfort, I got in the bed, said my prayers, and took my ass to bed.

Chapter Eight

Brigail Jenkins

"Are you sure?" I questioned, even with the proof right in my face. How could I let this happen?

"I'm certain." He paused looking at my leg that couldn't stop bouncing up and down. My nerves were all over the place. I couldn't help it. "Mrs. Jenkins this baby is coming in less than seven months." He assured me.

I bursted into tears as I thought about the mess I've created. Here I was, pregnant with someone other than my husband's, child. Cheating wasn't in my plan after I said those two words: I do. I made a vow to my husband that I didn't follow, but the choice I made would stay with me for the rest of my life. Abortion wasn't an option.

I didn't know how or when I became this woman. I let my husband's neglect turn me into someone else. I was slowly turning into the girl I was in my teenage years, heartless with an, I-don't-give-a-fuck attitude. He didn't show me any attention, so I found it elsewhere. I dialed up Damon, trying to get my nerves under control.

"What's up baby girl?" His deep voice resonated through the speaker.

"Hi." I said, drier than the Sahara Desert, not trying to feed into his sweet antics. I had a mission to accomplish. I was ridding myself of this adulterous affair. I took a deep breath, "I'm done fucking with you. I can't jeopardize everything I've built with my husband." I sighed heavily, cutting right to the chase.

"Oh, so now you wanna be faithful to your husband after fucking me for three years. You're a selfish ass bitch."

"Well you served your purpose for what I needed at that time but I feel God is speaking to me, and it's time to let this go. I can't keep sleeping around with you and I'm the first lady. It's only a matter of time before it catches up with me. Therefore, your services are no longer needed."

"I served my purpose, huh? Well let's see what purpose you'll serve, after I tell the pastor where you've been at every time he has a meeting with all the shepherds."

Before I could respond, he had hung up the phone. My blood was beyond boiling. Would he really go that far for a fling that was never supposed to happen? My brain was filled with so many different scenarios of how this shit would unfold but I had to cover my own ass.

I was excited to see my husband's car parked in the driveway. I pulled in behind him and put the car in park, before hopping out the car.

"Hey baby." I beamed, I had never been so excited to see my husband's face.

"Hey, where you coming from?" He asked moving swiftly around the bedroom.

"I went to see my brother." I lied, something that was inevitable these days. Lying was like my favorite hobby nowadays. Well, at least, it seemed like it.

"I haven't seen him in a while. We gotta get all the family over for dinner one of these days."

"That'll be nice." I said, setting my purse down on the nightstand. I got a glimpse of the back of the nightstand and there was a receipt from the Westin Hotel. My brows raised, "Babe, why is there a receipt to a hotel in your name?" I quizzed, waving the receipt in the air. My woman's intuition kicked in, sending a red flag.

"You don't remember me telling you I got my niece a room as one of her graduation gifts?" He asked nonchalantly.

"Oh yeah." I said remembering he did tell me that a few weeks ago.

I moved in closer to him, kissing his lips then his neck. I sucked lightly, making him let out a manly moan. I pushed him down on the bed and ripped his shirt off. My hands traveled to his belt buckle, releasing his manhood. I eagerly slid down on his rod. I had a plan that had to be executed perfectly. This baby was officially his. Mission completed!

***

"How you doing, first lady?" Maya asked me, the deacon's wife. Something about her rubbed me the wrong way, and I usually was on point with stuff like this.

"I'm fine, and yourself?" I put on a fake smile, engaging in the conversation like I really gave two fucks. I was good at pretending. Hell, I should be an actress with a lot of Oscars and Grammys under my belt.

"I'm doing well. Between the kids, my husband, and a few other things I'm so busy." She let out a sigh. "Have you and Jordan thought about starting a family?"

"You mean Pastor Jenkins." I quizzed with a raised brow. She was too damn comfortable for me.

"Yes, of course. My apologies." Her face almost looked like it was forming a smirk, but she quickly put on a smile instead.

I looked around for my husband and he was having a conversation with the guest speakers he had at today's service. I admired my husband and the suit that adorned his body, his chocolate skin glistening under the lighting. My husband is very sexy. I wish I could turn back the time and change the things I've done to my man. I couldn't, so I had to be on the straight and narrow, the path that God sought for me.

"Well to answer your question, we've definitely been practicing on it." A small smirk sat on my face briefly as I looked her up and down.

She chuckled lightly while rubbing her fingers through that stale ass weave. I mean, her husband needed to upgrade that cause there's no way in hell I could walk around in some weave that'll give me paper cuts every time I touch the shit. It was really pathetic, if you ask me.

"I guess that's good to hear." She replied while eyeing my husband lustfully. I don't know what she had up her sleeve, but if she kept that shit up, she was going to find out exactly who the fuck Brigail Renee Black was, and still is behind closed doors.

Maya Clark

~

I couldn't stand Brigail's uppity ass. She was they type of broad I stayed fighting in Junior High. Being classy and bourgeoisie is two completely, different things, and she took it to another level.

"Come on Mariah and Neriyah." I gathered up my beautiful little girls. They were my gift from God.

"I'll meet y'all outside in a second." My husband smiled his signature pantie dropping smile that gets me every time.

On the way out the door, Jordan brushed past me. "Same place, same time." He said, barely above a whisper.

Anybody who said you couldn't be completely in love with two men was a damn lie. My life was living proof that it was true. Ronald, my husband, is my everything but nothing could make me stop sleeping with my sexy ass pastor, Jordan Jenkins. Jordan filled in the areas Ronald lacked and vice versa. I was getting the best of both worlds.

Ronald came to the car as I was buckling the girls in their booster seats. Mariah was the oldest at five and my baby girl Neriyah was three years old. I swear they were meant to be twins, because they looked so much alike. Neriyah was the exact replica of her big sister.

"Daddy, can we get ice cream pwease?" Neriyah asked in the prettiest little voice ever. When she batted her long eyelashes, that sealed the deal. She had him. She got whatever she wanted because she was too cute. It was hard to say no and see her pretty self cry.

"Of course, baby girl." He nodded, getting off the freeway on the exit before ours to go to Dairy Queen.

I glanced out the window, thinking about a million things at once, but one thing in particular was weighing heavily on my mind.

"What's on your mind baby? You're so quiet."

"I'm just thinking about our little family. We're just so blessed." I lied, tearing up like I actually meant it. Really, I was daydreaming about how Jordan was about to make me cum multiple times, something Ronald couldn't do.

After we got our ice cream, we went to our neighborhood park. They ran around so much, they were asleep in the car before we got to our house, and that was only a five minute drive, maybe less. Ronald carried Mariah and I carried Neriyah up to their rooms.

"Babe, I'm heading out." I told my husband as I grabbed the keys to my Lexus and my duffle bag with my change of clothes and yoga mat.

"Okay, don't let them work you out too much." He laughed and so did I because little did he know, I was probably about to get the best workout of my life. He pecked my lips and I headed for the hills.

He thought I was going to my yoga class but I had a dick appointment that I couldn't ,or wouldn't miss for anything. I craved this man, I was addicted to him. I sped the whole way to the Westin, our meeting place.

I knocked on the hotel door, impatiently waiting on my other man to grace me with his presence. He opened the door with a towel wrapped around his waist. His small muscular body on display. I looked over his body lustfully. His body was wet and I licked my lips as so many nasty thoughts came to me.

"Well you gonna let me in?" He backed away, creating enough space for me to get by.

Before I could get all the way in the room, he pushed me roughly against the wall. He dropped the towel and got on his knees, lifting up my dress up in the process. The moment his tongue connected with my clit I moaned uncontrollably, basking in the incredible feeling. He moved his long tongue in a circular motion biting down lightly.

"Oh, baby, yes! I'm cumming!" I screamed loudly, I couldn't lower my voice if I wanted to.

He lapped up all my juices that were running down his beard. He picked me up with me still on his shoulders, and he continued licking my soul out as he carried me to the bed. I laid down so he could get between my legs. I let out a gasp as I felt the tip pressing at my opening. He eased himself in, yelling obscenities in the process. His strokes were so precise, hitting my g spot every time.

"Fuck. This pussy so tight. Damn." He groaned, quickening his pace. My pussy was running like a broken faucet. I lost track of how many orgasms I had.

"Oh my God!" I moaned, not trying to bring God into this fucked up situation, but damn. He sucked on my nipples as he beat it up. My eyes watered as he pumped into me slowly yet so deeply that I could feel him in my stomach. It wasn't long before he emptied his load into me. I laid there stiff as a board, my body restless. I was dickmatized, for sure.

Chapter Nine

~

Hazel Parks

I was the happiest I'd ever been. I was living comfortably in my beautiful, fully furnished home. Work was great. I felt great and I looked even better. The only thing I was missing was a love life, but I was fine without it, for now.

I pulled my thick, jet black hair into a ponytail. I let the curls fall freely, in its natural state. I applied mascara to my already long eyelashes. I looked at my appearance through my mirror, liking what I saw. I loved my new self.

I had my scrubs on already, so I grabbed my purse and keys. As I drove to work, I had my slow jams playing and sung along to every song. My pandora stayed on 90s R&B radio. 90's music was, and still is, my favorite. It had a way of making you feel good. The lyrics; always on point and the beat; always hot.

"Hey, Ms. Evans." I sung to my favorite old lady.

"Hey sweetie, you look like you're glowing and only two things can do that to you. Peace or a new man. Which is it for you?" She questioned with her brows raised. Ms.Evans knew she was a trip.

"Not the latter, I wish." I sighed. "But I'm at peace. I feel so rejuvenated."

"Is there a Hazel Parks working here?" Some guy came to the receptionist desk, holding a bouquet of roses.

I glanced at Ms.Evans who was staring at me with questioning eyes. I shrugged my shoulders, walking closer to the front desk. "That's me." I said, wondering who my secret admirer would be.

I read the note, *I miss you. Let me take you out, Ethan.* I rolled my eyes at the thought of me giving him another chance. I mean maybe it wouldn't be a bad idea if I let him see what he's missing. I sat the flowers in my locker and finished taking care of my clients.

The day had gone by extremely fast, but I had no complaints whatsoever. I packed up my belongings and said goodbye to all my patients before I exited the building. I found myself pulling into Planet Fitness. That had been my go to place whenever I felt I was about to get stressed.

I grabbed my gym bag out the trunk, that I always kept packed and ready. I probably looked crazy going into the gym with scrubs on but I wasn't about to drive all the way home to come right back this way. That wasn't an option. Gas wasn't cheap and that's what locker rooms were for. I quickly changed into my workout tank top that said, 'No days off' and yoga pants. My phone dinged with a text as I cleaned the treadmill with the some paper towels and cleaner that the gym provided.

Ethan: Are you going to let me take you out?

Me: Why should I?

Ethan: Because I love you and I miss you. I promise I won't hurt you again.

Me: One more chance...

Deep down, I missed Ethan more than I let on. I hated that I loved him as much as I did but I couldn't control who I loved. I've tried so many times to hate him, but I just can't. He always made his way back to where home was, back to me.

I stepped on the treadmill, getting into workout mode. I was determined to stay fit. Not the doctor's take on fit but my own. I loved being a size ten, thick in the hips. I had Beyonce's Lemonade album on. If Jay could cheat and Beyonce took him back, when she can easily get whoever she wants, working on my relationship with Ethan might not be so bad. Nobody was perfect, not even me.

I was thirty minutes into my workout when I felt someone staring at me. I looked around to see this fine, cocky nigga staring at me. His stare so intense, I felt he was looking beyond my physical appearance. Between the workout and the way he looked at me, my body was on fire. I was too damn hot.

I cut my workout on the treadmill short. I usually did an hour at least but the heat radiating from my body said otherwise. I damn near drunk my entire jug of water in one gulp to cool myself down.

"I hope I didn't scare you away. I just couldn't help it. Someone as beautiful as you, I had to stare." He apologized and just like that, I was hot again. It felt like the sun sat directly above my head, so close I could touch it.

"No, I umm..." I swallowed the lump in my throat. This guy made me so nervous, but turned on at the same time. My pussy thumping, wanting to be touched. "I just remembered I had somewhere to be." I politely smiled.

"Well I don't want to hold you up, beautiful." He said, flashing the sexiest set of teeth I had ever seen on any man. He had teeth like the movie stars, straight and pearly white.

I glanced around, looking for him as I walked towards the door. I spotted him on the bench lifting weights. I nodded in approval as I stared at the definition in his arms. Nigga was too damn sexy and he knew exactly what he was doing.

When I got home, I headed straight for the shower. My body was all sweaty from working out and I was at work for eight hours before that, so a shower was well needed. I stayed in the shower longer than I intended. Ethan was blowing me up with texts asking for my address. I had missed calls from his also. I let him know that I would meet him at his place instead. There was no way in hell I was telling him where I stayed. We weren't cool like that.

I lotioned my body with a new scent I was trying out from Bath and Body Works. I slipped into my hot pink bandage dress and my sparkly red bottoms. I grabbed my Christian Louboutin purse, that matched my heels, and I took a look at myself in the full body mirror. My hair was slicked into a low bun. I had applied a little makeup. I spritzed a couple more sprays of perfume to my body and headed out of my front door once again.

So many memories clouded my mind as I pulled in front of the home I once shared with Ethan. I texted him to let him know I was outside. He came outside looking even better from the last time I saw him. His hair was freshly done and was lined up. He was in dark Balmain jeans and a Ralph Lauren button up. He looked good enough to eat.

"Damn, you look beautiful." He smiled, running his tongue across his beautiful pink, suckable lips.

"Thanks, you don't look bad yourself." I complimented, nodding my head in approval.

He opened his car door for me before getting in the car himself. I smiled at the gesture. This is the Ethan I missed, the Ethan I loved, the Ethan I fell hard for. We made small conversation on the way to our destination. It was hard for me to hold a conversation, because things were different.

We pulled up to an expensive, five star restaurant in Farmington Hills. We took the seats that were on the rooftop. The view was breathtaking. I took in the romantic setting as he pulled out my chair. The night was going perfect, I wondered how long that would last.

Dinner was amazing as well as the service. I see why their ratings were all five stars. While we were eating dessert, a live band came on the stage singing my favorite song, Love by Musiq Soulchild. I felt this song explained my relationship with Ethan. I glanced over to where Ethan was sitting, but he wasn't in his seat across from mine. Instead he was on his knee on the side of me holding a small red velvet box. I felt my world stop as I looked at him staring back at me.

"Baby, I love you so much and I know I've hurt you so many times in the past, but I promise it won't happen again. It took for you to leave for me to realize how much you mean to me and the love I have for you. I promise to love, cherish, and protect you for the rest of my life. I promise to honor you and treat you like the queen you are," My face flooded with tears, a huge lump in my throat, the feeling in my heart indescribable. "I promise to put you first. Can I do that for you while making you my wife?" My eyes cloudy from the crying, I nodded my head, yes, as I took in this moment, the moment I've been waiting on for years. It took ten years, but I felt in my heart, I made the right choice. I deserved this.

Syan González

~

"You did what?" I screamed, hoping this was some type of sick ass joke. I had never been so mad in my life.

"I said yes. I'm marrying Ethan." She was so lucky I wasn't with her because I would've socked her dead in her shit.

"Hazel, why though? He don't deserve you. He don't deserve your love." I snapped. Hazel was more than my best friend, she was my sister. When she went through heartache, I went through heartache. I felt what she felt, we were just that close. I was pissed that she overlooked all the dirty shit he did and was going to marry his cheating, lying ass.

"Syan, he's different. I know he's going to do right by me this time." She sounded so damn stupid right now. 'This time' replayed in my head. This nigga has had too many times. He's all out of 'this times'.

"You know what, let me get off this phone. Let me calm down because I can't do you right now." I hung up the phone before she could protest.

I knew Ethan was full of shit. It was only a matter of time before he showed his ass again. I wanted the best for her and he damn sure wasn't it. I hated men like Ethan. Men who hurt women to the point where she didn't even truly love herself. Men who fed women *broken promises.*

"Bae, you good?" Hector came in the house, looking good as hell. His shoulder length curly hair hung freely. His goatee was freshly trimmed. He had on dark jeans, a white t shirt, and white and gold J's.

"Fire up that blunt I know you're hiding behind your ear." I simply stated, overwhelmed with too many thoughts. I had never smoked before but if it felt how people made it seem, I knew that's what I needed.

He sat beside me on the living room couch, firing up the fat blunt he pulled out from behind his ear. I knew my husband like the back of my hand.

"So tell me what's up. What's wrong?" He looked at me, staring deeply into my eyes. I hated when he did that shit, looking like he could see right through me.

"Hazel and Ethan are getting married." I said, taking a hard pull from the blunt. It only took a couple seconds for me to regret that. I started coughing and next thing I knew I was full blown choking. Choking more than the first time I tried deep throatin' Hector's anaconda.

"Slow down baby. You're a beginner." He laughed and I playfully mushed his head. Just like that, my husband had changed my mood.

"Syan you can't control people's' lives. Humans make mistakes. This won't be the first time Hazel has made a mistake and it damn sure won't be the last time, but you have to stand by her side as she makes them and as she learns from them. Love her through her flaws, you're the only family she has."

Before I knew it, I was crying. I was very sensitive about the people closest to me. Hazel had been through too much in her life to keep being dogged and disrespected by the same fuck nigga. Hazel deserved somebody who truly loved her and wanted what's in her best interest. Ethan's cheating, lying ass didn't deserve my sister. I just wish she would see it for herself. I wiped my tear. She will find out sooner than later that he isn't the one.

I got up and straddled my husband's lap. Jr. was gone with his grandma and I was going to make the most of it. I pecked his lips a few times before licking and sucking on his neck lightly. I trailed kisses up his neck and face until I reached his lips again. I tongued him down, placing wet, hungry kisses on his lips. I felt his third leg poking my thigh, ready to be freed. My wish was his command. I freed his dick and it sprung to life. I pushed my thong to the side and slid down his thick pole.

"Fuck." He groaned as I took him all in with no effort.

I rode him nice and slow, adjusting to his size. Regardless of how long we've been together, every time feels like the very first time. When the pain subsided, I sped up my pace riding his dick better than he'd taught me.

"Fuck. Baby you feel so good." I moaned, going even faster. The strokes becoming deeper, my pussy wetter. "Shit, I'm cumming." I whimpered, riding the wave to ecstasy. I slowed down my pace ready to tap out. That nut almost knocked the wind out my ass.

"It ain't over yet. Don't start no shit, it won't be no shit. Bend that ass over." He demanded.

I did what I was told and got in the face down, ass up position. He plunged into me, showing no mercy. His strokes deep, long, hard, and passionate all in one. He's the ultimate pleaser. My pussy wetter than wet. The sound of our skin smacking together and the gushy sounds from his dick going in and out of my sopping wet pussy was the only sounds that could be heard.

"Ohhhh.." My mouth formed in the shape of an o, that was the only thing I could moan.

"Tell daddy how he making that pussy feel." He groaned, slapping me on the ass.

"Fuck! Shit, it feels so good daddy. I loooove you baby." I moaned, barely functioning enough to even form words.

He quickened his pace and I felt his dick pulsating in my pussy as he kept thrusting his body into mine.

"Ahh." He groaned, shooting his soldiers into me. He stayed in a couple seconds longer, giving us both time to recuperate. This isn't the first and definitely not the last time he's fucked me into a coma.

Chapter Ten

~

Brielle Black\

"Jaden come eat." I yelled down the hall. I made parmesan crusted tilapia, mashed potatoes, broccoli, and dinner rolls. I knew how to cook thanks to my mommy. You couldn't live with Brenda Black and not know how to cook. No child of hers would ever go hungry, so she says.

I heard his footsteps as he neared the kitchen. Looking at my son, my creation, my gift to the world, I knew he was my everything. Always has been, always will be.

"Your plate's on the dining room table." I said, rubbing my fingers through the single braids he had in his head.

We sat down at the table and talked while we ate. We talked about school, his little girl crush he had, sports, everything.

"I'm going back to my room. I gotta finish busting the boys in 2k." He said to me while sitting his dishes in the sink.

"Okay baby." I laughed. My son swore he could bust anybody's ass at 2k. Basketball was his life. I could see him being drafted in the future. My baby was just that good.

After I washed the little dishes that were in the sink, I went upstairs to my room. I found a movie on HBO with my alcoholic beverage in hand. I got comfortable in my bed, snuggled in my comforter. It wasn't long before the TV was watching me.

I got up in the middle of the night with an eerie feeling. For some reason, I was sick to my stomach. I jumped out of the bed and walked down the stairs. Shaking my head, I heard Jaden's TV still on. I had told this boy time after time not to leave that TV and game going all night. DTE didn't need any extra money from me.

I walked into his bedroom to find no Jaden. What the hell was he even doing up at four in the morning? I knocked on the bathroom door, no answer.

"Jaden, where you at?" I called out, searching the house. I checked all the bathrooms, bedrooms, living room, dining room, kitchen, backyard, garage, everywhere and still no Jaden. That eerie feeling came back but this time ten times harder. I started to panic. I searched the house again and again and still no son.

"911, what's your emergency?"

"My-my son is missing!" I cried. My gut instinct told me something was wrong.

"Ma'am calm down. When's the last time you saw him? Can you describe him for me?" The operator said calmly.

"I just seen him around eight p.m. I fell asleep and now he isn't home." I said in one breath. I continued talking, rambling off his physical description.

"Well, we can't put an amber alert out yet because it hasn't been twenty four hours. Has he done this before?"

Now wasn't the time to be fucking with me. "I don't give a fuck about no damn twenty four hours. He's missing and I need him found now. My son don't make disappearing acts." I yelled, this bitch was about to get her ass beat. Cop or not, I don't play about Jaden.

"Ma'am, profanity is not needed. We're going to do the best we can to find him but it hasn't been –" Before she could finish, I hung up on her selfish, incompetent ass.

I quickly dialed my brother. He could fix everything. He fixed all my problems. My hands were shaking as I waited for my brother, my lifesaver to pick up the phone.

"Hello." He answered the phone, groggily. "What the hell you're–"

"Ja-Jaden is missing Xá. I don't know where he's at." I sobbed, reality was hitting me. My son was missing and I didn't know where he was.

"On my way." He said before the line went dead. My body slid down the wall, my baby was gone. How long had he been gone? Where did he go? Was he abducted? I had so many questions with no answers to either of them.

Not even fifteen minutes had gone by and my brother was walking into my house with my mommy right behind him. She rushed by my side and hugged me tightly.

"How could this happen? Where's my son?" I cried in my mom's arms.

Xá looked at me before opening the laptop he brought with him. He hadn't said a word since he walked in. He wasn't good with expressing his feelings. When our dad passed, he shut everyone out and no one had talked to him for a couple months.

He was focused on the computer screen, his eyes trained on whatever he was looking at. "Brielle, who the fuck is this?" Xá barked, making me jump.

Me and Mama walked over to where he was, staring at the screen just how Xá was moments prior. It was a recording of the house and I never knew I had cameras here, that's just like my brother. I watched a man in all black get the spare key I kept under one of the rocks that surrounded the garden I had in the front lawn, and walk into the house. He knew the place like he'd been here before. He walked into Jaden's room and walked back out with Jaden. His body was limp like he'd been drugged. The tears kept coming as I watched this man walk through my house with my son. On his way out, he unintentionally looked at the camera. I couldn't believe my eyes.

"Miguel. His name is Miguel." This nigga really went to the extreme and took my fucking son. He had sent threatening texts, but I paid it no mind. I just thought he was a nigga who got his feelings hurt. He was just supposed to get over it like any other normal man.

"Who the fuck is that?" He asked. I could tell by the look in his eyes that he was furiated.

"I messed with him for a minute. We had an argument and he was sending me threatening messages, but I blocked him and kept it pushing."

I heard a knock on the door and I ran to the door hoping it was Jaden. Maybe he had a heart and just decided to bring him back. Instead, I was met with Brigail. I didn't even know she knew where I lived, but it wasn't the time to go at each other's throats. Surprisingly, she greeted me with a hug, and I welcomed it.

My brother was on the phone talking to one of his old friends from the old neighborhood, telling them to spread the word that there was a bounty on that nigga head for five racks. Money talks so it wouldn't be long before we caught up with that nigga. I just prayed God kept my baby safe until then.

I dialed up my son's father, E, to let him know what was going on. He needed to hear from me and not from anyone else once the amber alert went out.

"What's up baby mama? Everything okay with Jaden?" He asked the million dollar question, even I wanted the answer to.

I cleared my throat preparing myself to tell him one of the worst things that you could ever tell a parent about their child. "Ja-Jaden was kidnapped. Somebody broke into my house." I cried. The silence, then his sniffles made me cry even harder. I just wanted my baby back. Too many hours had passed since I've known his exact location and it was killing me.

"How? Brielle, how did my son get kidnapped in your fucking care? How?" He screamed. I had snot running down my face along with the tears old and new. I couldn't believe my life.

"It's not my fault, E. You think I would intentionally put my son in danger?" I screamed, the tears faded away and now I was angry. Nobody can say I wasn't a good mother. Nobody. I put Jaden first before myself or anybody else. I was fuming with so much rage. How dare he say some shit like that to me?

My brother walked up to me and snatched the phone out of my hand and away from my ear. "Aye bro, what you not about to do is make my sister feel worse than she already does. Say some dumb shit again and that may cost you your life muthafucka." He gritted through clenched teeth. I had seen my brother like this once before, the day we found out someone killed our father. It wasn't pretty and I was scared for Ethan's dumb ass.

Ethan Rivera

I sat on the couch with a tear stained face. I never cried but to know that my son was in danger and I had no way of locating him or communicating with him was eating me up.

"What's wrong babe?" Hazel asked, coming down the steps.

"My son was kidnapped." I blurted out, I had to. There was no way to sugar coat that shit.

"Your son? What son?" She asked, raising her voice higher than my liking. I wasn't her damn kid. Her kids were probably in some landfill. Who knows what they did to the bastards that didn't make it.

"I have a son, Hazel. His name is Jaden, ten years old. My baby mama just called telling me, he was kidnapped."

"Don't you think I should've known about your son before you proposed? And how is it that I never seen him or heard you talk about him? We've been together over ten years Ethan. What the fuck?!" She screeched. I knew she was furious, but this was not the time to be getting on my fucking nerves, bombarding me with questions and shit. My son was missing and he's top priority over anybody.

"Hazel, I get that you're upset. Yeah I had a baby on you, but this conversation will have to wait until my son is back."

"Good luck finding your son, Ethan. Call me when you're ready to talk about everything. I don't need no more fucking surprises." She disappeared up the steps. When she returned, her bag was filled with all her things. She left out the door without another word.

I was glad she left, I needed time to myself. Time to come up with a plan to get my son back. Time to figure out my life. Whenever something tragic happened, you have the tendency to think of ways to better yourself and the relationships you have with the people you love. My son better return without a strand of hair out of place or the whole fucking city will be painted red.

Hazel Parks

~

Time after time, I let Ethan have another chance, he finds a way to shatter my heart into more pieces. A ten year old son, really? Am I really that stupid or could he hide an entire child for ten fucking years? Ten. I cried a thousand times before but this time the pain was worse. I killed my babies thinking he wasn't ready to be a father, thinking we weren't ready to be parents but all along he had a child.

At the back of my mind, I knew Ethan would never stop cheating. He had been doing it for so long. After a while I started to accept it. I was once told that all men cheat so just pick the best man you'll want to go through the motions with.

I knocked on Syan's door, hoping she was ready to talk. We hadn't talked much since I had taken Ethan back a few weeks ago. I needed my sister back. I stood at the door with tears running down my face. I'm sick of crying. Sick of hurting. Sick of revisiting the same problems. Syan swung the door open and when she got a good look of me, she pulled me into a hug and walked me into the house. I bet I looked all types of crazy. My hair all over my head with pajamas on.

I sat on the sofa with my head laid back. Syan went into the kitchen and returned with a bottle of wine and two wine glasses.

"You got something stronger?" I chuckled but I was serious as ever. I needed something that'll take away all the pain even if it was just for the moment.

She disappeared again this time returning with Hennessy and shot glasses. That's my girl. She poured us some shots and to my surprise she sparked up a blunt. I had never smoked but it seemed perfect for the occasion. She took a pull from the blunt, letting out a cloud of smoke then catching it just to let the smoke back out. Sis must have been holding out, because as far as I knew, she had never smoked either. Bullshit.

"Sis, this your new thing?" I asked taking a pull from the blunt myself. I had seen Ethan smoke a million times, so I kind of knew what I was doing.

"Girl, believe it or not, it's because of your ass that I'm smoking in the first place." She laughed taking the blunt from me.

"Bullshit." I said seriously, I didn't want my problems affecting her like they're affecting me. My problems were just that, my problems.

"For real Haze. When you called talking about you and Ethan was getting married, I was livid. So bae fired up that good shit." She giggled, making me laugh too.

After a while of taking shots and smoking two blunts I was feeling too good. Ethan was the least of my worries and I was fine with that.

"Bitch, I'm feeling too good." I giggled, I was somewhere between tipsy and drunk as hell.

"Hennything is possible." She raised her glass to take another shot. "But sis, what's up? What happened?" She asked, setting her shot glass back on the coffee table.

"Ethan has a son. He's ten years old." I blurted out while searching her eyes.

"What? How you find out?!" She screamed, yelling at me like I was the one with the secret child.

"He was crying and shit early as hell in the morning. His baby mama had called because he had gotten kidnapped." Saying it aloud just made it sound so much dumber.

"Shut the fuck up!" She screeched in total disbelief. Hell, I was shocked too. Never in a million years would I have thought he was hiding a whole fucking child from me and for ten years. Ten years, I had been living a lie. Ten years of my life wasted on a nothing ass nigga.

"I'm not bullshitting. How the hell has he been able to hide a child from me? That's what I can't understand."

"Haze." She paused looking me in my eyes, calling me by my nickname. "You can't put nothing past niggas. Nothing that a nigga does surprises me anymore. Some of the shit they pull is unthought of and it's not for us to understand. There's some good ones out there, but a lot of them are dogs. The right one will come searching for you." She smiled, spitting some real shit to me. I had never thought of it that way but I'm glad she shed that light for me.

"Girl, I need me a Marcus." I joked, making light of the situation.

"Who the hell is Marcus?" She quizzed but it wasn't even like that.

"Girl, from 'Love Without Permission'. You haven't read that novel by Kachet'?" She needs to get with the program. I mean I know she has Hector but it ain't nothing wrong with fantasizing a little.

Chapter Eleven

~

Harmony Woods

"So how does it feel to be free?" I smiled looking between Merci and the road. She was released today and I think I was more excited than she was.

We were on our way to lunch. I wanted to take her out to celebrate. I was able to sell my car for parts and I had enough money to buy a hoopty. As long as it got me to point A and B and sometimes C, I was okay with that.

"I guess I just feel free." She giggled. I was happy to see her with a smile on her face.

I pulled into Ichiban, this Japanese restaurant. I loved their food and I preferred to eat there more than Benihana. To me, that restaurant was overrated. Really, I think people just ate there for the name. I put the car in park and we got out the car to go into the restaurant.

We were seated with a black family and caucasian couple. I still felt it was weird to eat at a table with strangers, but it was different. Being open to new and different things wasn't a bad thing. It's okay to be outside of your comfort zone once in awhile.

"Do you know these people?" Merci whispered, making me giggle softly. This was new to her.

"No. This is just how this restaurant operates. I believe it has something to do with their culture." I answered while looking over the menu.

"You know what you want?" I asked her once I had picked the combination I wanted.

"No, what's my limit? It's kind of expensive." She asked, shyly. I hate that she didn't have parents to spoil her because she deserved it. She deserved to be loved, to be thoroughly taken care of, to be protected.

"There's no limit. Get what you want." I said knowing I could make a payment arrangement for my phone bill. That's what I loved about having Sprint's service. I wanted Merci to get treated how a princess should even if it was just for today. I didn't have all the money I wanted, but I had enough for her to get what she wanted. I had enough to make this day feel special.

"Why are you so nice to me?" She asked putting a spoonful of soup in her mouth.

"Because I love you. Actually, you remind me of myself. We're a lot alike in some ways. Everyone in this world needs to know what love feels like, what it looks like. If you don't know how love feels, that's not a good feeling to have and especially not for a child. I want to help you become that lawyer you want to be. I want you smarter than I was at your age. I know things that will help you and could possibly change your life forever. It's going to take time, hard work, dedication, self love, and learning how to humble yourself. Are you down?"

"Yes, I'm down." She smiled so hard her cheeks were rosy. "And I love you too sister. More than you know." She added.

I watched her face light up in amazement as the chef did tricks while he cooked our food. It was always fun to watch them do their thing. They need to tell us not to try this shit at home somewhere in the introduction. One time I called myself mimicking the things they do and almost burned the damn house up. Everyone had a calling for their life and I knew for a fact what they do, wasn't mine.

The moment he finished with the rice and sat it on our plates, I dug in without waiting on my steak and chicken. I didn't realize how hungry I was until I started smelling that garlic and my stomach started making all types of noises. I hadn't eaten anything since yesterday night and it was going on three in the afternoon. I was a day late and a meal short.

Halfway into our meal there was chaos from some of the patrons. I looked around to see Ivory in the middle of the commotion right along with the white bitch Kendrick cheated on me with, my former professor. I shook my head, remembering that day like it was yesterday. I could never forget it.

"What the fuck you looking at?" She yelled across the room, looking in my direction. I looked around to see who she was talking to because I knew it couldn't have been me. "Yeah, I'm talking to you black bitch."

Count to ten, I said to myself, counting in my head to calm myself down. I had Merci with me and I was setting an example for her so going across her fucking head with this plate like I wanted to, wasn't setting a good example. Woosah, I continued to tell myself as I waved down the waitress so we could get our to go trays and get the fuck on. I was not trying to go to jail fucking around with Canton police.

"Come on Merci, let's go." I said grabbing my purse out the chair that was next to me.

We got up and were heading out the restaurant and of course she was on some petty shit and she stuck her foot out and tripped me and I fell hard. One of those over exaggerated falls in the movies. When I noticed my food splattered all over the floor, the same food I was saving for my movie later, I lost it. Someone should have taught her ass not to mess with a black women and especially not her fucking food.

"You don't have nothing to put over my head this time bitch." I said, removing the big ass hoop earrings I had in my ear. I turned to Merci and gave her my things. "Go wait in the car, boo. This will only be a second." I said, giving her a reassuring smile. I didn't want her to witness me beatin' the brakes off this tired ass bitch.

Without warning, I hit her in her mouth. I went for that first since the bitch had a problem keeping that muthafucka closed. I rained punches all over her face. She had this coming, it was only a matter of time. Ivory called herself trying to get me off the bitter bitch but she was no match for me. She can't do shit with me. I flung her off me and she slid across the floor.

"Get the fuck off my mama!" She screamed as she ran back up on me, grabbing me by my hair. Bitches loved to grab hair in fights. I wasn't even surprised this was her mama. Ivory could be slick at the mouth but I swept it under the rug. The apple don't fall too far from the tree.

I pushed them both off me and I fixed my clothes that were out of place. I ran my fingers through my hair and I bet I looked like a wild lion out the jungle with my thick tresses all over my head.

"You bitches better stay away from me." I warned them. I looked at her mom again, her face all bloody and bruised. I knew I shouldn't be out here fighting my elders but that old bitch was exempt. Everyone had a breaking point and that was mine. I turned around to leave, I had enough of looking at their sorry asses.

"Bae, everything okay?" I heard a familiar voice. I voice I hadn't heard in years. That voice belonged to Kendrick. I turned back around to see him standing behind Ivory, arms wrapped around her waist. Her mom looked at them with a distasteful look.

I don't know what kind of sick shit they had going on but that shit was not cool. I scrunched up my face in disgust. I couldn't believe those sick muthafuckas. What mom and daughter you know fuck the same nigga knowingly?

"You know what, all y'all gone catch a fucking disease. Sick muthafuckas." I spat, leaving out the door.

I walked to my car with my face balled all up. This is exactly why you can't trust bitches, prime example. They were too damn sneaky. You can't tell them shit about your man without them wanting to go behind your back and experience the shit for themselves. I called myself having a tight circle with one friend and now I didn't even have that.

"That was longer than a second." Merci giggled, trying to smooth out my hair.

"That's not going to do anything." I joined her in laughter. The only thing that was going to tame this hair was some heat.

Ivory Peterson

~

I know I probably seem like a bad friend for sleeping with my "best friend's" ex, but I don't feel that rule applied to me. I've always got everything I wanted, my mama and daddy made sure of it. When I saw Kendrick, I wanted him. I wasn't letting the fact that Harmony and my mama had him before deter me of what I wanted. They didn't dictate shit in my life. That's not how it works in my world. Everything was fair game, nobody's nigga was safe.

"Look at my face!" My mama screeched upon looking in the mirror. I knew she was pissed because her face was fucked up. I would be pissed too if I looked how she was looking right now or even remotely close to it.

I had called a meeting for me, my mom, and Kendrick to have a real talk. My mama needed to understand that despite their fling or whatever they wanted to call it, he was my nigga and she needed to act accordingly. Of course it didn't go well because my mom was the older version of me, a brat. No wasn't in our vocabulary, cause who's gonna tell us no?

"Mom you're too old to be fighting so you need to get it together and act your age. How you gonna explain this to dad?" I asked, rolling my eyes. She swear she's young and hip until shit like this pops off. She didn't understand that we weren't the same age. She acted more like a friend than a mother.

"I'll come up with something. I can handle your father." She said with a little bit too much attitude for my liking as she dabbed her face with cotton balls soaked in peroxide.

"Well you do that then. I'm leaving." I told her followed by me slamming the door. She need to get her panties out her ass. I haven't done shit to her. She acts like I'm the one that beat her ass.

I got into my truck and headed to the west side of Detroit where I knew Kendrick was. I didn't even need to text or call him because I already knew. His ass was glued to the hood and that shit was starting to piss me off. I pulled up to the trap on Joy Rd. that he was always posted on. Of course he was outside with a group of niggas who didn't have shit better to do. I pulled down the mirror to check my appearance and to make sure I was on point. I applied lip gloss to my plump lips and fluffed out my curly, wild hair.

When I let the mirror back up, him and his bummy ass baby mama was hugged up like he didn't have a bitch. I guess my cousin Rayneka was right. As much as I wanted to believe he wasn't fucking with his baby mama, I knew he was. Please name a nigga who wasn't still fucking his baby mama.

"What the fuck is going on here?" I barked, catching them both by surprise. They both had me fucked up.

"Man, Ivory take your ass home." He said, pissing me off even more. I wasn't with showing out in front of people and acting differently when you're around certain people. Fuck all that.

"Oh, you want me to take my ass home so you can be hugged up with the next bitch? Kendrick you really got me fucked up." I yelled loud as hell. I needed him to hear me loud and clear. I wasn't with that boosting shit.

"Ivory go home. I'll be there after I'm done handling business."

"Naw nigga, stay where you at. And you," I said pointing to Carmen's money hungry ass, "I hope you didn't kiss this nigga. My pussy was in his mouth not even three hours ago and I know his nasty ass haven't brushed his teeth since then." I smirked, thinking about how good he ate my pussy in the parking lot at Ichiban. "That shit was bomb too. I needed that nut." I added, laughing at the shocked expressions on their faces. Yeah, he had the right bitch.

I sped off, heading to Carlos house, his best friend's house. Carlos was a pretty boy and a thug all in one. Light skin, blue eyes, with a curly fro and that body was nice as hell. All muscle. I parked my car on the street a couple houses down from his house. I was smart with my shit, never caught slippin.

I knocked on the door and he opened the door a few seconds later looking all daddyish and shit. I bit my lip as my eyes traveled down his chiseled chest to the print that was visible through the gray joggers he was wearing.

"What's up?" I asked, as he stepped aside to let me inside.

"You tell me." He said with a smirk on his face. He knew exactly what was up. I stripped out of all my clothing just in case he needed reassurance on 'what was up'.

"I take it your little girlfriend isn't here." I said stepping closer to him, filling in the gap that was between us. He nodded his head 'no' and I chuckled lightly. Like I said before, nobody's nigga was safe including my cousin Rayneka's.

Chapter Twelve

~

Brielle Black

It had been two weeks since I've seen my son, my everything. I knew I was slowly losing my mind. I couldn't eat, sleep, or function. How could you with your child missing? It was like this nigga Miguel fell off the face of the earth. No one knew where that nigga was.

"Baby, you need to eat something. Here Brielle." My Mama said, handing me a bowl of homemade soup, not taking no for an answer.

I put a spoonful in my mouth. My stomach was so empty I felt the soup traveling down to my stomach. All I could do was think about my son. Nothing else mattered. Not even the fact that I needed food to survive. I didn't even know if my son was alive.

My mom had been staying at my house making sure I didn't go bat shit crazy. I was glad she was here so I wouldn't be left alone. I never liked feeling alone. My mom sat on my side, rubbing my back like she always did when I was a child while I continued to put spoonfuls of soup into my mouth.

When I set the empty bowl on the table in front of me and rested my head against the back of the couch, the doorbell rang. I jumped up, hoping it was my baby. Without looking out the peephole, I swung the door open to find no one on the porch. Not Jaden, not anyone. When I stepped onto the porch to look further outside, I tripped over a cardboard box, neatly packaged. I didn't remember ordering anything. I thought hard about it, but nothing. I wasn't looking forward to any deliveries.

"Are you going to open it?" My mom asked in her signature stance with her hands on her hips.

I picked up the box and carried it to the dining room table. "It can't be anything in here mama. The box feels empty." I said as I began opening the package. There was so damn bubble wrap it wasn't even funny. It must have been some type of joke because it couldn't have been any merchandise in the box. I removed the last of the bubble wrap and my hand instantly went to my mouth, tears pouring out of my eyes like lava out a volcano. At the bottom of the box was my son's baby toe. I knew it was his because of the mole that covered it. That was one of the things Jaden had inherited from me.

"What the fuck?!" My mom screamed.

Under Jaden's toe there was a note. *Watch how you talk to people. Remember, Karma's a bitch.*

I read the note over and over processing what it said. Did he kill my baby? My world was crashing before my eyes. The room was spinning, colors started to merge together. I felt my breathing slow down as everything faded to black.

***

I woke up in the hospital bed surrounded by my family; mama, Xá, and Brigail. Everyone except my son.

"How you feeling?" Xá asked, standing at my side.

"I feel like my heart is broken. I feel like I don't want to be here another second without my son." I cried harder than I ever had. He had been gone way too long with no communication. I wanted my baby back, I needed him like I needed air to breathe.

"Baby don't say that." My mom said, wiping the tears from her eyes. It was true. My life would never be the same without my son. What's life without my world, my reason to live? If that was how my life was going to be, I didn't want it.

"It's true." I whispered, silently praying that my baby came back soon. I didn't know how much longer I could take this feeling, the pain that resided in my heart.

Brigail came to my side and rubbed her fingers through my hair that needed special attention. I hadn't combed my hair for two weeks. All my clothes were getting too big for me because of the stress I was undergoing. I couldn't keep any weight on me.

"He's going to be home soon sister." Brigail said, as she continued playing in my hair.

Without my son, I felt so lost. Jaden consumed all of my thoughts. I see things like this happening on the news or social media, but never in a million years had I ever thought I would be front and center, going through the motions of having an abducted child. I would never wish this feeling on anybody.

"Ma'am all of your results came back negative so you're free to go. It was a panic attack and that's understanding with your current situation. I'm going to draw up the papers so I can get you out of here to go get that son of yours." She smiled and somehow, I managed to smile back.

After I got my things together, I was wheeled to the main entrance. When my mom pulled her car around, the nurse helped me into the car. I was still dizzy and I was weak mentally, physically, and emotionally. I dreaded going back home because being home didn't feel right. Nothing was the same.

Once I was in the house, I went straight to the couch to lay down. I had the worst headache ever.

"Baby girl." My mom called me by my nickname she had given me when I was just a baby. She had a huge smile on her face.

"Yes Mama?" I answered, waiting to see the reason behind her smile.

"They found him!" She screamed, giving me a big hug. My heart rate accelerated and for the first time in a long time I felt happiness. I had almost forgot what it felt like.

"Oh my God, really?" I cried tears of joy. I missed my baby so much.

"Yes, Xá is on his way to pick him up now. He said something about him being in a vacant house on Seven Mile and Van Dyke," She turned up her nose after hearing herself say it aloud. That was not a good area at all. I didn't prefer anything on the eastside of Detroit though. Yeah, all towns had bad areas, but the east side of town ranked that number one spot.

Xá Black

~

"Okay, y'all ready?" I asked the boys before we hopped out the car. I had the realest niggas with me; Hunter, Eric, and Roger. Eric and Roger was in the streets, unlike Hunter and myself, but we wasn't green to the street shit by a long shot.

"Yeah, I'm about to light this bitch up like a Christmas tree." Roger smiled. He was the craziest nigga I knew, but the nigga was as loyal as they come.

"Do what you want when I get Jaden out this dump." I chuckled, I didn't give a damn about nobody else in that house. I understood what the pigs meant when they cried guilty by association.

Hunter and Roger took the back, while me and Eric took the front. We hustled in the house and searched the house. The first floor was clear. The other guys met me in the living area after they checked upstairs. I hoped this tip wasn't no bullshit. I heard movement coming from the basement so I signaled for them to follow me.

"Let me go first." Eric said stepping in front of me. "This is my expertise bro." He gave me a stern look and I respected that. It was the truth.

When we got down to the basement, I noticed my nephew tied to a chair. This big, cocky nigga had the nerve to pour a bucket of water over his head to wake him up. That shit pissed me off.

"Wake up little nigga." He barked. The look on my nephew's face pissed me off even more. He looked sad and afraid.

"POW POW." Eric let off two shots to his knees and his big ass collapsed to the ground. All you could hear was a huge thump.

"Ahh! What the fuck?!" He whimpered in agony, holding his knees with his hands.

My nephew's face lit up when his eyes landed on mine. I said a silent prayer to the man upstairs for keeping my nephew safe. I didn't need to go to church every week to pray. I rushed to his side to untie his wrists and ankles. I carried Jaden out of the house and into the car.

"Don't get used to this shit." I joked, setting him down in the back seat. I was just happy to see him and to know that he was safe. He had a bandage around his foot and all I could do was shake my head. What type of nigga cuts off a baby child's toe? That shit was unheard of.

As I closed the back door those familiar noises sounded off "POW POW POW". Moments after Hunter, Eric, and Roger came out of the house and a white van pulled up a couple houses down. Four men jumped out the van and they exchanged words with Eric and Roger before going into the house with all types of cleaning supplies in hand. I guess they were the cleanup crew.

"They're going to make sure there's no evidence left behind." Roger said, coming up to the driver's window that was partially let down.

"Shit, nigga you know you got hit?" I asked, trying to figure out how he was carrying on like his shirt wasn't leaking blood.

"Damn." He looked down at his stomach. "Some nigga was in there hiding in the basement and came out busting at our ass. I'm good though." He shrugged his shoulders nonchalantly.

"You want to go to the hospital? That need to be looked at and observed my nigga." My face balled up as I tried to imagine how that shit felt.

"Naw bro. One of my bitches is a nurse so she can patch me up, make sure I'm Gucci." He cheesed. I guess he had it all figured out. I laughed at this nigga. He was crazy as hell, but he was a thorough nigga.

The ride back to Brielle's was one to remember. I smiled the whole way there. We were really blessed to have Jaden back in our care. There aren't too many cases where your loved ones that have been missing for weeks are found alive and well.

When I pulled into the driveway, Brielle came running out the house before the car was even in park. My little sister had been going through it the last couple of weeks. I was happy she could finally be herself again. She opened the back seat and scooped Jaden's big ass up like he weighed the size of a penny. That lil nigga was heavy as hell but I knew why, his ass didn't know how to say no to food, but then again look at who his mom is. He wasn't fat, but he was solid as hell.

"Hey baby. I've missed you so much!" She cried, as she carried him into the house. I backed out of the driveway so I could drop these niggas off. Today had been a long day. I'll check Jaden out tomorrow. My sister needed this time with her son.

Chapter Thirteen

~

Hazel Parks

"Here's your meds Ms.Brown." I said, handing my patient her daily medication along with a cup of water.

I had been at work for twelve hours out of the sixteen I had signed up for. I loved my job, but I was ready to go. I wasn't feeling good. After I took the tray, put it where it belonged, and disposed of the trash, I went to the lounge room to get a bottled water. I felt dehydrated and nauseous all in one.

I grabbed some crackers out the vending machine to put something on my stomach, because I hadn't eaten in awhile. Usually that helped me feel a little better. Two crackers later, I was running into the employee bathroom throwing up everything I had ate today. Must be a virus, I thought, or something I ate just didn't agree with my stomach. After I let it all out, I started to feel so much better, I was relieved.

After I retrieved the travel mouthwash I always kept in my purse, and I rinsed my mouth out a few times, I went back to work, ready to get my shift over with. My bed was calling my name.

"Hey baby." Ms.Evans called out to me as I passed her room.

I smiled because I hadn't seen her all day. I had taken someone else's shift, so I was dealing with new patients. "Hey Ms.Evans. How you doing today?"

"I'm making it. How about yourself?" She asked trying to reposition herself in the bed as best she could.

"I'm okay." I responded, feeling my mouth get all watery again.

"So you gonna come to my appointment next week?"

"Don't I always take you to your appointments?" I laughed, she had to be joking with me right now.

"Yes but I mean come to my appointment with me meaning I want you to sit in on my visit."

With my brows raised, "If that's what you want Ms.Evans, I'll be happy to." I smiled, Ms.Evans and I had become so close over the past few months that she'd been my patient.

"Okay, I'm going to hold you to that." She smiled.

"You do th-" Before I could respond, I ran to the nearest trash can so I could throw up. I was sick to my stomach. "Virus." I assured Ms.Evans before she said what I already knew. I grabbed the can and ran into the bathroom. After I rinsed my mouth out again all I could do was cry. Yeah me and Ethan were engaged, but I didn't want to be pregnant with his child. We still hadn't even talked since he told me about his secret child. I didn't know why this kept happening to me. I never believed it when people said they were too fertile but damn it, I believed it now.

I told my supervisor I was leaving for the day. I got into my car driving in the direction of the home Ethan and I shared once upon a time. His car was parked out front and I didn't know if that was unusual or not because I'm usually at work and he makes his own schedule. You can do that when you're the boss. I used my key and let myself in.

"Ethan?" I called out. No response. He had to be here because his car was parked outside and I saw his wallet on the table when I first walked into the house.

I started up the stairs and I heard noises. Noises that you only hear when you got the dick so deep in your throat, the only sound you can hear is your man moaning and groaning. My face was instantly balled up. I was disgusted beyond words. Not only did he have the bitch in the house he's been begging me to come back to, but he has her in my bed. I paid for that shit to be custom made. He had me all kinds of fucked up.

"So this how we doing it now?" I screamed, stopping him and the bitch dead in their tracks. I wanted to get a good look at the girl he just threw everything away for but she didn't turn around. I hope she was worth it.

"Man, Hazel get on with that shit. You know I never been faithful to your ass." He had the nerve to say it, like that validated this fucked up situation but in the fucked up head of his, maybe that dumb shit actually made sense to him.

"Yeah you right but this the last time nigga."

"So, what you thought all that shit I said and that ring meant something to me?" He chuckled, I hated his arrogant, ignorant ass. "Well it didn't, as you can see." He smiled. I couldn't help the tears that fell on their own without my permission. I was supposed to be done crying over this worthless son of a bitch.

The girl finally turned around and I felt like all the oxygen in my lungs vanished. It was like looking at my reflection. It was my twin, a twin I never knew I had. I looked at her and she looked at me with both our mouths hung open. I threw the ring at his head and walked out of his house and his life for good.

I never knew niggas could be so damn trifling. Instead of telling me about my twin, that I was oblivious to, he fucked her. He's not going to be satisfied until he catches some shit medication can't cure. Dirty dog ass nigga.

Harmony Woods

~

"Really nigga?" I screamed as I hurried to pick up all my belongings. I had never in my life met a nigga as sick as him.

"Yeah, you can go now. I already sampled the pussy." He chuckled nonchalantly.

With all my belongings in hand, I slapped fire out his ass on the way out. His arrogant ass had an ass whooping coming his way. Why the fuck would he pursue me and have sex with me if he was engaged to my twin sister? Niggas these days were a new breed. Fuck the niggas my age, I needed a sugar daddy. I'm going to find my next man at a golf club event. I'll have all type of grandaddy options, fresh out of retirement.

I cursed myself when I got outside and remembered I didn't drive. I walked a couple blocks to get to some type of business so I can have an address to send to my Uber. I got dropped off at my house and hopped right into my car. I drove in the direction of my mom's house. Although I hadn't talked to her in so long, I needed answers to all these questions in my head. She was the only one who could answer them.

Being in that neighborhood brought out so many memories;good and bad. I fingered through my long, jet black hair that I had silk pressed, remembering when I wasn't allowed to wear my hair down. I was only allowed to wear my hair in buns. As long as I lived with my mama, that was the only hairstyle you would ever see me in, even in school pictures.

I knocked on the door nervous as hell to see my mama after all these years. She swung the door open and her ass looked high off something. "Look what the cat dragged in." She laughed, opening the door up wider. Kenya, my older sister was sitting on the couch drinking a forty.

"What you doing here? You lost or something?" Kenya asked rolling her eyes and neck all at the same time being extra as always. All that fake shit wasn't even necessary.

"Naw, I just got some questions. And you," I said pointing at my mama, "are the one with the answers," I continued.

"Girl, what the fuck you want?" She asked, lighting up a cancer stick. I hated that shit and she didn't need any more habits. She looked a hot ass mess. Her hair was all over her head. Her clothes were filthy with big ass holes all over. She even had the nerve to have those saggy ass titties flopping all over the place.

"Why you never told me I had a twin?" I quizzed with my hands planted on my hips.

"What the hell are you talking about?" She asked like she was stuck on fucking stupid.

"I have a twin sister. I saw her today. Why you acting like you don't know? This is not the time to be acting clueless!"

"Girl, cause I don't. You really thought I was your real mama?" Her and Kenya engaged in a fit of laughter. I hated when people laughed at me. That was the quickest way to piss me the fuck off and have me flying off the handle.

"I should have known I didn't belong to this bummy ass strung out family. Y'all some fucking haters too. I'm glad you not my mama and if I didn't have the little respect I do have for you, I would beat yo fucking ass. Stupid bitch." I turned to leave this nasty ass house to get the fuck on before I reassemble their fucking faces.

"What you running from bitch? Fight me then scary hoe." Kenya stood on the porch like she was tough when really she didn't want or need this smoke. Just looking at her weak ass, I knew she was no match for me.

"Ain't nobody scared of yo stale face ass. Bitch please." I laughed at her dumb ass as I walked to my car.

When I grabbed the handle to my car door, I was pulled by my hair. I expected nothing less from a bitch of her caliber. I fed into her direction so she wouldn't pull my hair out. Once I got a hold on her neck, it was over. The little control she did have was gone, just like Mariah Carey's career. I punched her in the nose then her mouth. I continuously hit her in the face until she fell to her knees in surrender. I kicked her in the face before getting in my car successfully. I figured she had enough of Harmony Balboa. If she didn't know before, she knew now to not fuck with me. I hated when people tried me. That brought out another side of me that should always stay locked up.

I drove to the bar that wasn't too far from my job. I was in dire need of something strong. I needed the type of liquor that put hair on your chest. The type that made you feel numb to all your problems.

"Let me get a triple shot of Remy V.S.O.P and a double of 151 Bacardi." I told the bartender who was so kind to fetch me my order. She set the glass on the counter and I quickly threw back both glasses with no hesitation.

"Can I have another round, please?" I giggled, already feeling the affects of the liquor.

"Make sure you put that round on me." I looked up to see that sexy ass caramel God that took me home a few weeks ago.

"You really don't have to." I said pouring the contents in my shot glass down my throat. My face twisted up at the nasty ass taste.

"If you gone make that face you don't need to be drinking it. You probably can handle one of them girl drinks." He smirked, I guess he got jokes.

I playfully mushed his arm and his shit was brick hard, all that damn muscle. "Boy bye." I laughed it off.

"Baby, there ain't nothing boyish about me. I'm all man." He said in a serious tone although his lips held a smile the entire time. Between him and this liquor, my body was hot as hell and my center was pulsating.

"Is that right?" I countered, I'm an active learner. You gotta show me, all that talking is unnecessary.

"I'm sure I can show you better than I can tell you." He smirked, talking the thought right out of my head. The sexual tension between us, there was no denying that.

"Prove it." I mumbled under my breath, taking another shot to the head. Yeah, I was fasho feeling the liquor, and I was loving every minute of it.

When I tried to get up and ended up plopping right back down, I knew I had enough. I ordered some chicken wings and fries to try to sober up enough to make it home. Hunter kept me company until I was able to drive home.

Hazel Parks

~

"Ms.Parks are you sure you understand the risks if you go through with this?" I sighed heavily, because, honestly, I was tired of him asking me the same damn thing like he was a tape recorder.

"Yes I understand that I may not be able to conceive in the future. I understand that totally."

Here I was sitting in the abortion clinic I had been too many times before. After having three miscarriages and going on four abortions, I would be a fool to think otherwise. I hated that I kept coming down the same road expecting different results, but there was no way I could carry a child with the same bloodline and genetics as Ethan's ass.

It was all my fault though. I take full responsibility because I didn't have to stay but for some reason I couldn't leave. I gave him all of me when I knew he didn't deserve it. Silly me, I guess that's where I went wrong. I gave him my 'virginity' knowing he was fucking every bitch in our high school, hoping that would make him faithful. Even after that, I moved in with him after we graduated. He continued cheating and I stayed.

I stayed because I was taught to deal with the hoes as long as he took care of home, which he did financially. My foster mom assured me that I take whatever came along with Ethan, because he's the only nigga who would waste their time on a lost cause. Taking care of home may have gotten me seven unsuccessful pregnancies, Gonorrhea, Chlamydia, and a few bruised necks but I still stayed. I stayed even though I wanted more from a man than what he could offer. I made sure the house stayed squeaky clean. I made sure his dinner was ready in the microwave every night for whenever he decided to show his face. I did all the right things, but for the wrong nigga. The old naive, stupid for love me stayed, but this new strong, fierce, beautiful me knew it was time for me to leave, and forever.

"Go ahead and do the procedure." I said with finality in my voice. I wasn't changing my mind. The decision was made when I walked through the doors of the clinic.

The procedure didn't last long, but the fact that you have to be observed for a couple hours made the process even longer than it really was. I laid there on the cold bed, lost in my thoughts, thinking about the twin sister I didn't know I had. It was like I was living in a movie. Nothing made sense anymore. It's crazy how I've always wanted someone blood related to be in my corner and all the while I had a twin sister.

"You're free to go Ms.Parks." The nurse's assistant stuck her head in the door and I was so happy to hear those words.

With a faint smile on my face, I replied, "Okay, thank you."

I got up from the bed slowly. I was a little sore from the procedure. Unfortunately, this was a pain that I could tolerate because I had gotten it time after time, so I was almost just immune to it. After I called my job to let them know I wouldn't be at work today or tomorrow, I went home and got into bed.

***

My first day back to work, I wasn't feeling like myself. I hated to sulk in depression or dwell on the things I had no power of controlling, but

I had feelings, I was human. I don't know how it feels to truly be happy, and it was sad that I kept getting dealt bad hands and I was tired. I'm tired of being tired.

"What's wrong sweetie?" Ms.Evans questioned as I drove her to her weekly appointment.

"I'm just tired Ms.Evans. It's almost like I can't catch a break." I answered truthfully. It was no secret that I was sad, hurt, and depressed. Anyone who looked me in my face could see that.

"Well baby, I've been there before. It takes time for the mind to heal. You're a smart, beautiful, strong woman and I wish you weren't feeling this way. Just remember God gives his toughest angels the strongest battles. It won't always be like this." She smiled that smile that made it seem like everything was going to be okay. I couldn't help the tears that fell. I needed those words more than she knew. I wiped away my tears and went inside the office building with her.

When they called for her to go to the back, she looked at me, "Come on." She smiled, waving me over. I had forgotten she wanted me to go back with her. My mind was all over the place.

When I walked into the room, I froze up. I was met with Mr. Sexy from the gym. My eyes traveled down his muscular physique in the expensive suit he was wearing so well. It had to be tailored made just for him. He look so damn good.

"If it isn't my lucky day." He cheesed, showing off all the thirty two of his perfect teeth.

"Lucky?" Ms. Evans asked with her brows raised. This lady was a mess.

"Yes, lucky. I ran into her before, so yes this has to be luck that I've ran into her again."

All I could do was blush. My words were stuck in my throat. I hated he had this affect on me and I didn't even know his name.

"So you two have met?"

"Well not formally." He said, never taking his eyes off me. He had been staring at me since we made eye contact when I walked in.

"Hazel, this is Dr.Black, my psychologist." Ms.Evans introduced us while I stayed in the same spot, not saying a word. I couldn't. My vocals had given up on me.

"Please call me Xá." He extended his hand out to mine and I shook it.

After the introductions were out the way, they got started with their session and I sat back quietly in the recliner chair in his office space.

The room was decorated nicely. The office was painted and designed with a welcoming feel.

"So Ms.Evans we've covered everything except what bothers you most. Are you ready to to talk about it now?" She looked away and I could tell whatever it was really did bother her.

"When I was fifteen I was raped by a boy I had a crush on for the longest time. Of course with the way my life was, that one time was all it took for me to get pregnant. I didn't believe in abortion, but I also didn't want to look the child in the face with any malice in my heart because of the father and the circumstances. So I did the next best thing," She sighed and wiped the tears that slid down her vanilla skin.

"I gave them away. I was fifteen. I was a baby myself. I was still my mother's responsibility. When I told my mama I was pregnant, she acted like I was beneath her. She was disgusted with me. She didn't understand that it wasn't my fault and that I was a rape victim. I pushed my pregnancy to the back of my mind and I carried on like that wasn't my reality. I didn't go to any appointments, no ultrasounds. It wasn't until I was in labor that I found out I was having twins. Twin girls to be exact, they were so precious, but yet a constant reminder of the worst day of my life." She paused to wipe another set of tears and so did I. You would never be able to tell that she's gone through all that by taking one look at her.

"Have you had any contact with them since that day?" Xá asked her, leaning further back in his desk chair.

She sighed heavily, "I don't even know where to start. I don't know how my babies look. That was almost thirty years ago. All I can remember is the big birthmark one of my daughter's had on her back. It sat directly in the middle and it was in the shape of a slice of pizza." She laughed but I sat there with my mouth hung open. I had enough surprises to last me two lifetimes. I don't need or want anymore.

"Are you okay?" Xá spoke up, looking me into my cloudy eyes. As much as I cry, I shouldn't have any tears left. I should have been ran out, I wish it did work like that. I just lifted up my uniform shirt and no words needed to be spoken. That was more than any words could say.

"Oh my God." Ms.Evans who was now known as my mother, cried, and I just stared at her with my mind cluttered with so many thoughts. I got up from the couch I was sitting on and walked out the room.

Why couldn't my life just be simple? There were a million pieces to my puzzle, a lot of pieces were missing, but that may be a good thing. I don't want to know anything else about my life that I don't already know. I just rather be blind to it all.

Chapter Fourteen

~

Brielle Black

Time stood still as I stared at my baby. I never wanted to take my eyes off him. When I saw his handsome face, I couldn't stop crying. I was happy he came back in decent condition with nothing major wrong. The doctors assured me that his toe wouldn't affect him or his basketball career and we were both happy about that.

"Ma, stop crying." He said and I didn't even realize I was crying again. No one knew how happy and grateful I was. I thought my baby was dead. Once a child goes missing, that's usually it. By the time you see they're missing, it's too late, they're already gone. "I'm okay, everything's taken care of." He smiled, so I had to smile back at my little man. He was growing up so fast, I wish that time could slow down.

"You know you're my everything. I love you so much son." I was crying even harder now, I couldn't help it. I was just so happy he was home with me.

"I know ma. I love you too. Now stop being a cry baby." He joked and I laughed. "You're not even ready to go yet." He sighed, and I knew he was ready to have some fun.

"Okay, okay. I'll be ready in thirty minutes."

"Thirty minutes? You were supposed to be ready over an hour ago but you're a woman, so I get it. Uncle already put me hip." I stood there with the shocked face. That boy and his uncle had their damn nerve.

I shook my head and chuckled lightly on my way up the stairs to my bathroom. I cut the shower on and stepped under the hot water and lathered up with my Victoria's Secret Pure Seduction. I washed over my body thoroughly before stepping out the shower.

After ransacking my closet to find something to wear, I chose the simple look, plus we were going to Zap Zone and I liked to have fun too. I'm not that mom that stands to the side and look cute. I put on a pair of jean shorts, a baby tee, with some Puma slides. My hair was down in wand curls.

I applied red lipstick to my plump lips and grabbed my purse and I was ready to go.

"Come on baby." I told Jaden, who was sitting on the couch watching TV.

"Finally." He said, getting up. I followed him out the house and into the car.

When we pulled up to Zap Zone, I think I was more excited than he was. I needed this, I needed fun. I was a big ass kid at heart. When we went in, we went straight for the go-karts after we got our tickets. Jaden was already tall for his age, so he had no problem meeting the height requirement.

"Ma, I hope you know I'm about to dust you." He laughed, and it was funny that he actually thought that. As a child, I loved go-karts and because I was my brother's shadow, I did all the things that boys did.

"Yeah, okay Jaden. You don't have no faith in your mom, huh?" I had a fake pout on my face, but I was dying laughing inside because he just didn't know how bad I was about to dust his ass.

"Get ready ma." He said, before taking off really fast.

He was so determined to beat me. I passed him up quickly and he stayed close behind but even still, he was no match for me. Maybe in 2k or Call of Duty, but driving? No baby, I had that in the bag.

"One more lap." The conductor yelled to the drivers and I weaved in and out passing up everybody until I got back to the starting point. Of course I won, but it's no surprise to me because I already knew that would be the outcome.

"Fix your face baby." I smirked, looking at my son's face. He hated losing but he talked so much shit, I had to show him that mama can drive better. Hell, I was the one with the driver's license, not his ten year old ass.

"Well if it isn't Ms.Beautiful Brielle in the flesh." I turned around to see Christian's fine ass dressed casually in jeans, a t-shirt, and Jordan's on his feet. I could feel the moisture between my thighs as I continued staring at this sexy chocolate.

"Yeah, it's me." I smiled. Jaden stood at my side, staring at him like he was sizing him up. This little boy was going to be the death of me. "Christian, this is my son Jaden. Jaden this is my friend." I introduced them so it wouldn't be weird. Christian spoke while Jaden only offered a head nod. He was so much like his uncle it wasn't even funny.

"You're a hard woman to get in touch with." He said seriously and I thought back to all the messages and calls that went unanswered. It was nothing against him personally, but my son was missing at that time. I didn't have time to think about a nigga when I didn't know my child's whereabouts.

"Not on purpose. I had too much going on." I said, bringing my son closer, giving him a side hug.

"Well I'm glad you're feeling better now. Will I be able t-"

"Daddy." A little girl came running in our direction. She was the prettiest with her two pigtails in her head.

"Yes baby?" Christian answered and they started conversing. I admired the interaction they had. Seeing a father actually being a dad to their child always did something to me. Too many children in this world had no relationship with their fathers and that had an impact on their life, whether we cared to admit it or not.

"Can we get ice cream?" She asked with the prettiest smile on her face. With that smile, no one could tell her no.

"Yeah, we'll go in a little while. Go play, Bailey." She ran off and played at the arcade.

"So that's your little girl?" I asked, already knowing the answer.

"Yes, that's my daughter, Bailey." He smiled, looking back at her playing some monkey game.

My son had went off to play some arcade games himself, so we continued talking about life, about everything as we watched our kids play. Who would have thought?

"Ms.Brielle, when will you let me take you out?"

"When would you like to take me, Mr.Christian?" I quizzed, mimicking him.

"The sooner the better." He smiled, staring directly into my eyes."What about tomorrow?" He asked and I should have known it would have been immediately.

"Tomorrow's fine."

" I can pick you up at seven. How's that?"

"Sounds like a plan to me." I smiled, already planning out my outfit in my head. I always liked to be prepared.

***

"Mama, how do I look?" I whined, I had already gone through ten different outfits within the last thirty minutes. I wanted to look perfect, walking out the house half stepping wasn't my thing.

"Brielle Nicole Black, now I done told yo ass you look fine a million times. You look perfect."

I didn't even know why I told her to come over here. I didn't have any friends because I didn't fuck with bitches, at all. "Mama, you sure? I don't know." I said smoothing out the imaginary wrinkles in my dress.

"Girl that tight dress don't have no damn wrinkles in it."

I glanced in the mirror again for the millionth time today. I was in a Fuschia bandage dress and black strappy heels that I would pair with the matching clutch. I let out a frustrated breath of air and decided this would be the outfit I would go with. I didn't have much time, because he would be here in less than thirty minutes. I applied little eyeshadow to my eyes and pink lipstick to my lips.

I gave myself another glance in my full length mirror, just as the doorbell sounded. I fluffed out my hair and grabbed my clutch, then I headed for the door.

"Hey beautiful." He smiled and at the same time handed me a bouquet of Orchids, my favorite flower.

"These are my favorite. Guys usually go for roses." I smiled, sniffing the beautiful flowers.

"Yeah, but you have to take a different approach for a different, unique woman. I can tell you're not like any other woman in this world." He smiled and I knew my face was rosy, because I was blushing hard as hell.

I simply nodded and I followed him to his Jag. He opened the door and I sunk into the comfy plush seats. My body immediately relaxed.

"So, where are we going?" I quizzed with a slight attitude, because he had been avoiding the question all day.

"You'll see soon." He smirked, turning up the volume to the radio. I laughed at his antics. This man was something else, but I liked the way he operated.

We pulled up to a low key restaurant downriver. It was dimly lit, giving a romantic vibe. The restaurant was decorated in black and gold, with hints of red here and there. It was decorated very pretty.

"Mr. Byrd, where would you like to be seated?" The hostess asked with a lustful glare that didn't go unnoticed.

"We'll take a booth with a clear view of the water." He said sternly and she grabbed two menus and lead us to the back of the restaurant.

"This is nice." I cooed, looking at all the decor around the place.

Moments after we were seated, the waitress came to take our drink orders. I liked how they were quick paced.

"Iced tea with lemon for you, Mr.Byrd, and what can I get for you Miss?" She looked to me.

"I'll have water with lemon." I said with a smile on my face.

"You must be a regular here. They treat you so nice." I turned my attention to Christian who looked damn good in his navy blue suit. It should be a crime to be that damn sexy. It was truly a hazard for women.

"They better." He chuckled lightly before the waiter returned with our drinks.

"Are you ready to order?" The waiter looked from Christian to me.

"I'll have the stuffed Salmon with mashed potatoes and broccoli." Christian stated while handing her the menu.

"And for you?" She turned towards me,ö as she finished scribbling down his order.

"I'll have the Filet Mignon, loaded mashed potatoes, a side salad with a half order of shrimp scampi." I said, giving her my menu as well. My stomach was surely talking to me and I needed to answer in a timely manner before everyone in this establishment heard what was going on in my insides.

Christian Byrd

~

"You sure you didn't want to order the rest of the menu?" I joked and she laughed the prettiest laugh showing off her deep ass dimples. Brielle was the most beautiful woman I'd ever laid eyes on. I had to have her sexy ass. It's something about the way her beautiful brown eyes sparkled when she smiled.

"Don't tempt me. I done told you, I like to feast even though it may not look like it." She giggled, and I nodded my head in agreement. Her body was sick as fuck. She had the flattest stomach but that ass poked out and stood up just how I liked it.

The waiter brought out our food and Brielle dug in, wasting no time. She talk all that shit, but I bet my last dollar she'll be leaving with a to go box.

"This is so good." She over exaggerated, putting another forkful of potatoes in her mouth followed by a piece of shrimp.

"I'm glad you like it." I said, stuffing my face as well. She wasn't the only one who could eat.

"Mr.Byrd, do you need anything else?" Amber asked me with her hand gliding across my shoulder. Shorty was being disrespectful as hell. I glanced at Brielle and she gave Amber the side eye. From the few times I had been around her, I knew she was crazy as hell and it was only a matter of time before she showed her ass.

"No, I have everything I need right in front of me." I said, and I could tell I had hurt her feelings.

"I think that's your cue to leave." Brielle spoke up, because Amber was still lingering around like she didn't get the hint. "What's up with these chicks all up your ass? Don't bring me here again." She sassed, rolling her eyes. She had the prettiest pout on her lips.

"Maybe because I'm their boss." I chuckled, watching her pout form into a smile.

"This is your place?" She smiled.

"Yeah, it's been up and running for about two years now." I stated proudly. Being an entrepreneur had its perks but it wasn't easy. It takes blood, sweat, and tears to have a successful business. Any business owner will attest to that.

"That's so good. I love to see our black men doing their thing and not in the streets." She smiled and I could sense that she was genuinely happy for me.

"Would you two like dessert?" Ashley asked, while taking both our empty plates. Good thing I didn't make that bet aloud. True to her word, lil mama could definitely eat.

"I'll have the strawberry cheesecake." Ashley wrote her order down, then she looked to me. "I'm all set." I gave a friendly smile. Any other time I would have gladly had some of our molten chocolate brownie cake, but my tooth hurted like a bitch. I had waited thirty years to get a damn cavity. I didn't even have cavities as a child, now ain't that some shit.

After she finished her dessert, I paid the bill and left Ashley a hundred dollar tip. I knew how those college days were, broke as hell, plus she had a son to care for.

I knew what it was like to be a single parent. I was a full-time dad while Brittany, Bailey's mom, was out in the sunset with some white man in London. She couldn't be down with me when I was struggling to make it, so she took the opportunity to get out the hood, even though that meant leaving her one week old child behind. Brittany was selfish as hell. She just better stay where she at because if she tries to come around after not being around for four years, I'll fuck around and lose all the sense I do have.

"I don't want the night to end." Brielle pouted and I could honestly say the feelings were mutual. I was feeling shorty, for real.

"That makes two of us. You wanna watch movies at my place?" I asked. Bailey was with my sister for my niece's sleepover this weekend, so we would have the house to ourselves.

She looked hesitant at first, but I would be on my best behavior unless she wanted differently. Yeah, I wanted her legs up in the air with her screaming my name but I didn't mind the wait to what was eventually to come anyways.

"Yeah, you better have some good movies." She joked.

We talked the entire ride to my house out in Farmington Hills. We could never run out of things to talk about. I could see her being my best friend and wife in the future. So far, she had everything I was looking for and more.

I parked my car in my four car garage right alongside with the rest of my precious babies.

"Wow. All of these are yours?" She asked, admiring my diverse selection of cars.

"Yup." I boasted proudly.

I worked my ass off in college and after college, so I could have all the things I wanted growing up. My mama was a single parent raising seven kids by herself. She was able to make ends meet because she worked three jobs but anything extra was out of the question and I understood why. To this day, my mama wanted nothing from me, or either of my five sisters.

I was the only boy and I had been since I was ten years old. My brother was killed by a stray bullet that came flying through our kitchen window. I stayed kicking ass for my sisters after my brother passed. Having five sisters was challenging as hell. Being around all that estrogen made me wanting to jack their smart mouthed asses up every day.

We went in the house through the garage and after giving her a tour of the house, we stationed ourselves in the movie theatre I had built into my home. It was a nice size, enough to fit about thirty people comfortably.

"I love your house Christian." She complimented as she took a seat in one of the recliner, theatre chairs.

"Thank you." I said, taking a seat next to her. I watched her as she flicked through all the movies. She ended up picking White Chicks. That movie could never get old, it was a classic.

As she watched the movie, my eyes stayed glued to her, watching her face form into all different expressions. I couldn't take my eyes off her, so I studied everything about her. I wasn't no soft ass nigga but it was just something about her. She had me in a trance. She glanced over her shoulder and caught me staring at her and out of habit, my tongue glided across my lips.

I motioned for her to come to me so she got up and straddled my lap. We looked into each other's eyes and I kissed her lips hungrily, something I had been wanting to do all night. The kiss got more intense and I knew she had to feel my dick pressing against her thigh. My hands landed on her zipper and I pulled it down as she fumbled with my belt buckle on my pants. I pulled her dress over her head and I was met with her perky breasts. I wasted no time putting them into my mouth, taking my time to give both breasts the same amount of attention.

"Mhmm." She let out the sexiest moan I had ever heard from any woman. I slid my pants along with my boxers down while she was still positioned on my lap.

"You gone ride this dick?" I groaned as she sucked on my neck hungrily.

She grabbed my dick and glided it into her wet, tight pussy that gripped my dick tightly. I bit the inside of my jaw to keep from crying out like a lil bitch. Lil mama's pussy was lethal, shit held a death grip on my dick.

"Oh shit." She moaned sexily as she sped up after adjusting to my size. I didn't want to bust prematurely cause I wasn't a minute man, but that shit was coming, it was out of my control.

"Christian!" She screamed out my name and at the same time I felt her juices covering my dick. Her body was trembling something serious.

"Fuck.." I groaned, as I shot my soldiers inside her. It wasn't until now that I noticed I had went in raw. Yeah, shorty had my mind gone. "This shit is a long way from over." I whispered in her hair as I carried her to the master bedroom with my dick still pulsating inside her. I hope she was ready for this dick lashing that was coming to her.

Chapter Fifteen

~

Hazel Parks

"Hey boo." I said, giving Syan a big hug. It felt like we hadn't seen each other in ages. We were living our own lives.

"Hey sis. What's up with ya?" She quizzed, switching Jr. from her right to left side. He was getting so damn big, time waited for no one.

"Girl nothing. I'm just taking one day at a time." I sighed, thinking about the past few events of my life. I've said it before and I'll say it again, my life was like a damn movie.

Coming to terms with Ms.Evans being my mom was weird at first, but after I saw the DNA results that she was 99.9 % my maternal parent, I was coming to grips. The idea of having a mom that truly loved and cared for me is an indescribable feeling. I just wished she was apart of my life from the start.

"How's your mom?" She asked and I could tell by her facial expression that it sounded funny rolling off her tongue.

"She's doing okay. I just wish I could get her out of there and take care of her from home, but I have bills to pay." I retorted, feeling myself getting upset. The love I had for my mama had grown exponentially since I found out that she was my mom, if that makes any sense.

Giving us up was what she felt was best. Being a rape victim is not easy to deal and cope with and it'll be forever embedded in your memory. I understand her more than she knows. I would never hold that over her head.

"It'll all work out sis. I told you I would handle the bill to hire a caregiver for her." She sassed, knowing I would never let her do that. I had people coming to my rescue for as long as I remember. I just wanted to be my own hero and figure things out on my own, without the help of anyone.

"I'll find a way," I said, stuffing a potato chip in my mouth. "What's been going on in your world? I feel like we're out of touch." I quizzed, trying to get the scoop on what was happening in Syan's World?"

"Girl, I've been so bored, trying to stay busy since I quit my job. I've rearranged all the furniture in the house, I don't know how many times, even in my bedroom, trying to busy myself." She explained, all in one breath. I already knew she was going to do that because her ass can't stay still. She has to be actively doing something. I kept telling her ass she had ADHD.

"Why you can't just sit your ass down somewhere?" I laughed, knowing she wouldn't be able to sit still even if you paid her to.

"I got five racks for you right now if you can stay still for an hour." Hector came into the living room laughing.

"What's up brother?" I gave him a hug. It had been a minute since I'd seen Hector and I missed all of them. They were my only family for years.

"Shit, just tryna keep that cash coming in so my family can stay eating good." I had so much respect for him. His dedication to taking care of his family was so strong. He worked so hard to keep them living the lifestyle that they had.

"I wish more men were like you." I smiled, watching him take Jr. out of Syan's arms.

"Girl, no you don't. We don't need no more Hector's walking around." She joked, prompting me to join her in laughter. Together, they were a hot ass mess.

"Well, I have to take my mom to this grand opening, so I'll see y'all later." I waved them goodbye and walked to my car.

I wasn't in the mood to be around people, especially not Xá. Every time I was in his presence, he had the power to make my whole body quiver. The way his eyes looked into mine had my center hot and my pink pearl thumping. I wasn't ready to be around a man who already had a way of controlling me and my body. But I had to suck it up because I had already promised her that I would bring her.

"Hey ma." I said, shocking the hell out of me and her by the look on her face. I felt weird as soon as the words left my mouth.

"Hey baby." She smiled harder than she ever has.

We rode to the center in silence with us probably in our own thoughts. When we arrived, it was jam packed. I had to park down the block. It looked like everyone in the city had come out and were in attendance. I loved to see black people support one another. That wasn't something you see everyday, but when you did, you were genuinely happy.

When we walked to where all the patrons were standing around, I spotted Xá looking GQ fine, dressed to impress, in a tailored made Gucci suit and standing alongside him was another fine ass nigga that matched his fly.

"So who's ready to see the inside?" Xá asked the crowd. Everyone made their own cheering sounds simultaneously. "Before we go in, I just want to thank everyone for coming. Our mission is to give back to the community and to help our youth get on the right track. Everyone needs that one person in their corner, but in this case you'll have two. Now that, that's out the way, let the party began." He chuckled lightly and I laughed too. He looked around the crowd and when our eyes connected, butterflies filled my stomach and a chill went down my spine. See that's that shit I'm talking about. He graced me with his pearly white smile before he turned towards the door and him and his partner, I assumed, grabbed either of the doors and pulled them open.

As I walked through the building, I was taken back of the decor all over. The lobby was filled with couches and lounge chairs. Behind the front desk were two comfortable looking office chairs and two of the newest Macbooks. The walls were painted mint green with colorful abstract paintings strategically placed around. There was a gym, auditorium, offices for therapists, game room, movie theatre, library. It had everything youth needed and wanted.

"Hey beautiful." I could never forget his voice even though I hadn't even had that many encounters with him. His deep baritone voice was everything and unforgettable.

I spun around and faced the sexiest nigga in Michigan. He had to be. "Hey." I smiled, taking in his appearance. He looked even better up close and personal. His hair looks like God himself lined it up.

"How have you been?" He asked, his pretty brown eyes staring into my hazel ones.

"I've been doing okay. I see you've been doing good. Congratulations are in order." I cooed. I was very proud of him even though I didn't know him that well. Seeing black men overcome the everyday stereotypes and obstacles that are thrown their way from damn near every direction should have been enough to put a smile on everyone's face.

"Thank you. So be honest, how does it look in here?" He asked, rubbing his sexy long beard that he wore so damn well.

"I love the decor. I'm impressed Dr.Black." I smirked, already knowing what was next to come.

"Call me Xá. Let's keep it as unprofessional as possible." He smiled, showing all thirty twos. I could feel my thong moistening and my nipples hardening. I was long overdue for some dick and the sexual tension between us was very tense. I'm positive that he could feel it too. "So, with that being said, when you gonna let me take you out?" He continued. My body screamed now, but my heart yelled never. I wasn't ready to open up my heart so fast.

"Job well done." My mom said, interrupting my response. I was jumping for joy in the inside because I didn't know what to say. I didn't need my heart broken again when it was never even healed completely.

"Well thank you Ms.Evans. I only paid top dollar for this outcome." He chuckled, making me and my mom laugh.

"No problem sweetie. I give credit when it's due." She said looking around to admire the decor. Her beautiful smile turned upside down as she stared at somebody in front of us. I followed her gaze and there was a tall, dark skinned man with specks of gray hair. He was older but good looking to say the least.

"Who's that?" I quizzed, wanting to know who this man was that altered her demeanor so quickly.

"That's him." She looked off to the side. "The man who raped me...Your father."

I looked back in his direction for a second time and my mind had to be playing tricks on me. Him and my twin sister were conversing like shit was sweet. Rape was a very sensitive subject for me for obvious reasons. I had been a victim of rape since I was the tender age of ten. Before she could say anything else, I rushed towards his sick, nasty ass. My stomach turned in knots as I envisioned the shit he did to my mama.

"You're a sick muthafucka." I grimaced, giving him the meanest mug ever, pointing my finger all in his face. I know that gesture was disrespectful but he clearly wasn't thinking about disrespect when he forced his nasty dick inside my mama's youthful, innocent vagina.

He glanced between me and my twin but that wasn't the topic of discussion. Unfortunately, it was his nasty ass.

Harmony Woods

~

I stared at my newfound twin as she called my boss out on his shit. Before we were interrupted, he was offering me a promotion that had better pay, more benefits, and more hours. I was all ears but this confrontation peaked my interest just the same.

"Do I know you?" He asked, never changing his demeanor.

"Naw, but you're the nigga that raped our mother. Nasty ass." She snapped, pointing in the direction of a pretty older lady in a wheelchair.

When she saw all eyes on her, she wheeled herself towards us. When she got to where we were, she mugged Mr.Robinson so hard that I could feel her anger.

"I thought I forgave you after all these years but seeing your face disgusts me. Why Timothy? To impress your friends?" She snapped, tears coming down her face.

"I-I-I was young and dumb. If I can go back in time, I would take all that shit away. Kim, I wasn't thinking. I'll apologize a billion times, but that'll never change what happened. I'm sorry." His eyes glistened as he apologized. I felt the sincerity in his voice but that wasn't for me to judge.

"Wait a minute." I joined in, realizing what the fuck was really going on. "Y'all are our parents?" I looked into both their eyes.

"Yes." My *mom* said and Timothy's shocked expression told me that he had no idea. I'm glad he didn't.

I felt sick to my stomach as I thought about all the times he had came on to me, tryna shoot a shot he would never land, when all along I was his damn child. This is some ole Jerry Springer type shit that I didn't want to deal with. I couldn't catch a break from the bullshit. It was one thing after another coming at me like a raging bull. My life was more complicated than Lebron James' hairline and the uncertainty of the sex of Wendy Williams.

"Well neither of you are no parents of mine. Where were y'all when I needed you most?" I yelled louder than I intended. It's like everyone had stopped what they were doing and conversations had ceased as they looked in our direction. I didn't come to cause a scene, but with the way my life was set up, anything was bound to happen.

"It's not the time nor the place for this discussion so let's leave it at that." My *mom* stated sternly. I looked at them all once more before I walked away in search for Merci. She was the reason I was in attendance in the first place. I had done my research on this new center and I knew it would benefit her in more ways than one. She needed more than just me in her corner.

"Why everytime I see your beautiful face it's always balled up?" I turned around and was met with Hunter's sexy ass.

"Probably cause you're only around when I' in a sour ass mood." I retorted, trying to act more pissed than I really was.

"Well let me sweeten that up for you." He smiled, as if my panties weren't already soaked.

He had the type of vibe that made you smile. No matter how mad I was, he found a way to break down every barrier I had up. "I don't know Hunter." I smiled, matching his.

"At least let me do that more often." He said, taking a sip of whatever was in his cup.

"Do what?" I asked with my brows furrowed. There was no telling what was going to come out of his mouth next.

"Make you smile." His eyes stared a hole through mine as he waited for a response, something. But in return, he got nothing. I had comebacks for days but in this moment, I had nothing to say. I hated how my mind and my body reacted to him. I was wide open for him and I didn't like that shit at all. But no matter how I tried to front, the effects he had on me were something serious.

"Hunter, could you come to the front please?" Some guy spoke through the microphone with sex appeal all in his appearance.

He looked at the guy who was calling him to the front then back to me. "Let me get your number at least. I let you slip away too many times, but not this time." He handed over his phone and I keyed it in, smiling so hard on the inside. I didn't like the fact that I was falling for the idea of him and I didn't even know his last name. He swiftly walked away as he stole glances at me on his way to the front.

"Who was that?" Merci asked, standing at my side with a plate of fruit in hand. Her ass was always eating. She was the type who could eat all day without gaining a pound. See me, I had to frequent the gym to keep my body to my liking. If it wasn't for the gym, I know for a fact that I wouldn't be the size twelve that I am, thick in the hips and slim in the waist. I'm as slim thick as you can get.

"Just a guy that I met some time ago." I stated nonchalantly, avoiding eye contact with her. I didn't want her to see the silly grin that appeared on my face whenever I thought of him.

"Can I have your attention?" He tapped the mic lightly so all the patrons would look at him. "I'm Xá Black and this is my partner Hunter Williams. We're the guys behind this master plan. We couldn't do this without the help of Sasha, out interior designer, and the people who helped get this place up and running, our sponsors..." He trailed off as he gave thanks to everyone who helped with the great establishment.

I stared at Hunter with so much respect. To know he wanted to help the youth and give back to the community as much as I did, made my insides smile. Having support from positive people as a young adult can benefit the youth greatly. You have to really embed positive things in their heads in their teen years, so they can take heed in the knowledge you're giving them. With that fruit, just watch how they'll grow and succeed.

As the place started to clear up, Merci and I prepared to leave. The grand opening was very nice and I'm looking forward to the positive impact they will have on our youth. I saw my twin on the way out and I had to say something. At the end of the day, she was my sister. I had gone long enough without knowing her, twenty eight years to be exact.

"I know the circumstances aren't ideal, but I need to at least know my sister. I'm Harmony." I said with a friendly smile on my face.

"I'm Hazel, take my number down so we can talk and link up soon." We exchanged phones so we could put our phone numbers in each others phones.

We went our separate ways, but I planned on hitting her up ASAP. I always wanted someone in my corner but they all turned out to be temporary, part-time. Meanwhile, I had a whole ass twin sister. Shit was beyond crazy.

Chapter Sixteen

~

Syan González

"Hey mommy's man." I cooed in my mommy voice. The smile on his face always brightened up my day.

"Mama." He said, as clear as day, and I was so happy that I felt a lone tear trailing down my cheek. This was his first word and I hated that my husband was out working, missing this special moment.

I dialed up his number, hoping that he wasn't busy and could talk. Monday was always his busiest because that's when his shipment came in. I hung up the phone and called right back, but there was still no answer. Because he didn't answer, I called the next best thing.

"Girl, I swear I was just about to call you." She laughed into the phone. It's crazy how we always try to call each other at the same time.

"What's up with you?" I quizzed, pushing my exciting news to the back burner.

"No, you first."

"Okay, okay. Sonny boy said his first word." I smiled, calling Jr. by the nickname I gave him, fresh out the womb.

"Yayy. What he say, TT?" She asked seriously. She swore up and down that she's his favorite lady. That's not even the case, but she could take the spot right after me.

"Girl, no." I laughed at her silly, delusional ass. "He said mama." I continued, my cheeks were hurting because I couldn't stop smiling.

"He's so smart. He gets that from me though." She joked, well at least I hoped she was. He most definitely took after his mommy, but you couldn't tell her that.

"Yeah, you keep believing that." I chuckled. "But, what's the tea on the life of the infamous Hazel Parks?"

"So this guy is trying to take me out but my guard is up but I wanted to give him a chance. He seems like a nice guy." She continued to ramble about the uncertainty of opening up for another guy. I understood where she was coming from, but all guys aren't the same, although most of them are.

"I say give him a chance Haze. Every guy isn't like Ethan's dirty ass." I sighed, feeling sorry for all the shit Ethan's put her through. Her twin, though? That was the icing on the cake. Fuck him and everything associated with his stupid ass. "How he look though? That's the real question." I pried, as best friend that was a key component and I needed to know what we're working with.

"Sy, let me tell you. He looks good enough to eat and you know I don't even fuck with that kind of meat." She joked. Her ass claimed she didn't like sucking dick, but I didn't know why. I liked knowing the fact that my grade A head is the reason for my husband's nut. A lady once told me, a nigga can't cum off head, and I looked at that bitch like she was crazy. Sis, you just don't know what you doing, that's what I should have told her ass. You can't keep it cute, they like that shit sloppy.

"Well if it's like that, hurry up and date his ass so I can see him." I laughed, but we both knew I was serious as hell.

"Yo ass is crazy." We both fell out in laughter. "But I think I will go ahead and follow your advice."

"Good, you get to that cause I gotta go. Hubby's calling." I said, seeing that Hector was trying to Facetime call me.

"Hey baby," I sung into the phone, I was missing his ass something serious.

"What's up bae?" His deep voice resonated through the phone, causing the hairs on my back to stand.

"I miss you and your son said his first word." I pouted, I was real life sad, cause I was missing my other baby.

"Word?" He asked, smiling harder than I was. I knew he was going to do that though. He was all about his kids, nobody could deny that.

I nodded my head yes. "He said mama. I wish you were here to hear it for yourself. When are you coming home?" I whined, acting like a brat, but I missed my husband. What else was I supposed to do?

"We wrapping this shit up now, but I'm going to check on Gabby when I leave. Lisa been blowing my shit up like she fucking dumb. I'm trying not to kill her ass." He snapped, rubbing his temples. I could see the stress on his face. But what did he expect to happen? That's what his ass get for fucking with a lazy, needy rat bitch.

"Well, hurry back to me. We need you." I seductively said, so he could know for sure the tip I was on.

"Okay baby. I love you." He said, trying to kiss me through the phone.

I puckered my lips to match his. "I love you too boo, now hurry." I ended the call and continued playing with my baby boy.

I had to have cleaned up the house over and over about a thousand times. Dinner was done, I had prepared baked chicken, loaded potatoes, and broccoli. The baby was asleep and I was bored out of my mind. Me and Hector ended our call two hours ago. He should have already been back, or at least called me to check in. I dialed his number back to back with no answer. He better have a superb reason to why he let my calls go unanswered or his ass is mine and that's guaranteed.

Hector

~

"Daddy!" Gabby screeched, upon seeing me coming through the front door.

"Hey pretty girl." I said, picking her up in the air. I held her up in the air so that she was pretty much kissing the ceiling. Her crazy ass liked that shit. She loved when I did that.

"Umm, I am sitting here." Lisa irritating ass said, probably thinking that would make me speak to her. Little did she know, I had spoke to her enough to last me a lifetime.

I looked over Gabriella and noticed she still had her ballet clothes on. "Aye, what time is it?" I looked at Lisa, I had left my phone in the car because I didn't plan on staying long.

"It's ten, why? You gotta run to your perfect wife?" She asked, rolling her eyes and neck all at the same time. Sometimes I look at her and I want to smack my own ass for fucking her trifling ass. But at the same time, I wouldn't have my daughter if I didn't.

"So why the fuck has she not taken a bath yet?" I said, covering up her ears so she wouldn't hear me. Her bad ass already be trying to sneak curse words in her vocabulary.

"She can take one in the morning, damn." She snapped. It took everything in me not to choke her ass up. I don't know how the dumb shit she says registers in that big ass head of hers.

I looked at her ass disgusted that she was even my daughter's mother. I didn't even have no words for her simple ass. I carried my daughter to her Frozen themed bathroom, that was in her room. I had copped them this crib cause she was a damn fool if she thought she was going to continue staying in the King Homes with my seed. I ran her a bubble bath and sat her in the tub after she undressed herself.

I smiled as I watched her innocent face light up as she played with her toys and splashed bubbles every fucking where. Whenever I bathed her, she never wanted to get out.

"Come on baby girl. It's time to get out." She had already been in here damn near an hour.

"Already?" She whined, batting those pretty lashes. She was six but had the manipulation skills of a grown woman. Lisa was her mama, so that should have been expected.

"Yes, baby girl. Daddy has to go." She looked at me with sad eyes and grabbed her towel and stepped out the tub. I hated that I couldn't come home to her, but she needed her mommy. If it was up to me, she would be under the same roof as me, Syan, and her baby brother.

"Good night baby." I said, tucking her into bed.

"But daddy, I'm hungry. Mommy hasn't made dinner yet." I felt like Lisa was trying to get murked. She stayed trying me.

I grabbed my daughter up and walked in the kitchen to see Lisa standing over the stove. Who the hell eats dinner at eleven at night when you have a kid to feed. You can do that shit when you're not a parent. She didn't understand the responsibilities that came along with being a mother.

"What you making, mommy?"

"Fried chicken, mac & cheese, and cabbage."

"Daddy, can you eat dinner with us please?" She begged with her hands pressed together like she was waiting on her prayer to get answered. She was a piece of work.

I shook my head and just walked over to the dinner table. "Anything for you princess." I smiled, giving in to her manipulative ass. She's lucky because I didn't want to spend any more time around Lisa than I had to. I started to just take her with me and just order some pizza, but the way her face lit up as she asked me to stay is the reason why my ass is sitting down at the table.

"Well if she's the Princess, I have to be the Queen." She smirked, setting the plates in front of us,

I paid her ignorant ass no mind, as I said my grace over the food and dug in. To my surprise, it wasn't bad and didn't taste like dog food how I remembered. We ate in silence with a weird vibe in the atmosphere.

"What do y'all want to drink?" Lisa asked, getting out of her chair. Her ass was gonna fall off by the way she was switching so damn hard in those little ass shorts. Shit wasn't necessary, because I damn sure wasn't checking for her ass.

"Can I have apple juice, mommy?" My daughter's eyes lit up when Lisa shook her head, yes. She loved that damn juice. Me personally, I wasn't drinking shit that could be passed for piss. I didn't even drink beer.

"And for you baby daddy?" She grinned, knowing I hated when she called me that dumb shit.

"You got lemonade or pop?" I asked with a raised eyebrow. I was sick of water, I needed some shit with some flavor.

"I have Mountain Dew." I nodded my head and she went into the kitchen to get our drinks.

When she returned with our drinks, I drunk mines in one gulp. I was beyond thirsty. My body started feeling off almost immediately. I looked at my daughter as she continued eating her food without a care in the world. Lisa stared at me with an unreadable expression and that's when I realized what was happening, but it was too late. I thought of all the ways I could kill her ass if I made it out alive and then eventually my vision faded completely.

Lisa Mitchell

~

"Why is daddy sleeping?" My daughter looked at me with questioning eyes. "Daddy, get up," She yelled, and I silently laughed. It was going to take more than that to get his ass up.

"Go to your room now." I hollered at her and her cry baby ass started screaming at the top of her lungs like I was killing her. If she kept that shit up, I just might. I didn't have em' all and she was trying the little patience I did have. "Shut the hell up before I give yo ass something to cry about!" I retorted, saying the bitch who I call mama, favorite's line. She said it so much, I could have easily mistaken it for my damn name.

Once she stumped her way to her room, I made sure her door was closed so I could proceed with my mission. I dragged Hector's heavy ass to my room. It took all the strength I had to get him in my bed. Because he was unconscious, his dead weight almost made it impossible for me to maneuver his body. I laid him in my bed and I unbuckled his jeans to release the beast I'd been craving for over six years. I took him into my mouth, so I could get him nice and hard.

This may seem over the top. Yeah, if he wanted me in this way, I wouldn't have to go through these extreme measures. But in this world, you have to do what you have to do to get what you want. And right now, I wanted to have his baby. Surely, that wife of his won't be pleased with him having a baby on her so that'll send him back my way, the next best thing.

"Oh shit", I moaned as I rode his thick dick. I had forgotten just how good it was, I wish he was enjoying it as much as I was. I bounced up and down fast and steady with one hand playing with my nipples and the other toying with my clit. I was riding the wave to a bad ass orgasm.

"Daddy, you like how my pussy feel?" I moaned, speeding up the pace. His dick was brick hard, so I knew he was about to release as well. "Fuccck." I screamed out in pure pleasure, releasing my juices all over his dick.

I smiled as I seen the cum still oozing out his dick. I grabbed a small container especially for this occasion and I jerked him off and the cum flowed freely into the cup.

"Come get him." I roared into the phone. When his ass woke up, I didn't want to be nowhere in sight.

I cleaned us both up and put his pants back on then waited on my cousin's arrival. It took him all of thirty minutes to get here.

"Where the money at?" He asked before he was even all the way in the house. Reggie had just gotten out of prison a couple weeks ago, which is why I knew he would do this favor for me as long as I threw him some cash.

I rolled my eyes at his money hungry ass and searched Hector's pockets. The years that I've known him, he always has a couple stacks on him at all times. That shit was dumb to me, but whatever floats his boat. I smiled as I pulled out two stacks of Benjamins. I gave him one and took the other for myself. Somerset Mall, here I come!

"Here nigga." I barked, handing him over the bills and his face lit up like the Fourth of July.

"So where to cousin?" He smiled, counting out his money.

"Drop him and his precious car somewhere in Brightmore." Hopefully that nigga gets a chance to wake up, it's some dirty skeemish niggas that way. "Oh, and if this shit come back to me, I'm killing you and that bitch." I said, pointing towards the door. His ass didn't have a whip, so he had no choice but to involve somebody else in this shit. All I know is, they better keep their mouths closed or they'll be casket sharp, cousin or no cousin, I don't give a fuck.

Chapter Seventeen

~

Brigail Jenkins

"What is this?" Jordan barked, coming into our bedroom. I sighed heavily as I looked at him holding the ultrasound of *our* baby. I wasn't in the mood for any bullshit. I had a banging ass headache and my body was weak from me going to the bathroom countless times, throwing up everything I had left in me.

"It's the ultrasound of *our* child, Jordan. I'm pregnant." I said, trying to suppress the urge to throw up again.

"And when did you plan to tell me? Huh, Brigail?" He yelled, his tone louder than I anticipated. I looked at him with my brows raised, because this nigga officially had me fucked up.

"Whenever I got around to it. What's your issue? We've been married for seven years and we have no kids."

"I just should have found out the same time you did. How far along are you?" He asked, softening his tone. He better had for his own damn sake.

"Only a couple months. We have a long way to go." I sighed, already dreading this pregnancy but it was only the beginning.

"I bet I have a little junior in there." He smiled, rubbing on my still flat stomach.

"Or we have a little princess." I smirked, crushing his dreams. In order to have a junior, it has to be his right?

"Whatever, y'all not having family dinner today?" He asked me, as he typed away on that damn phone.

"Oh my God. I totally forgot!" I screeched as I jumped up, heading straight for the shower. I had been in the bed all day except whenever I had to regurgitate.

I took a quick shower, trying my best to really make it quick. I already knew my mom would be down my throat because of my tardiness. After lotioning my body with Michael Kors lotion, I threw on some ripped jeans, a peplum top, and my Giuseppe heels.

I applied a little foundation to my caramel skin and I put on bright red lipstick to my perfectly shaped lips. I took my bonnet off my head and let my shoulder length hair fall into place. I was fine ass hell and I knew it too. Not to mention I was stacked like a Video Vixen. Excuse my language, but I'm a bad bitch. I spritzed some perfume onto my body, before I grabbed my keys and purse and headed for the door.

I hopped on the highway in my freshly waxed BMW and cruised all the way to Brann's Steakhouse and Grille in Northville. I pulled up to the restaurant forty minutes later, mentally preparing myself for the tongue lashing I was about to get from my mom.

As I approached their table, I could see my mama glancing from me and her Apple watch repeatedly. I bet that's all her non-technological ass could do, was look at the damn time. "Do you know what time it is?" She snapped and I could see Brielle and Xá laughing in my peripheral. They had always been childish as hell starting from when we were babies.

"Yes mama, I totally forgot. I've been in bed sick all day."

"Well you should have at least called. You know this is very important to us." She sassed, dismissing the fact that I was sick. That had to count for something, but to Ms. Brenda Black, late was late, reasonable excuse or not.

"You right, sorry mama." I sighed, agreeing with her just so she could get off my back. It was bad enough I was throwing up my whole damn life.

"Damn it." She mumbled under her breath. She had to have the last word, it never fails. No matter if she closed it off with saying a number, she was gonna be the last one talking. Mama is a piece of work. I don't know how my dad put up with her ass all the years that he did.

"Brielle...Xá." I huffed, taking my seat next to Mama.

"Wassup sis." He spoke without looking up from his phone. By the way he was cheesing, I already knew what was up. Smiling like his life depended on it.

"Hey sister." Our relationship was better than it had ever been. Honestly, I think my nephew's kidnapping made us closer. A child can take your vulnerability to another level and her going through that, made her grow up and mature in a way. She was more mindful of the things she did and said. Well her overall disposition as a whole.

"Did y'all order yet?" I asked, looking over the menu. I didn't realize I was hungry until I started reading the menu.

"No, we were waiting for your grand entrance." My mama said, obviously still feeling some type of way. She was the Queen of petty.

The waitress came moments later, and we were all set to order. My stomach was growling something serious, so I even ordered an appetizer. When she came back with the wings, I got straight to it.

"So, who is the woman behind that smile?" I asked my brother. It was no secret that that was the case. He paused and looked up from his phone to make eye connection with me.

"We not official yet, but it's coming. Her name is Hazel." He smiled, showing all thirty twos. Sis had to be a force to be reckoned with, the way he was carrying on.

"Hmm...I see." I said and switched the spotlight on Brielle. "So, who's the new man in your life?" She was a fool if she thought for a second that I didn't know she had gotten some act right.

"Umm, I have a man now. His name is Christian." She nervously smiled, probably assuming Xá was gonna have a slick ass comment. Sometimes, he acted like he was our damn daddy and I was the oldest.

"What that nigga do?" Xá asked, setting his phone down on the table. I'm guessing he was all ears now.

"He's actually a businessman." She smirked, feeling confident in her answer.

He chuckled lightly, that was his way of not going off. "You know usually when a nigga says that, he's in the illegal business. That's not what you want Brielle."

"Naw, he's legit. He has restaurants and everything." She smiled and I could see that she was truly happy.

"You talking about Cocky Christian, last name Byrd?" He asked with a sly grin on his face.

"Yeah, how you know him?" She, quizzed and I too, wanting to know his answer.

"College. Those were the wild days. We called him Cocky Christian cause that's a big nigga." He laughed. We always say the world is small, but you never know just how small it really is.

Xá Black

~

Brielle looked at me like she wanted to say something but she didn't. Whatever it was, I'm glad she thought twice about it, because I didn't feel like getting in her ass today.

"Mama, we'll be having a little meet and greet dinner at your place real soon. I give it a month. We can bring our dates." I said. It sounded like a plan to me. I hope Hazel was ready to be somebody's wife. I was too old to have girlfriends and shit.

"You good?" I asked my sister who looked like she was about to throw up. She held up her finger signaling for me to hold on and she jetted in the direction of the bathroom. Everyone started looking at one another, giving each other that look. We were always on one accord.

When she came back to the table, we all stared at her waiting for some type of explanation.

"Stomach flu." She mumbled once she saw everyone looking at her.

"It's safe to call bullshit on that one. Spill it." Brielle demanded, saying what we were all thinking.

"Okay, Okay. Jordan and I are expecting." She replied and I could tell by her expression and body language, she wasn't jumping for joy how most married women would be.

"About time." My mama blurted out because she wanted a bunch of grandkids and she only had one. In her mind, she was long overdue.

After we wrapped it up with family dinner, I headed to Hazel's place. This was our official date and my grown ass was excited to see her sexy ass. It took me a little minute to get there. She had a nice little house in Rosedale Park. I shot her a text letting her know I was outside.

Me: Outside

Future: Be out in a sec.

Moments later, she came outside dressed in a sundress and even though it wasn't skin tight, you could still see all those damn curves and dips the good Lord blessed her with. Her jet black hair was blowing in the wind as she approached the car. I hopped out the driver door and opened the passenger door and I helped her into my custom Rose Gold Chrome s550.

"Hey beautiful." I said, lusting over her and that sick ass body of hers.

"Hey, you don't look so bad yourself." She giggled, as I rounded the car to get in on the driver's side.

"How was your day, beautiful?" I asked, heading in the direction of Downtown.

"It was good. What about yours?"

"Better now that I'm with you." I smiled, spitting game like a muthafucka. I had her right where I wanted her.

"Is that right?" She giggled that pretty ass soft laugh.

"Yeah. You know what yo moms told me at our last session?" I asked, pausing as I looked at her. She motioned for me to continue. "She said she like me and all but if I fuck with her baby, that's my ass and after the ass whooping, I would just have to get over it cause she's going to continue seeing me as her psychologist ." I laughed all over again. That lady was funny as hell and crazy too.

"She's a mess." She said, shaking her head. If you were to look at their bond and see their connection, you wouldn't be able to tell they found out they were mother and daughter a few months back.

We continued to make small talk about everything. It was so easy to talk to her. I hated when I had to force a conversation out of people. In this case, it just flowed naturally. I found a parking garage to park my whip. I grabbed my duffle bag and mini cooler and we found a spot on the Riverwalk.

"This is so nice." She complimented as she watched me lay down the blanket and I even scattered some rose petals all over. Yeah, ya boy got sisters, so I was hip to all the romantic, girly shit women fantasize about.

"I try." I chuckled, patting my own self on the back. "Have a seat, sit back and enjoy the view." I said, pulling her between my legs. With the connection we had, I felt like I've known her my whole life.

"Is this an act, Dr.Black, or you're like this all the time?" She asked out the blue, catching me off guard.

"Baby, what you see is what you get. I'll never switch up, if that's what you want to know. You'll see once I make you my woman."

"You sound so sure." She smirked, looking up at me, her hazel eyes sparkling like diamonds. I saw an opportunity so I had to take it. I leaned down and planted a kiss on her soft ass lips.

"That's because I am. Are you hungry?" I asked, opening the cooler filled with chocolate, strawberries, mini sandwiches, and wine coolers.

"Sure am." She laughed, popping a strawberry into her mouth.

I looked at her admiring her true beauty. She was beautiful, inside and out, and that was hard to find. I know this is just the beginning of Hazel and Xá. Stay tuned because we still have a couple of forevers left, I can feel it.

Chapter Eighteen

~

Harmony Woods

Ever since I found out my dad was my boss, coming to work wasn't the same. I hadn't ran into him since then, but the point that it was going to eventually happen had me feeling some type of way. I needed to find another job, and quick.

"If it isn't the Sour Patch Kid in the flesh."

"Sour Patch Kid?" I questioned with raised brows. The feeling I got whenever he was near was almost scary.

"I know you're sour and sweet. I guess I'll be the one to bring it out though." He smirked. Hunter's sexy ass was going to be the death of me.

"I'm starting to think you're stalking me." I smirked, changing the subject. My body started to get hot, he was already bringing out too much shit and he didn't even know it.

"Not at all Ms. Harmony. I have an appointment for my cleaning and whitening." He stated firmly.

I looked down at my computer and I'll be damned if I didn't see a Hunter Williams for an 11 a.m. "Mr. Williams?" I quizzed, knowing damn well that was him.

"Yes, but Hunter is just fine Harmony."

"Dr. Schneider will be right with you, he's finishing up his last client." I said, checking the progress checker our office used to better serve our patients. "You can have a seat over there." I pointed to the leather sofas we had in our lobby. The lobby was set up like the living area in a house with sofas, ottomans, coffee tables, and more.

"Or I could just stand and talk to you. Or is that a problem?" He questioned, wearing that sexy ass smile.

"Of course not, Mr.Williams." I teased, knowing he had just corrected me minutes prior of what he preferred to be called.

"If you insist on going that route, at least call me Dr.Williams." He smirked, pulling out his work badge.

"I see you got jokes." I retorted. He was a trip, but I was too.

"Dr. Williams, you can come on back. I see you found your way to my new location." The dentist said, leading him through the double doors.

"I sure did." Hunter said, looking over his shoulder at me. He gave me a wink just before he turned his head in the opposite direction.

I got back to work. Answering calls from snobbish patients, doing paperwork, setting up upcoming appointments for our patients and sneaking on my phone periodically to pass time and lurk, my second job.

"Let me take you to lunch." I looked up and there he was again. I loved a nigga who was persistent.

"I am working in case you didn't know. I can't just get up and take my lunch." I sassed. I wouldn't be me if I didn't add a little attitude with it.

"You're ri–"

"Harmony, you can go ahead and go to lunch. I'll cover for you." Vanessa, one of the college interns said, wiping the smirk right off my face.

"Well I guess you're free now. Come on." He ordered, not giving me an option to decline. I wanted to scream "Okay daddy", well at least my inner freak 'Lashae' wanted to.

"I only have an hour and thirty minutes."

"You would have only had an hour and thirty minutes had I not let them know you were leaving for the day." He assured me, avoiding eye contact with me. Instead, his eyes were glued to the road.

His alpha mannerisms had me turned on in every possible way. Being in his presence was the only time I had no come back, nothing to say. I was indeed, speechless.

The rest of the ride was quiet with the music playing the background. We occasionally stole glances at one another. We pulled up at Black Rock and my mouth watered as I thought about the bomb ass ribs they had.

He helped me out the car and he held the small of my back as we walked to the door. He held the door open for me so I could walk in. I couldn't help the smile that came at the true gentleman he was. If he kept this up, there's most definitely going to be many more dates to follow. I loved his energy and the way he moved.

***

I paced the floor, heart feeling like it was going to beat out of my chest, as I waited for my sister to answer the phone.

"Hello." She answered, sounding like she was skeptical about picking up the phone.

"Hey Hazel, this is Harmony."

"Hey girl. How are you?" She asked, softening her tone once she found out it was me that was calling, which made me relax.

"I'm good. How are you?"

"Good. I'm glad you called. Mama and I were going to the beach to enjoy the last of this hot weather. You know how that go." She laughed and I nodded my head in agreement like she could actually see me.

"That sounds great. Which beach?" I questioned, I hope it wasn't too far because I was not trying to be on the side of the damn road. I wasn't even trying to drive to Dearborn in this piece of shit of a car.

"We're just going to Bell Isle." I silently thanked the man above for being on my side. Now that, I could make it there.

"Are y'all on the way there now?" I asked, starting the shower so I could get ready.

"We're going to be leaving out in like twenty minutes."

"Okay, I'll see y'all there." I said just before I ended the call.

I stepped in the shower, letting the hot water run down all over my body. I washed my body over and over in my Magic In The Air body wash from Bath and Body Works. I stayed in the shower until the water started to get cool. After I lotioned my body, with the identical lotion, I put on my matching pantie and bra set. I stepped into my jean shorts and put on a cami. I kept it cute and simple and put on some gold gladiator sandals. After I was completely dressed, I got into my hoopty and made my way east to the beach.

Hazel had already sent me a text with her location, so I knew exactly where they were. I spotted them at a picnic table right off the water. As I walked towards them, I couldn't help but to be taken back at the fact that I had a sister, and a twin at that. She's the exact replica of me and vice versa. It was almost scary, but I was glad that I could finally have someone in my corner. That was a breath of fresh air.

"Hey." I called out, getting their attention.

"Hey." They both said in unison in a sing song voice. I was glad to see they were just as excited as I was to be meeting up with them. Little did they know, I had been waiting on this moment ever since I knew they existed. I needed this.

Kim Evans

~

Looking at both of my daughters was nothing but the work of the Lord. Only God knows of how many times I've prayed for their safety. Never in a million years did I think he would give me a second chance at being their mother. I am beyond blessed to be the mother of two beautiful women.

"Hey baby. I know this must feel weird." I said, trying to lighten up the mood.

"Not really." She shrugged, sitting down across from Hazel.

"I just wanted to apologize. I never would have stepped to E-" Harmony started, but Hazel stopped her by raising up her hand.

"Let that be the last time we even think of mentioning his name." She laughed. "Excuse my language ma, but fuck that nigga. You're my sister." She smiled and that put a smile on Harmony's face as well.

"I just wanted to tell you both that I'm sorry for giving you away, but I felt that was what was best for y'all. I've missed your childhood and so much of your life and I regret that but I'm glad we were reconnected and that we can have a fresh start and start over. I'm so sorry girls." I stated again, wiping the tears from my eyes.

I was fifteen when I gave birth to them and nine months prior to that, I had never been the same. He took everything from me. I was stripped to nothing and no longer even loved myself. I couldn't look at myself without feeling disgusted. It's taking for me to go to therapy weekly to regain my self esteem and self love back.

I remember that day like it was yesterday. It's so memorable because that was my worst birthday and I have yet to celebrate since. Because it was my birthday, my mom let me stay out later with my friends. We were hanging out at the park, eating cake and just having a good time.

" Hey Kim. You look nice." Timothy said, looking over my developed teenage body. I was wearing my new Guess overalls with the steel toe Adidas, I had practically begged my mom for. She didn't have much money coming in, but she made do and got me what I wanted for my birthday.

"Thank you." I cheesed, looking off to the side. I couldn't keep eye contact with him if my life depended on it. I was a freshman in High school and he was a freshman in college. All the women in my family had their thing for older men, so I guess the apple didn't fall too far from the tree.

"Follow me. I got something for you." He said and I followed without question. Little did I know, me following his lead would change my life forever. I smiled the entire time I followed him to the back of the vacant school.

"Here." He said, handing me a small box with some type of jewelry inside. My hands were shaking as I fumbled with the wrapping around the box. My nerves had gotten the best of me.

I finally opened the box to find a diamond tennis bracelet with my initials on it. My hand went up to my mouth, surprised was an understatement. No one had ever bought me something so expensive.

"Thank you." I smiled, pulling him into a hug.

When he pulled back, he kissed my lips and I didn't know how to respond. His hands started to roam my body and something felt off.

"You know, everything comes with a price." He barked as he yanked my overalls off my body. My cries for help went on deaf ears as I screamed for someone to rescue me. But no one ever did.

"Mom, you don't have to apologize, yeah I wish you were apart of my life from the beginning, but as long as you're in my life now, that's all that matters." Hazel spoke up first and I let out a breath of relief, I didn't even realize I was holding in.

"Just promise me you're here to stay. Both of you. I need permanent family in my life." Harmony said, wiping away her tears.

It felt good to be reunited with my girls without any ill feelings. I always thought that if somehow I ever got reconnected with them, they would deny and resent me. Hearing their acceptance of me, meant everything to me. They were my only family.

Hazel Parks

~

Sitting on the beach with my mom and sister had to be the best feeling ever. I never knew how it was to be surrounded by genuine love but I knew now. I was happy. This was the happiest I'd ever been. We talked, we laughed, we enjoyed each other's company.

Xá: Am I seeing you tonight beautiful?

I couldn't help the smile that adorned my face. At times, he seemed too perfect. He's everything there is to want and need in a man. I just hope he remains the same and won't switch up on me.

Me: Only if you want to deal with me three days in a row, lol.

Xá: I might want to deal with you for the rest of my life, you never know.

I was caught off guard with his response. This is what I meant, when I said he seems too perfect. There was never a day that Xá didn't cross my mind. It's crazy how I was already falling for him. Our connection is at an all time high.

"Who you over there daydreaming about?" Harmony quizzed, bringing me back to reality.

"You remember Xá? The owner of X&H Recreation Center?" I asked, smiling from ear to ear. I found myself doing that every time I mentioned his name.

"Yeah, I remember him."

"We've been talking for a minute now and he just asked me out on another date. This is the third day in a row."

"Bro putting a smile on your face like that, though? I need to meet him." She smirked. "You're talking to one owner and I'm talking to the other." She announced and I was surprised.

"As long as you don't sleep with Xá, we're good." I joked, it was actually kind of funny now. Well funny enough to joke about anyway.

"Trust me, Hunter is enough for me." She laughed and I felt the same way about that damn Xá.

We all engaged in a fit of laughter. Being with my family was like a breath of fresh air. There was no way I was going a day without talking to either of them. Too much time had already passed by as it is. I never felt or even knew a love like this. Without even knowing them completely, I loved them with all my heart.

"I can't express how happy I am to have y'all in my life. I had a terrible childhood but I made it through so that's all that matters." Harmony said, revealing both are truths. "I should have known that snag-a-tooth bitch wasn't my damn mama." She sassed, rolling her eyes.

"The feelings are mutual. We'll have to swap horror stories about our childhood at a later time. I don't need that killing my vibe." I chuckled, trying to avoid all negative thoughts. Today was going to be a good day. Being around my Mama, I'm learning to start speaking things into existence.

"I know that's right. Y'all are so strong and beautiful." My mom smiled, looking between me and Harmony.

We spent the remainder of the day talking and catching up with everyone's lives. Mama wanted to know everything there was to know about us, her girls, and I didn't blame her. She had the right to know, and I didn't want to hold anything back from her but some things that I've been through, it's best I just keep it to myself.

***

I had been picturing what to wear for tonight all day, but here I am, twenty outfits later with nothing on, and I was expecting Xá any minute now. I let out a frustrated breath as I went into my closet to search high and low for something in between sexy and slutty. I was going for the kill, the wow factor.

After what felt like a million hours, I found a deep v-neck dress that had a cut so deep that it stopped just above my belly button. It was a rose gold in color with sparkles all over. I paired it with my nude Jimmy Choo peep-toe pumps.

I had my hair curled in spirals. I applied little makeup to my face and right after I put my final coat of lipstick on, my doorbell was going off. Perfect timing, I thought to myself. I grabbed my clutch off my nightstand and headed for the door.

"Damn." His eyes lustfully roamed all over my body, admiring the way my thick body filled out my dress. "I don't even think you realize how beautiful you are." He smiled, now staring into my hazel eyes.

I couldn't help but blush as I stared at his sexy ass. "Yes, I do and thank you." I smiled, moving my hair from my face. "Shall we?" I asked, because we were still standing in the same spot, lost in the moment.

"Of course." He grabbed me by my hand, helping me down the porch steps. He led me to his sexy ass Porsche and opened the door. As long as I'm with him, I don't even have to think about touching a door handle. It's just the little things that he does that have my whole body on fire.

"Where we going?" I asked, as I put my safety belt on. With the way he drives sometimes, I can never forget to do that.

"You remember how I told you it was a surprise earlier, I meant that." He chuckled and I had to laugh at him and that slick ass mouth of his too.

"I guess." I sassed, playfully rolling my eyes. I turned the radio up, liking his taste in music. I was an eighties baby, but nineties music had my heart.

Forty-five minutes later had passed and I didn't notice until I got a text message from my sister asking me if I was I still buried in my closet. We had to be jamming tough as hell for me not to notice how much time had passed.

"We're almost there." He said, switching to the far right lane. As we came up on our exit, he handed me a blindfold. "Put this on."

I was hesitant for a brief moment, because you can't trust a nigga as far as you can throw em'. Syan had my location if some shit was to go down, which I doubted. We were riding for about five additional minutes before we came to a stop.

I heard Xá get out the car and seconds later, my door was being pulled open. He grabbed my hand and he lead me to some mystery place. "Watch your step. We're going up three steps." His deep voice tickled my neck, making the hairs on my back stand at attention. Something as minute as that shouldn't have had my panties wet, but it did. His body heat, from him being so close, radiated on mine as he tugged at the blindfold I was wearing.

My mouth hung open at the sight in front of me. We were on a yacht and before me was a table set for two, decorated beautifully. There were candles, flowers, everything you can imagine for the perfect, romantic date.

I took in all the decor, the scenery, just everything. He always knew how to put a smile on my face. It's these things that made my feelings for him grow deeper and deeper. As I continued to look around, there was a massage table setup with massage oils sitting on a stand alongside it with a robe hanging on it as well. He really did the damn thing.

"You decorated this yourself? I've never seen something so beautiful." I beamed, remembering the time we were on a picnic, our first date.

"This is only the beginning," he paused, handing me a small gift bag and a bouquet of Sunflowers, my favorite. "I see you have faith in me but no I could never do anything as close as this. I hired Omega Decorates for the job. She overdoes it every time. I kid you not."

"Well I'm very impressed and definitely Team Omega." I giggled, the decor was just really out of this world.

"Have a seat." He pulled out my chair, and I happily took my seat. "Are you ready to eat?" He asked as he took his seat at the table, across from me.

"Yes sir." I couldn't stop smiling, because I couldn't believe he had all of this setup for me. I never thought I was worthy of something remotely close to the excellent treatment he gives me on a daily.

"Waiter, we're ready." He called out to the foreign lady dressed in a black and red uniform. She rushed right over and took our order in record time.

"How long do we have to be on here?" I asked, already not wanting the night to end.

"Whenever you're ready to end it. It's mine, but I'm on your time. This your world, I'm just living in it." He smiled with so much sincerity and seriousness laced in his voice. Where has this man been all my life? He's like ten years late.

"Who raised you?" I asked, really wanting to know who helped mold him into the man he is.

"Mom and dad. I was raised in a two parent household. Why'd you ask?" He stuffed a forkful of salad in his mouth.

"I just want to personally thank them for having such an amazing son."

"My dad made sure he taught me how to properly treat a woman. I'll never forget all the talks or just watching his actions, the way he worshipped the ground my mom walked on, and just how he interacted with my mom. Damn, I miss that man. Can't believe it's been almost eight years since he's been gone."

"I'm sorry. I know he's proud though, looking down at the man you are and that you've become." I gave him a reassuring smile, because I could tell that him talking about his dad was a touchy subject.

We spent the remainder of the night talking, laying down and looking up at the glistening stars and the moon in the summer's night air. Perfect night with the perfect man for me.

Chapter Nineteen

~

Syan González

"Oooh baby...fuck.." I moaned in my sleep. Getting woke up to my husband in between my legs was the best shit ever.

He gave my clit a passionate tongue kiss as he played with my titties with his hands. He precisely ate my pussy, licking, biting, and sucking wherever he saw fit. He was hitting places I never knew were there. You would think his ass had a degree in Pussy Eating. With every lick, he took a piece of my soul with him. I grinded my pussy on his face, intensifying the pleasure I was already receiving.

"Shit, I'm about to cum. Hectorrrr." I cried out as he lapped up every drop of my sweet nectar with his thick, massive tongue.

"Good morning bae." He said before softly pecking my lips.

"Good morning baby." I cooed, feeling so rejuvenated. Bomb ass head will do that to you. I be in this bitch singing Kumbaya every time my husband bless me with his wicked ass tongue game.

"Wait, where you goin?" I asked as he got up from the bed. "You can't start something without finishing." I smirked, grabbing him up and roughly pushing him into the bed.

I slid his boxers down and I positioned my body on top of his. I rubbed my pussy against his dick and tongue kissed his mouth and his dick sprung to life completely. Once he was inside of me, I wasted no time riding, bouncing up and down on my dick. I kept my pace steady as I pleasured my man, the best way I knew how.

"Damn mamí." He grunted, when I dropped down into the splits while still maintaining the same speed. There wasn't shit I wouldn't do to please my man.

"Oooh, you like that papí?" I moaned, quickening my pace as I bounced up and down still in the splits and tightening my pussy muscles all at the same time. That was multitasking at its finest.

Before I knew what was happening, Hector picked me back up and gave me long deep strokes while standing up. "Bend over and touch them toes baby." He whispered in my ear, juices steady flowing down my leg. I followed his orders and bent my ass over. He wasted no tie ramming his dick in my dripping wet pussy. He pounded me hard and fast, just the way I liked it, pussy leaking like a broken faucet.

"Baby, I'm about to cum!" I shouted, trying not to fall. My equilibrium was all fucked up.

"You gonna cum all over daddy's dick?" He groaned, picking up the pace a little.

"Fuck....yes!" I cried, releasing all over his dick.

"Damn." He grunted, shooting his soldiers inside me. "If you not already pregnant, I know you are now. You might fuck around and have triplets." He smirked, going into the bathroom then turning the shower on.

"Whatever man." I brushed him off and stepped into the shower behind him. Any other time, we would've kept going, but instead we washed our bodies a few times before we got out the shower.

As I threw on a pair of leggings and a t-shirt, I saw that Jr. was up on the baby monitor. I went down the hall to his nursery and there was my little man with drool dripping from his mouth. This teething phase had my baby slobbing on every damn thing.

"Hey handsome." I cooed, kissing him all over his face and tickling him. His little laugh was so cute and soft. "You want food?" His eyes lit up. It's a shame his greedy ass knew what food was, by hearing the word.

I carried him down the steps and put him in his walker so I could get breakfast started. I quickly whipped up pancakes, grits, cheesy eggs, and bacon.

"Baby, you ready to eat?" I asked Hector who was playing with our son putting him in the air and Lil Hector was cracking up so hard.

"Yeah baby." He said, walking into the dining room. He put the baby in his high chair and he started crying his lungs out, with his spoiled ass. He was about to cut up until I sat his food in front of him and his fat ass started stuffing his face immediately.

"Your son should not be this damn greedy." I chuckled, setting my husband's plate and glass of orange juice in front of him.

"Shit, we can't help it with you cooking the way you do." He said, shoving pancakes in his mouth. I smiled, thinking of my mom. That's where my love for cooking started.

"I need to go grocery shopping today. You know my family is flying in, in a couple days." I smiled excitedly. I was happy that we resolved all issues. Sometimes it takes a tragedy or a loss to come together. "So I need you to keep your son." I continued as I took a sip of my coffee.

"You know that's not a problem." He said, finishing the last of his food.

I grabbed my ringing phone to see that it was my dad calling. "Hey dad." I smiled into the phone.

"Surabhi, how's my grandson?" He asked and I was kind of jealous. That's all he thought about. My damn phone bill was so damn high from the international Facetime calls. Jr. loved talking to his grandpa in his baby talk.

"He's doing great. He's in there with his dad playing the game." I smiled looking at my three favorite men. Two sitting in front of me and the other looking at me through the phone. "Are y'all all packed up?" I asked, they were leaving in two days.

"Yeah, I am. You know I'm simple. Your sisters are the ones to worry about." He laughed and I nodded because I knew how Zoya and Aadhya were. They took their time doing every damn thing.

"Tell them I said to hurry. I hope y'all don't miss the flight because they like to slow poke around." I sassed because that was a strong possibility, with the way my older sisters were.

"I'm going to make sure they're on time. See you soon, baby girl." He blew me a kiss through the camera and I caught it and put it to my heart, something we always did when I was a kid.

As I was setting my phone down on the table, my phone lit up with several messages from Facebook Messenger. I blew out an irritated breath, when I saw it was Lisa, Hector's trifling ass baby mama. Against my better judgement, I opened it up to see pictures of her and Hector in bed butt ass naked. I could see his outfit from a couple weeks ago in the background. The same day his lying, cheating ass wasn't answering the phone. As I continued flicking through the series of pictured, I stumbled across a photo with ten different positive pregnancy tests. To top the cake, there was also a video attached with her sucking my husband's dick.

I can't begin to explain the amount of rage I feel flowing throughout my entire body. I took my marriage very seriously. I thought he did too, but I guess that's what my ass gets for thinking. I meant my vows when I said for better or worse but damn it. Hector González had me all the way fucked up. Not only did he fuck the bitch, but he got her stupid ass pregnant again as if his dumb ass didn't learn the first time.

I looked between him and the knife stand that sat on the island in the kitchen a few times, contemplating the idea of chopping his dick off and forcing it down his throat but when I looked at my baby sitting in his lap, I erased the thought from my head. That wouldn't be the best approach with him in the middle of the crossfire. Becoming a mother calmed me down a lot. When Hector cheated on me in the past, it wasn't a pretty sight. When I found out about his cheating, he happened to be with me so I grabbed the first thing I saw, a pair of scissors, and I had to have stabbed his ass twenty times. I wanted to hurt him, not kill him so when I saw all the plugs of missing skin, I drove him to the hospital. When the doctors asked who did it, I dared him with my eyes to snitch. I'm not the one for bullshit and he should definitely know that by now.

To avoid killing his ass, I had to get the fuck out of dodge. I jogged up the stairs to collect my purse, shoes, and the fat ass pre-rolled blunt out my nightstand. Once I had all my things, I jetted out the front door without saying a single goodbye. To say I was hurt, was an understatement. I am broken.

I found myself pulling up in front of Hazel's house and I was glad to see her car parked in the driveway, cause I hadn't bothered to call to say I was coming. I hopped out my truck and knocked on the door, once I made it up the stairs. She came to the door with a smile on her face, but that quickly changed when she saw my face. I had tears running down my face and I knew my eyes had to be bloodshot red between me crying and facing that healthy ass blunt.

"What's wrong sister?" She grabbed me into a bear hug as I sobbed in her arms. "Talk to me." She said, walking me to the couch. I had to stop smoking because I was seeing two of Haze in two completely different spots.

"Syan, by the way this is Harmony, my twin. Harmony, this is Syan, my best friend." Yeah, it was confirmed that I was losing my damn mind. How I had forgotten Hazel had a twin was beyond me. I waved at her and looked back to Hazel. I didn't want to come off as rude, but talking to Harmony was the last damn thing on my mind.

"Hector's cheating on me." I blurted out and my heart sank into my chest as I spoke my truth aloud. Hearing myself confess it made it worse. My heart was aching and filled with so much pain.

"No, he can't be." She said and I would've said the same thing had someone just told me what I just told her. I wish that was the case, but I had already seen the proof with my own eyes. I handed her my phone with the messages already on the screen and her eyes almost bulged out her head and she had her hand over her mouth.

"So what's next? We go kick his ass?" She jumped up, putting her hair up into a bun and Harmony followed her lead. I guess she was cool too.

"No, I want to think all my options through first. You already know, had this been the old Syan, I would've shot his dick and balls off with the chopper." I stated calmly as I lit another blunt. So many thoughts were flowing in and out of my brain, all surrounded by Hector.

"You don't have to remind me. Remember the time that random, disrespectful hoe tried to make a move on Hector in front of you, and set her synthetic ass weave on fire." She laughed and I did too. Those were my badass days, when I swore up and down my little ass was untouchable.

"Yeah, I remember that shit like it happened yesterday. He knows I'm crazy, so why he decided to fuck with me is his own damn problem." I said, taking a big pull from the blunt then blowing the smoke out of my nose. I was damn near a professional smoker now.

"So, what are you gonna do? You want to stay here?" She offered, taking the blunt I was passing her way.

"Hell naw. That nigga needs to find him somewhere to stay. I'll be damned if I leave and his ass is the stupid muthafucka who fucked up." I fussed, feeling myself getting more irritated. Never in a million years did I think I would go through this with Hector. Those childish ass games were over once we both said I do.

I stayed kicking it with them for a couple more hours before I headed out. All I wanted to do was cuddle with my son, until we both fell asleep. When I pulled into the driveway, I saw Hector's right hand man Dex's car parked in the driveway as well. I sighed heavily because the confrontation had to be put on hold. I don't like having people all up in my business.

When I walked into the house, they were all staring at the TV. I spoke to Dex, grabbed my son, took my ass straight to my bedroom, and closed and locked the door.

It wasn't until I was in my deep REM sleep before I heard Hector banging on the bedroom door, damn near about to break it.

"What the fuck is your problem?" I snapped, snatching the door open. He had his damn nerve.

"Before we continue this conversation, I'm gon' need you to change that damn tone." He gritted through clenched teeth. He hated when I raised my voice at him, but that shit went out the window when he stuck his dick into that scum bucket hoe and implanted his seed into her.

"I don't give a fuck about none of that shit, but what I do know is you need to get your shit and find somewhere to live." I yelled, getting up all in his face.

"What the fuck is your deal? I haven't done shit wrong Syan." The fact that he thought I was going to believe that pissed me off.

I pulled my phone out of my bra, brought up the messages, and handed him the phone over to him. "Like I said, get the fuck out. Matter of fact, you can get your shit when I'm not here but you can either leave willingly or unwillingly, but you're gonna get the fuck out." I barked, snatching my phone from his grasp and lamming the door in his face.

I heard his heavy footsteps fade as he went down the staircase. I slid down the wall and cried my eyes out. It took a lot for me to cry, I wasn't no weak bitch. When I heard the hemi engine start up, I knew he had left. I'm glad he did leave on his own or shit was going to get real ugly. "Get yourself together bitch." I told myself as I dried my eyes. I didn't have it in me to let no man break me down.

Hector

~

I felt undefeated as I sat outside of Lisa's house with no signs of her or my daughter. The day I woke up after that bitch did that fuck shit, I had been searching all over Detroit for her ass. I should have followed my first mind and told Syan when it happened, but honestly I didn't want anyone to know how she got down on me. I never let nobody get the opportunity to catch me slipping, but I didn't see that coming. The shit was really fucking with my mental. I sped off her block and drove to my warehouse.

"So ain't nobody seen this bitch? So she just fell off the face of the Earth with my fucking daughter and no damn money?" I barked, punching a hole in the wall. I had called a meeting with all my men and to hear that they still didn't know shit was pissing me the fuck off. It had been damn near a month with no lead on their whereabouts. Before I knew she was pregnant, I was just going to off her ass and get custody over my daughter. Although she did some foul shit to get pregnant with my seed, I couldn't kill her ass knowing my bloodline was in her. I'm crazy, but killing children wasn't my thing. I'm not a heartless ass nigga.

"We thought we had a lead on them, but it was a no go." Chris, a young cat had the nerve to say. I pulled out my gun and shot his ass in the knee.

"What the fuck man. It ain't my fault you can't keep up with your damn baby ma-" Before he could finish his sentence, I shot him in his other knee then his foot. His ass would permanently have a limp to his walk.

"There was no point in opening your fucking mouth if you didn't have shit I want to hear. You could've kept that bullshit to yourself." I was sick of all these niggas coming up empty handed. "Ain't none of y'all niggas getting paid until you bring me some information." I turned my attention to all the other men before me. I could see the distasteful looks on their faces. Some even had the nerve to smack their lips like bitches. "Put your fucking ears to the streets." I gritted, before leaving their asses looking stupid. If they didn't already know, they were about to have front row seats to my crazy side. Nobody was safe from my wrath.

I dialed up Syan for the fiftieth time today. Surprisingly, she answered the phone.

"Hello." She roared into the phone, not trying to hide the attitude in her voice. I knew she was upset and she had every right to be. Hell, if the shoe was on the other foot, she would be six feet under.

"I know you mad but can I atleast see my son? It's already been three days." I sighed into the phone, I missed my little guy and I was used to seeing his face every day.

"I don't have a problem with you seeing your son. Get him from your mother in an hour and take him back there when you're done spending time with him." She hung the phone up before I could even respond. I needed to catch, with Lisa ASAP so I can have my wife back.

I decided to take inventory to kill time, until I could pick up my son. I went over the numbers a few times, because shit wasn't adding up. I felt like niggas were purposely trying me. I had fifty guns missing which meant I was missing over thirty racks. I don't know who would have the balls to cross me but all I know is somebody's mom was about to plan their son's funeral. Niggas must have thought since I was home more with my wife and son that I had turned pussy, but shit just got real. I had a feeling a few bodies were going to be dropped and I would bet my last dollar, it won't be mine.

Chapter Twenty

~

Brielle Black

"Good morning baby." I cooed into my man's ear. It had been so long since I had a man, it almost felt unreal.

"Good morning bae." His deep ass, sexy voice had my pussy thumping in the silk panties I had on. I got on top of my man and kissed his lips passionately. It was as if I got a high when my lips touched his. I was falling hard and I wasn't ashamed to admit it.

"Ew, stop kissing my daddy." Bailey busted into the bedroom. Her pretty face was balled up as if we disgusted her.

"I told yo ass to start locking the door." I mumbled under my breath, but at the same time, smiling at Bailey with my arms out, reaching for a hug. I had told Christian's ass about leaving the door unlocked, especially because both of our horny asses wanted to fuck every five minutes. "Hey beautiful." I smiled, squeezing her tightly. We had formed a special bond over the past few months Christian and I had been together.

"Are you going to cook breakfast? I'm starving." She said, rubbing her belly, with her overly dramatic ass. I told Christian we needed to put her in acting classes like yesterday.

"Anything for you princess." I smiled while grabbing my robe and making my way downstairs.

"Good morning big head." I said, peaking my head through Jaden's second bedroom. He had just as much stuff here as he did at home. We might as well have lived here as much as we were over.

"Good morning Ma, you about to cook?" He asked, and I couldn't help but to laugh at the greedy ass kids Christian and I had. I simply nodded and continued downstairs to the kitchen.

I plugged up the waffle maker and started mixing the batter from scratch. You would never catch me using shit from a box. I quickly whipped up belgian waffles topped with strawberries and whipped cream, and what I call a breakfast scramble. It had eggs, roasted potatoes, onions, peppers, cheese, bacon, and sausage. It was a bunch of shit, but they loved it. Of course, they were all making their way to the table as I sat the last plate down. It never failed. They always had the perfect timing when it came to eating.

"O-M-G, this is so yummy." Bailey said, stuffing strawberry after strawberry into her mouth.

"Thanks, eat up so we won't miss our appointment." It was a must that we hit the nail spa to get our manicures and pedicures every Sunday. Today we were even getting a facial.

Once everyone had finished with their food, I washed the dishes and wiped down the counters and table. After that was taken care of, I headed upstairs to take my shower. I stayed in there all of twenty minutes. I was trying my best to hurry so Irene, our nail technician, wouldn't be up my ass about always being late.

I slid my thighs into my white ripped jeans that I paired with a white off the shoulder crop top. On my feet were my custom Gucci furry slides. I rocked my all white attire whenever I was feeling Godly.

"You ready boo?" I asked, walking into Bailey's bedroom. She was putting on her Michael Kors sandals. She was dressed in a floral maxi dress. I was impressed because she had completely dressed herself without my help.

"All done." She said, as she finished strapping her right sandal. She was so pretty. Her hair was freshly done in two braided ponytails with beads.

"We'll be back in a few babe." I pecked his soft lips a couple times before we made our way to get pampered.

We had Bruno Mars 'That's What I Like' on repeat. You would think she would be sick of this song by now but nope, their relationship was still going strong. As the end of the song neared, she got my attention.

"Can I ask you something?" She asked and I glanced at her through the rear view mirror.

"Of course. You can ask me anything." I told her, stealing glances at her while still looking at the road.

"The girls in my class talk about all of the things they do with their mommy and you do those things with me, so can I call you mommy?" Her question caught me off guard and broke my heart all at the same time. Christian told me about her trifling ass. I would never understand how a mother, the same woman that pushed their baby out can abandon them, their own creation. I really didn't know what to say or how to approach the situation. I could never take the place of her mommy, but I knew she must have felt some type of way that she was the only one who didn't talk about the things she did with her mom.

"Bailey, that's something you have to talk to daddy about. I don't mind. We just have to get his permission first." I smiled, trying to say it the best way I could to a four year old. Her pretty face looked defeated as she held her head down, twiddling her fingers.

"You're my best little friend though, remember that."

"Okay." She said, her little pout she was wearing turned into a smile.

Bailey was the smartest four year old I'd ever encountered. She could hold a conversation like no other child her age. Her language and ability to form sentences was superb, because her dad only had her in the best private school and she stayed on her iPad watching learning videos on YouTube. I remember one day I was bathing her and she told me every damn bone in her little body. She never ceases to amaze me.

When we got to the salon, of course, it was packed with bitches gossiping about any and everything. Irene wasted no time taking us to the back of her shop to her private studio. I was surprised she wasn't getting in their ass about keeping it professional. Irene was crazy as hell, so I couldn't understand why they even tried it. If they keep it up and they would be out a job and lose their pride with the ass whooping she'll gladly hand out.

"Ms. Bailey, go ahead and pick out your color. Don't act like you don't know the drill." She joked.

"I know, I know Ms.Irene. We go through this every time." She even had the nerve to have her hand on her little hip. Little Miss Diva was going to be her nickname from now on.

Bailey decided to get pink and she had Irene put white polka dots all over on every single toe. Me on the other hand, I kept it simple and got red on my hands and feet. After we got out our facials, we were on our way back to the house.

"Can we get ice cream?" She pleaded, batting her long, pretty eyelashes. That reminded me of the first day we met all those months ago.

"Sure little Miss Diva." I giggled and she looked at me with wide eyes.

"I am so not a diva." She had the nerve to say. I had never laughed so hard in my life. All I could do was laugh and shake my head.

I made sure to stop at the Dairy Queen closest to Christian's house, because both him, and Jaden would act a fool had I came in the house with ice cream for just me and Bailey. I would never hear the end of it. After I had everyone's favorite ice cream, we were pulling up to the house five minutes later.

"Thanks Ma." Jaden said, putting a big ass spoon of Oreo blizzard into his mouth.

"Daddy, can I call Brielle, mommy? She does everything mommy's do for me." She blurted out as she continued licking her ice cream, dripping shit everywhere.

Christian looked my way and I shrugged my shoulders and mouthed 'It's your call'. I honestly didn't mind, but I understood if Christian wanted her to call me Ms. Bri or Bri. like she's been doing.

"Will that make you happy?" He asked, tickling her. She laughed uncontrollably, while trying to wiggle her way out of his big, muscular arms.

"Yes daddy!" She managed to scream in between laughing.

"Well you already know I love to keep you happy and see that beautiful smile of yours."

"Thank you daddy. You heard that mommy? He said it's okay." She smiled with the biggest grin on her face, running in my direction. When she was in arms reach, she leaned in for a hug and I gladly accepted it. I guess it's safe to say, I'm a mother of two!

Jordan Jenkins

~

"Are you fucking serious right now?!!" Maya's small ass voice boomed through the phone, making me draw the phone away from my ear.

"Yes, I have to be there for my wife. She's pregnant, remember?" I barked, growing irritated with her needy ass. Sometimes, I hated I even dealt with her ass in the first place.

Maya is just one of the hoes I messed around with in the church, who just happened to get pregnant with my two beautiful girls. Maya was bad as hell. She had chocolate colored skin, like myself, with pretty gray eyes that her father passed down to her and both my girls. She was what most people called a BBW but I didn't mind the extra meat here and there.

I know y'all pretty much already have y'all mind set about what type of nigga I am and I'm pretty sure you're right. I'm a typical nigga that likes to eat his cake and have it too. I tried to be on the straight and narrow by being faithful to my wife, but I just didn't have it in me. Yeah, I'm the pastor of one of the biggest churches in Michigan, but players fuck up all the time. As long as I keep preaching those powerful sermons and showcase my *perfect* life, I can do no wrong in my congregation's eyes.

"Yeah nigga, I remember. Do you remember that you have two kids by me though? Neriyah is sick to her stomach, throwing up all over the place, crying for your stupid ass and you telling me you can't come to the hospital to check on her cause that bitch wants you to come to her appointment. Do for the fucking kids that's already here, first."

I rubbed both my temples to keep my composure. This is the side of Maya that I couldn't get with. She knew damn well I had a pregnant wife, but yet she wanted me to leave her and tend to her. She didn't understand her place. I thought she would though, considering she was married as well. I guess fucking around with married women, they still get attached and start to buggin' just like the single women.

"Okay, I'm on my way." I quickly hung up on her ass and mentally prepared myself for the argument that was to come with my wife. Between the both of them, I was going to have a head full of gray hair.

Before I could sit the phone down on my desk, my phone was ringing again, but this time it was my wife.

"Hey baby. You're on your way?" Brigail asked as soon as I accepted the call.

"No. I have to do the conference call. I won't be able to make it baby." I lied through my teeth, effortlessly.

"Jordan, why can't it wait? I've been talking about this day for weeks. This is the day we find out the gender of the baby. You haven't been to a single appointment and still you bail out at the most exciting one. I'm tired of you putting your work before me and our child that's growing inside of me!" She yelled and I could tell she was on the verge of crying. This pregnancy had her ass on one hell of a roller coaster. If her belly wasn't poking out the way it was, one would think her ass was bipolar.

"Brigail, you know just as well as I do that these conference calls is what's going to keep that cash flowing in that bank account of ours. You like being laced in Gucci and gold but you can't accept the work that goes into this shit. You know what, fuck it, I'll skip it but keep in mind, you won't get that hefty lump sum of money that you get in your account every month if I skip it." I roared, flipping the script on her ass, just like a typical nigga would.

"Just go ahead. This not the first appointment you've missed." It had gotten quiet, I couldn't hear her moving around in the background, so I looked at my phone that was on the home screen. Sure enough, she had hung up on my ass but of course, her money hungry ass had taken the bait.

I locked up my office, got into my car, and sped to Providence Hospital. My phone kept going off with phone calls and threatening text messages from Maya, so I just turned it off. She was really working my damn nerves. She even had the nerve to ask how can I put the bitch that I faithfully cheated on before my own daughter. I swear her mouth had me wanting to jack her ass up a little. I think the suits and my occupation has made a lot of people forget who I am. Ain't shit changed about me but the numbers in my bank account.

"Daddy." My little girl managed to say just above a whisper upon seeing my face. I could tell she wasn't feeling well by the way her face was flushed. She just didn't look like the energetic, bright little girl that she was. Laying in the bed with IV's hooked to her little arm.

"Hey princess." I said, leaning over the railing to the hospital bed to place a kiss on her forehead. "Have the doctors said what's wrong?" I turned my attention to Maya who was staring at me with hate in her eyes. If looks could kill, I would be six feet under.

"Nope." She snapped, crossing her arms over her breast and rolling her neck. I couldn't believe her grown ass was really throwing a tantrum like that.

I looked back over to Neriyah and she had fallen asleep, so I pulled my phone out and handled a few things to kill time.

"So you really got that bourgeoisie bitch pregnant?' She asked angrily with her face frowned up.

"Yeah, that's my wife. Why can't you get that through that big ass head of yours? You want to be her so bad, but for what though? I'll do the same shit to you but you would never have that opportunity because I love her, not you." I yelled louder than I wanted but not loud enough to where I would wake Neriyah.

She didn't say anything else but I saw her quickly wipe the tears off her face. She knew exactly what she was doing, messing around with a married man. Moments later, the doctor came in and informed us that she had the stomach flu and not to hesitate to bring her back if she got worse, including having a fever.

We walked through the lobby and I had a sleeping Neriyah in my arms with Maya walking alongside us. From the outside looking in, we looked like the perfect family not like a married man, his married mistress, and their child.

"So this is the conference call you mentioned earlier?" I almost jumped out my skin at the sound of my wife's voice. I cursed myself for not knowing where her appointments were. Shit was about to get real.

Brigail Jenkins

~

For the first time in my marriage, I really felt like killing Jordan's black ass. I had my suspicions about him, but I gave him the benefit of the doubt. And out of all the bitches he could have chosen, it had to be the bitch I hated, Maya's sneaky ass.

I wanted to slap the taste out his mouth but he had that bastard baby in his arms so I decked Maya in her shit because she had tried me for the last damn time.

"Stupid bitch." Maya yelled, and at the same time she swung wildly and I blocked every hit she tried to land. The fact that she kept trying to throw punches at my very pregnant belly, let me know she had it out for my unborn child. But she had another thing coming if she thought she was going to intentionally hurt my baby boy. Yes, you heard right.

I punched her dead in the eye with my right hand and I followed it with a punch to her nose with my left. Blood was leaking everywhere. Once she fell to the ground in surrender, covering up her face, I kicked her a few times in her stomach. I felt my body being lifted in the air and I looked in the eyes of Damon, my child's *biological* father, who was dressed in a security uniform. This situation just went from bad to horrific. Things couldn't possibly get any worse.

"You wildin' like this and you're pregnant?" Damon gritted through his teeth and I could tell by the way he was looking, he was disgusted with my behavior. I was now feeling stupid for fighting and putting my baby at risk.

"Get off me!" I snapped, I was embarrassed for acting this way like I wasn't out here doing the same shit Jordan was doing.

"Baby, I'm sorry. I didn't mean for –" I waved him off to save him the trouble. I didn't want to hear that shit.

"Please, stop. You're only sorry because you've been caught. Let me save you the trouble of that bullshit ass lie you were getting ready to tell."

"Fuck all that, is this baby mine?" Damon chimed in and if looks could kill, his ass would be dead with the death stare I was giving him.

"What the fuck is he talking about?" Jordan glared at me and I honestly didn't know what he expected me to say. He had been cheating on me since we were married. I was in denial, because I never had proof until now.

"Is it mine or not?" Damon asked again and I felt he already had the answer to his question.

"Yes!" I yelled because I was fed up and I was ready for the truth to be out. We had both made our beds and it was time for us to lay in them.

"I'm filing for divorce, muthafucka." I scoffed and turned around. At the same time they were putting Maya on a stretcher, she had loss a lot of blood. I couldn't give a fuck even if I wanted to.

When I got into my car, I let out a scream. This isn't the way I wanted my life to go. In my heart, I knew Jordan is where home is. We had too much history and so much at stake, a reputation to uphold but was he willing to raise another man's child? That was the million dollar question.

"Are you home?" I spoke into the phone after hearing my sisters voice seep through the phone.

"Yes. What's up sister?" She asked and she wasn't ready for that answer. I had painted this picture, like I had the perfect life but it was far from it.

"I'm on my way." I quickly said before I ended the call. We had a lot to talk about.

I pulled up to Brielle's house fifteen minutes later. I parked in her driveway and carefully removed myself from my truck. The bigger my stomach got, the harder it was for me to maneuver and do certain things.

"Hey sis." I said, giving her a hug. My sister had a glow to her like never before. Whoever was hitting that, was doing a damn good job.

"Hey boo. Look at that belly." She smiled, rubbing my stomach and as soon as she did that, I felt him moving around.

"Where's Jaden?" I asked, because it was quiet and there was no sign of him being here. No matter what, my nephew always makes his presence known.

"Girl, he's with his daddy. Do you know this nigga had the nerve to ask me if my pussy still taste the same?"

My face was scrunched up like he had just said that disrespectful shit to me. "I know he didn't." I said, rolling my eyes. I was in disbelief. He had his damn nerve.

"Girl, yes. So what's up? Do I need to beat somebody's ass?" She asked with her brows raised. Brielle had no problem beating nobody's ass. We stayed fighting bitches and niggas in the projects we were living in when we were younger. You can ask anybody about them Black sisters.

"My life is just falling apart, Bri. Today, I had an appointment to find out the baby's gender and Jordan couldn't make it because he had work, but tell me why I saw this nigga with a bitch and their child about to walk out the hospital. The crazy part about it though, it's the deacon's wife from our church." She gasped loudly with her hand covering her mouth. I knew she was shocked.

"That's not all though, I was up in there fighting, pregnant and all and I was pulled off the girl by the security guard, my child's father."

"What the fuck!!" She shouted, jumping up from her seat, doing the most.

"So I don't know how to handle this situation. I've only known Jordan, damn near my whole life, so should we try to fix this mess because we've both cheated?" I asked, searching in her eyes for an answer. I'm the big sister but here I am, looking for some advice, answers to my problems from my little sister, the baby.

"Sis, you have to follow your heart on this one. Do you feel like you can come to terms with the fact he's had a baby on you?"

"Two." I mumbled and she looked at me with an unreadable expression.

"Sis, sometimes you just have to throw the whole nigga away." She shrugged her shoulders and I understood where she was coming from.

It took me an hour to explain all the details about my infidelity and the fact that I knew Jordan had been cheating on me our entire marriage. I had a lot to think about and I really didn't know what to do, but at the end of the day, I had my baby boy to think about too. It wasn't just about me anymore.

"But what's up with you though? Enough about my shitty life. I need excitement." I laughed, to keep from crying, like I was on the inside. When I was alone, the tears that I've been forcing to stay bottled up would fall, but for now, I had to keep it together.

She gave me a sympathetic look before she started talking. "I have no complaints right now. Christian is damn near perfect, but I can't help the voices in my head saying it's too good to be true."

"You can't think like that and be truly happy. You shouldn't live your life in doubt and most certainly, don't let the guys of your past mess up what you're trying to build with him."

"You're absolutely right, sister." She said as she texted away on her phone, smiling ear to ear.

I was happy to see my sister happy and falling in love. Love was a beautiful thing, you just have to find the right soulmate to enjoy the journey with.

Chapter Twenty-One

~

Hazel Parks

My palms were all sweaty as I continued to get ready to meet Xá's mom. This was a big step, so hell yeah, I was nervous. Syan always told me I care too much about what people think about me. All I wanted was to make a good first impression, that's all.

I had on a black fitted leather skirt with an off white tank paired with an olive green blazer. On my feet were some olive green strappy over the knee boots.

"You still not ready?" Xá came into my bedroom, looking good enough to eat. I pushed that to the back of my mind, trying to focus on one thing at a time.

"How long you been here?" I asked while putting on my diamond hoop earrings and the matching necklace.

I had given him the spare key to my place and he did the same, because we were always at each others house. It made a lot of sense and plus it was convenient if the other was running late getting home.

"I just got here." He said, pecking me on my lips, sending butterflies throughout my entire body. "You look beautiful as always." He hugged my body tightly, while his hands were planted on my ass, where they always found themselves.

"Okay, give me five more minutes." I pulled away from his embrace and went into the bathroom to apply light makeup on my face.

"Good thing I told you to be ready at four." He said, rubbing his hand over his waves. "You would've been getting cussed out for showing up late." He laughed, but I didn't find that shit funny. I shot him the bird as I applied my M.A.C shimmer lip gloss on my lips.

"You could say thanks for saving your ass." He playfully mushed my head, but I paid his ass no mind.

I ignored his ass and grabbed up my bag, phone, and keys. "I'm ready. Come on." I fussed, ready to get this over with now.

The ride to his mom's house in Wyandotte was a little over a thirty minute drive. We pulled into the driveway of her beautiful property that sat off the water. I could only imagine how the inside looked. When Xá parked the car, my nerves returned, but this time, ten times harder. He came around to the passenger side, and I grabbed his hand so he could help me out the car.

"Don't be nervous bae. I know she's going to love you." He kissed my lips passionately while he held the small of my back. He gave me a reassuring smile before he proceeded in opening the door with the key that he had on his ring with all his other keys.

"Mama, we're here." He called out, searching each room for her, with me following behind him.

When we reached the kitchen, I saw her standing over the stove with her back to us. I could already smell the food when I came into the house, but now that I was standing in the kitchen, the soul food aroma hit my nostrils full force. All of a sudden, I felt like I was starving. My mouth watered at the crispy chicken she turned over in the cast iron skillet .

"Hey Ma." Xá spoke again, walking further into the kitchen, closer to her.

She jumped back, frightened. "Boy, you liked to got shot." She said with her hand on the holster she had planted at her side. Her pretty face was frowned up. His mom's face looked so youthful. You wouldn't be able to look at her and say she had three fully grown ass kids with grandkids. Her complexion was like vanilla. She didn't have any wrinkles in sight. Her body was fit, giving me a run for my money.

"Ma, so you really was gone shoot me?" He laughed, shaking his head. She gave him that look like 'hell yeah', "Well this is my woman, Hazel. Hazel, this is my mama Ms. Black."

"Girl, you better not listen to his ass. Don't call me miss anything. Mama B or BB will be just fine." She smiled and welcomed me with a hug.

"It's nice to meet you BB. You have a wonderful home, might I add." I said, admiring her kitchen and all the artwork portrayed all over the walls.

"Thank you. Son, you got you a beautiful lady. I was starting to think you had switched to the other side." She joked but Xá didn't find it funny. However, me on the other hand, was cracking up along with his mother.

"Ma, you know better than that. And you think that's funny?" He asked, pointing at me.

"You laugh when something is funny, right?" I sarcastically countered because he was getting too defensive for my liking.

"Ain't nobody worried about that man. He'll be alright. Matter of fact, go up in that nursery and set that baby crib up for me."

"All that's not even necessary." He fussed.

"I'm getting ready for my grandbaby, so yes it is. You not giving me any, so shut up. I need to get to know my daughter anyway." She dared him with her eyes to say something back and in seconds, he disappeared somewhere in this big ass house.

"My son don't bring just anybody around to meet me and that's for whoever, friends included, so I take his word and I know you're a good person. What I want to know is, do you plan on building a future with my son and most importantly, do you plan on having my grandchildren?"

I sat at the bar and processed everything she said. She was crazy for sure. Having children were the last thing on my mind and from what the doctors are saying, I won't be able to conceive in the future. It's probably sad to say, but that might not be a bad thing. After all the things I've been through, it may just not be meant for me to have children. I didn't know how Xá would take that information which is why when he mentions having children, I change the subject or give an indirect answer. I'm learning to accept it because I have to, it's me, it's my life. Xá didn't have to accept it and that was killing me. I didn't want him to leave me because of that minor issue. It may be selfish, but I will hold on to that information as long as I could.

Brenda Black

~

Meeting Hazel was just how I thought it would be. I know Xá so I knew he wouldn't bring no hoochie, or in other words, no rat ass bitch to my house to meet me. She's the most prettiest lil chocolate thang I'd ever seen with the most beautiful hazel eyes. Together, her and Xá will make me some beautiful grandbabies. All my kids were grown as hell, in their thirties or damn near kissing them, but I only had one grandson. I lucked up and had one in the way as well by my oldest girl, finally.

"I'm pretty sure we're going to last forever and when the time comes, I don't have no problem giving you grandchildren." She smiled, and it amazed me of how drop dead gorgeous she was. I don't even think she realized it.

"I can roll with that." I nodded my head as I got up to take the last batch of chicken out the grease. "Do you have any children?" I asked, pulling my macaroni out the oven. I did that, stirred the greens and candied yams and she still hadn't answered my question.

"No ma'am, I don't." She finally said with uncertainty laced in her voice. My son hadn't mentioned her having any children so I would just leave it alone. Besides, the truth always comes to the light anyways.

"Now, I like you and all but call me ma'am again, we're going to have some serious problems." I raised my voice just a little, so she could know just how serious I was.

"Okay, okay. I got it Mama Black." She said with her hands in surrender, as if I was going to arrest her.

"Girl, you're alright with me." I laughed, while taking my corn muffins out the oven and at the same time Brielle and her date came in the kitchen hand in hand.

"Hey mama, this is my man Christian. Christian this is my mama Ms. Black, just don't call her that." She joked and I nodded my head in agreement.

"Nice to meet you." He said, extending his hand to shake mine, but I pulled him into a hug instead.

"Likewise, and this is Hazel, your brother's lady."

"Hey." She said, waving to them both with a smile on her face.

"Wassup man. It's been a minute." Xá said, coming into the kitchen, speaking to Christian. They gave each other a brotherly hug.

"Yeah, you been smooth though?" He asked, taking a seat next to Brielle.

"Yeah, yeah. I'm glad to see you doing good too, with the restaurant and all."

"Bri, where's my grandson?" I questioned, I missed his bad, smart-mouthed ass.

"He's with Ethan, it's his weekend." She said, trying to open the lids to my pots with her greedy ass. I popped her hands like I always did when any of my children did that shit, knowing that it irked my damn nerves.

"Help me set the table." I nudged her and I glanced at Hazel who had been tense ever since Brielle mentioned Ethan's name. I pay attention to everything, thanks to my late husband, my kid's father. He kept me on my toes and made sure I watched everybody and everything, especially with more than two niggas in one room. I'm always ready for anything, which is why I kept Bambi at my hip. Bambi is my 9mm that I kept with me at all times, no matter the occasion. That was the first gun my husband had ever bought me. Lord knows, I missed my baby. He was what kept me whole.

Hazel Parks

~

I had zoned out upon hearing Ethan's name. Shocked was an understatement. There was no doubt in my mind that they were talking about *my* Ethan. I had heard Xá mention his nephew Jaden's name several times so I just put two and two together and that had to be the grandson she mentioned.

"You okay bae?" Xá asked, rubbing my thigh. We were at the dinner table and I had been picking over my food and in and out of the conversations that were going on. I was out of it and didn't know how to feel about this crazy situation.

"Yes." I put on a fake smile and started to eat my food. Somehow, I no longer had an appetite, despite how good the food looked.

I put my acting skills to use, putting Ethan in the very back of mind. The fact that we were no longer present, yet he kept lingering around; it pissed me off. I didn't want to come off as rude or anti-social for a first impression, so I engaged in the conversations that were flowing throughout the table. They were all so funny, and keeping me laughing. I had laughed so much, I was scared I wouldn't e able to laugh anymore.

"Where's your other sister?" I asked because I was looking forward to meeting everyone today.

"Girl, she's at home being pregnant as hell, stank ass attitude and all." She laughed and I shook my head. With all the hormonal changes your body goes through, carrying a child, I don't blame her.

"And she's entitled to that stank ass attitude, as you call it." Ms. Black chimed in.

"OMG, sorry mama. You know I get carried away sometimes." She whined, rolling her eyes. Without knowing them, anyone could sense that she was the baby.

"I'm just going to start carrying around a bar of soap and bottle of water like I had to when you were younger." She fussed, removing herself from the table. I could tell she was annoyed, by the expression her face held, and by the way she moved around the kitchen.

"Ma, we going to head out." Xá announced, grabbing both our plates. After he dumped the remaining contents of our plate in the trash, he put our dishes in the dishwasher.

"Not before dessert, you won't." She sassed, taking out the triple fudge cake, she made from scratch, out the oven. Either he was going to stay a little bit longer or he was going to be waiting for me in the car, because if it was the last thing I did, I was getting some of that cake. I hadn't eaten sweets in a couple weeks and the fact that it looked like it should be on the cover of some food magazine just ignited my urge to devour the chocolate goodness. It looked that damn good, I wouldn't lie to you.

When I bit into the cake, the chocolate fudge oozed out, bringing so much moisture into my mouth. This was by far the best thing I've ever put in my mouth. After I ate the cake, she wrapped me up a slice, and after thanking her a thousand times, we left with Brielle and Christian following behind us.

"Hazel." Brielle got my attention as I was getting into the car.

"Yes?" I answered, wondering what it was she had to say. I couldn't read her face, so I just waited to hear what it was.

"Do you happen to know my baby daddy Ethan?" I looked at her long and hard to try to see where she was coming from, so I could know how to respond.

"Yes, he's my ex." I could feel Xá's glare on me. We've talked about him before, I just never felt the need to mention his name when he's a non-factor in my life.

"I've heard about you before but for some reason I just never saw you around. I just want to clear the air, because I don't want it to feel weird when we're around each other. Especially when my child will be around you. I just don't want no bad blood." She smiled, walking closer to the car.

"I'm not going to lie, it's gonna be a little awkward for me at first but as far as me acting or being a certain way towards your son, that's a negative. He can't help who his father is. We're good and plus we've both moved on to bigger and better things anyway." I joked, and we were both laughing.

"Damn right. See you later sis." She gave me a hug, before she got into the car and left with Christian. I was just glad that conversation went the way it did and that it's out the way.

"Are you coming to my place tonight?" Xá questioned as we hopped on the expressway. I nodded my head, yes, and got comfortable in my seat for the ride.

I hadn't realized I fell asleep, until Xá nudged me to get up, because we were at his house. I stretched out my arms before getting out of the car.

"You can't even stay up for the car ride." He had the nerve to say, while shaking his head.

"Man, whatever." I laughed, playfully mushing his head.

"Got slob and shit all over my seat belt." He laughed, turning the lights on in the living room.

"I'll get your car detailed, that's what you want to hear?" I joked, taking a seat in the recliner chair.

"Nope, I got it." He plopped down on the sofa and flicked through the movies on Netflix. My eyes were glued to him. I still couldn't believe I could call him mine. He was so damn fine and perfect.

"So what we about to watch?" I quizzed, breaking the stare I had on him.

"You mean what I'm about to watch? I give you a good ten minutes, before you're snoring again.

"I'm up, I swear." I said, climbing into his lap, pecking his lips.

"You taste so good." He pulled me back closer, this time kissing me hungrily. My body was reacting, my pussy wet, and nipples standing at attention. I unbuckled his pants, shocking myself, but it was time. The wait was over.

"Not here." He whispered against my lips. He got up with me still on him. I wrapped my legs around his waist as he continued up the stairs to his bedroom. When we reached his bed, he gently laid my body down and he dimmed the lights and turned the stereo on. 'It Seems Like You're Ready' boomed through the speakers. He seemed to be walking in slow motion, as he neared me.

He pulled my shirt over my head then he unsnapped my bra. He kissed my lips again and trailed kisses down my neck, collarbone, and when he reached my breasts, he took my left nipple in his mouth. He took his time licking and sucking on it, so hungrily.

"Mmm." I lightly moaned, as he switched to my other breast. He flicked his tongue over my hardened nipple multiple times as he roughly pulled down my skirt, ripping my lace thong off in the process. He trailed kisses down my stomach until he reached my honey pot, sucking and biting along the way.

The warmth of his tongue invaded my pussy as he took his time pleasuring every part of my vagina. My body trembled as he sucked the life out of me, becoming one with my pussy.

"You gone feed daddy that good shit?" He asked in between placing wet, sloppy kisses on my clit. I could feel my orgasm nearing.

"Oh my God! I'm cumming Xá!" I shouted as my body started shaking uncontrollably. No man has ever made my body feel the way that it does now.

Before I had time to recuperate, my body stiffened up as he slid his meaty dick inside my wetness. He pumped in and out of me nice and slow, giving me deep and passionate strokes. A lone tear traveled down my cheek from the sensual dick down Xá was giving me.

"Xá.." I moaned barely above a whisper, feeling another orgasm coming.

"You like when daddy fuck you like this?" He sped up the pace, stroking me faster, deeper, and longer. "Or like this?" He slowed his pace down, not missing a beat. He kept hitting my g-spot all the while. My pussy got wetter, sounding like macaroni and cheese. All you could hear was him moving in and out of me and my cries out for help because he was murdering my pussy.

"Babyy, I'm cumming again. Fuckkk!!" I cried out, this orgasm more powerful than the last. I couldn't take any more, or my throbbing pussy, so I took him in my mouth, using it as a suction as I sucked his dick and gently massaged his balls. His light moans motivated me even more, so I continued sucking his dick like my life depended on it, taking note on the way his toes would curled up.

"Damn girl." He grunted, pulling on my hair as he fucked my face. It wasn't long before he unleashed his kids down my throat. I swallowed with no hesitation.

Unable to move my body, I laid my head on the pillow. He had officially fucked me to sleep. Moments later, I could feel my eyes getting heavy so I closed them, not putting up a fight and let sleep take over me.

Syan González

~

When I found out I was pregnant with Hector Jr., I was jumping for joy. Now that I just found out about my current pregnancy, I couldn't be happy. I didn't want to bring a child into our drama. Not only that, but I damn sure didn't want to be pregnant at the same time as Lisa. I just didn't know what to do. I hadn't seen Hector in weeks. We had been co-parenting and for the most part, it was going well. Either his mom or sister would be the middleman.

"Good morning baby." I cooed to my son, watching him make spit bubbles with his mouth. I don't know how$ his ass learned that shit, but between him being his dad's son and watching YouTube all damn day on his iPad, there was no telling.

"Dada. Dada. Dada!" He screamed at the top of his lungs. It broke my heart that, he too, was suffering from the seperation just like I was. I was so upset that I'd been living like a single parent when I had a whole ass husband.

Life had a way of showing you things about people that you would never think one is capable of. In this case, I've learned that Hector doesn't respect me like I once thought he did. If he did, we wouldn't be in the place that we're in now. I wouldn't be feeling the way that I feel and neither would my son. I really wanted to kick his ass, but that wouldn't solve shit.

I grabbed my ringing cell phone and saw that my dad was Facetime calling me. I had gotten used to hearing his voice at least four times out the week.

"Hey dad." I gave a forced smile. I never liked for anyone to see me sweat, not even family. Showing any type of vulnerability wasn't my thing.

"What's wrong baby girl?" He asked, staring deeply into my eyes.

"Nothing, everything's fine." This time, I gave a more convincing smile, but he looked as if he could see right through my bullshit.

"Surabhi, you don't have to lie to me. Let me help you."

I sighed heavily, already over this conversation that hadn't even started yet. "Hector's cheating on me."

"Are you sure baby girl? In marriage, you can never assume, and never take an outsider's word over your husband's." He said sternly, his accent thick like the hair on my head.

"Daddy, I seen it with my own eyes. There are pictures." I sobbed, feeling myself getting worked up. This is what I was trying to avoid. Lately, I had been on one hell of an emotional roller coaster.

"I'm sorry baby girl, but you have to sit down and talk to him like two grown adults. I know Hector loves you and sometimes, us men, we do stupid shit to the women we love. Me and your mom has been there before. Save your marriage while you can because Brahman knows, I miss your mother, my beloved wife." His voice cracked and I couldn't imagine losing Hector. Although, I hated his ass right now, I loved him even more. "Kiss my grandson for me and remember everything I said." He added, before disconnecting the call, leaving my thoughts to invade all the empty space in my brain.

Chapter Twenty-Two

~

Harmony Woods

"You're such a cheater." I pouted, staring into Hunter's eyes. I was the biggest sore loser ever.

"So I'm a cheater just, because you lost?" He chuckled, but I found nothing funny. My expression held the resting bitch face. I had talked big cash shit on the way to paint balling, and I had lost to his ass. I would probably feel better had we not made that bet.

Before we started the game, he told me he would buy me a car of my choice if I won ,because beating him, is like trying to knock out Mayweather. And if I lost, I would have to cook his lunch during the week for two whole months. On top of me losing the game and the bet, I would hear him bragging all damn day.

"You could have at least let me get you one time." I rolled my eyes as I followed him in the parking lot in search of his car. Before we got changed, I was wearing every color of the rainbow while this nigga looked like he was fresh out the shower.

"And that would be cheating fasho, so just take this L baby, we all have them. You can't win all the time." He joked, making me want to slap his ass.

The ride to his house was unique. I ignored his ass, like the plague while continuously turning the volume up every time he tried talking to me. I could be Petty Betty like no other, I had that shit down pact.

When we pulled into the parking garage, we rode the elevator up to his place in silence. I paid it no mind as I engaged on my phone, catching up on drama amongst other irrelevant, but interesting shit. I took a seat on the couch and flicked through the channels while he disappeared to the back.

In the middle of me cracking up, watching Tamar's crazy ass on her TV show, I felt Hunter's presence and his intoxicating scent explored my entire nasal cavity. I glanced over my shoulder and sure enough, he was leaning on the wall, staring through my soul.

"Come here." His voice demanded, sending a shockwave through my body. He had Morris Chestnut in 'Not Easily Broken' beat when he said those same two, short but strong, powerful words to Taraji P. Henson.

I eased off the couch and, slowly, strutted to this man. I could feel my pussy pulsating more and more as I got closer to him. When I was in arm's reach, he grabbed me up roughly, backing me up against the wall he was just leaning on seconds ago. The moment his lips connected with mine, I tightened up my legs because I could feel my juices building up, on the verge of sliding down my legs.

His hand traveled down my body and his fingers found my pussy. His fingers toyed with my clit as I bit down on my lip, trying not to cry out from the pleasure I was receiving.

"Stop ignoring me over petty shit." His husky voice whispered against my neck. The warmth of his breath caused the hairs on my back to stand. He stuck three fingers in and out of my tight, soaked pussy as he continuously flicked his thumb over my throbbing clit.

"Shit." I softly moaned, trying not to slide down the wall. It was so hard to keep my balance.

"You hear me talking to you?" He groaned, quickening his pace and my eyes rolled to the back of my head. This man's fingers had voodoo on them, I swear.

"Yesss!" I screamed as I creamed all over his fingers. I had never came so hard from getting fingered before. He brought his hand to his mouth and licked his fingers clean.

He picked me up bridal style and carried me into the master bedroom where he had ran me a bubble bath. The bathroom was barely lit, the only light was coming from the few candles he had placed around his massive jacuzzi tub and throughout the bathroom. He stripped me out of my clothing and he placed me in the steamy, hot water, just how I liked it. I could feel the soreness from our activities earlier, leaving my body as the jets in the bathtub hit the pressure points all over my body.

"Are you getting in?" I cooed, looking into his tantalizing eyes.

He shook his head, no. "I'm going to watch you.' He smirked, lustfully looking over every detail of my naked body.

After our stare down that only lasted about eight minutes, he grabbed a washcloth from the cabinet and lathered it with my body wash. He gently washed every crease and fold of my being. He washed my body multiple times with his soft and gentle touch. After he helped me out the tub, he lead me to his luxurious king size bed, directing me to lay on my stomach. I quickly obliged, anticipating what was to come next.

I felt something warm being drizzled over my body. I closed my eyes as he rubbed in, what I assumed to be, oil as he gently caressed and massaged my body. I shocked my damn self when I started moaning uncontrollably at the sensational feeling.

"Turn over." He ordered and I wasted no time following his command.

When his hands groped my breasts, I bit my bottom lip watching him, watching me as his hand roamed freely all over my hot, glistening body. He placed a kiss on my lips followed by my neck, shoulders, left breast, right breast, belly button, thighs, legs, and feet. He sucked on every toe before he traveled back up my body, stopping at my most precious treasure. He placed a soft, delicate kiss on my lips. Once his mouth was met with my clit, he marked his territory, writing his name all up and through there, putting some pornstars to shame with the skills he had.

"Ooooh baby. I can't fight it!" I shouted to the rooftops from my second orgasm.

"Don't hold nothing back." He coached as he slurped up every drop of my sweet juices.

After regaining my composure, I slid his boxers down his legs, using my teeth. The amazon between his legs greeted me, and I gladly opened wide to give him a warm welcome. I let the tip of his dick touch the base of my throat, while making it sloppy for him, how most men liked it. I built up saliva in my mouth and spat on his dick, using my hand to massage it in. His dick disappeared back down my throat and I took my left hand to caress his balls.

"Fuck. Damn, girl." He growled as I sucked the skin off his thick rod, making smacking sounds with my mouth.

I took my mouth off his dick and I positioned myself to straddled him, reverse cowgirl. I planted my feet on both sides of his legs and eased down. As he guided the head of his dick at my opening, my mouth formed the O shape. I inched my body down until he filled me up with all he had to offer. As I bounced my ass up and down, his hands found my breasts, once again, and he played with my hard nipples while sucking on my neck.

"Baby, you feel so damn good!" I cried out from the euphoric pleasure I continuously felt with every stroke.

"Daddy about to bust." He grunted and that was all the motivation I needed to quicken my pace. I took my right hand and played with my pussy as I continued to ride the wave to another orgasm.

"Fuccck." We both shouted in unison as we creamed together.

I was fresh out of energy, as I stiffly laid in the middle of the bed as he washed my body then his with the warm washcloth he'd gotten from the bathroom. When he got in bed behind me, I cuddled close to him and it didn't take long for my eyes to close and heart rate to slow down, until I was asleep.

Hunter Williams

~

"What up old man." I gave my pops a quick hug before taking my seat across from him in the booth. I had met him at Red Lobster, my mom's favorite restaurant, for her birthday. She would have been sixty today.

"I done told you about that shit man." He joked, taking a sip from his water.

"I miss her so much man. I just wish she could see the man I've become." I confessed, I had been feeling this way a lot lately.

I had done a complete turnaround from back in the day, when I was in the streets. While in high school, I gave my mama hell. She spent so many nights worrying about my whereabouts. She had already lost one son to street violence. She didn't want to lose me too. When my pops got out of jail, I had to straighten up because he was on my ass. I got my grades up and graduated high school and I surprised myself when I enrolled in college. Now that I was a certified doctor and had my business up and running, she wasn't here to celebrate my accomplishments with me, and it broke my heart.

"She's smiling down at yo ugly ass now." He joked, bringing light to the situation.

"I bet my ugly ass can take your girl." I laughed, watching his smirk turn into a frown. I knew that would get his ass started.

"Nigga please. You can't give her what I can give her. She needs that ole school loving and yo young ass don't know how to put that shit down playa."

"Man, whatever. When am I gonna meet this woman anyway?" I asked, he had been talking about her heavily so I was just curious to know when the introductions would come around.

"I'm gonna put a little dinner together and you bring your lady and we'll all meet then." He stated, I guess he had it all figured out.

"You want us to bring a dish?"

"Now you know better than that." He waved me off. His ass swore he was Gordon Ramsey in the kitchen. I remember when I was younger, him and my mom would go head up in the kitchen and would throw me in the middle of their shit and have me judge and pick the best dish.

After we kicked it over lunch, I headed to X&H Recreation Center. It was still surreal to me that I had my own business. Helping the youth is what I always wanted to do. I had been there before, so I knew how it was being in the streets. My Mama was a single parent while my pops was locked up, so we didn't have it like we did when he was out. That's why I decided to take matters in my own hands and started hustling in the streets. I'm just glad pops got out when he did, because I know I would've been deep in the streets and everybody knows nothing good comes from the fast life. Either you'll be casket sharp or cage ready.

"What's the word Xá?" I peeked into his office. He had paperwork scattered all over his desk and his eyes trained on the computer screen.

"Shit, just trying to get all these resources in motion." He replied, not taking his eyes off the screen. Focused wasn't even the word.

"Did you get the files I put in your mailbox about the housing commission that we're partnering up with?" We were about to start up a program where we helped young adults get on their feet, whether it be they have no family or good living conditions or they were fresh out of juvenile or jail. Our number one goal was to keep the streets clean of teens because our future is in the hands of the youth.

"Yeah, I sent that through this morning."

"Cool, cool. Well it's something I wanted to run by you." It had been on my mind lately, so I was glad I caught up with him in his office.

"What's up bro?" He questioned, with his eyes trained on me and his arms folded across his chest.

"You know Harmony and Hazel's birthday is coming up, so I wanted to know if you was down with planning them a surprise party?"

"Hell yeah. That shit gonna be dope. I'm just mad my dumb ass didn't think of it before you." He joked. "We better get Sasha on the decorating and planning now then."

"You ain't never lied. I'll hit her ass up in a few."

"If you mentioning black folks time 'few' expect her to get in yo ass." He laughed. "You better be in her DMs or however y'all communicate by tonight."

"I already know bro. That girl is crazy as hell." I agreed, thinking about how far she was in our ass the whole time we were getting the center together.

I handled more shit at the office, before I headed to the crib to cook my girl a good meal. I had a lot more free time on my hands because I had the company and we had overly competent workers, who could run the business just like we would with no problems. I still had my clients that I would see. My lady was working hard, so it was only right she came home to dinner, dick, and company.

Chapter Twenty-Three

Syan González

I sighed heavily upon hearing a knock, followed by the sounding of the doorbell. Before I even got up to check who it was, I already knew it was Hazel's persistent ass. Her and Harmony had been adamant about getting me out the house. It was Hector's weekend, so finding a babysitter wasn't the problem. I just wanted to be left alone.

"Why aren't you dressed?" The smile that she had faded away as she looked at my attire. I had on my Hello Kitty onesie, with a cup of coffee in my hand.

"I told you I wasn't coming." I mumbled, and stood aside to let her in.

"But you are though." Harmony snuck up behind us. I might as well put my clothes on and get over it. It was no winning against them two.

Without responding, I rolled my eyes and stormed upstairs. like a kid throwing a tantrum. I took a quick shower and threw on Puma leggings and the matching hoodie and gym shoes to match. I had no one to impress, and dressing comfortably had been my motto. If I wasn't in sweats, I was lounging around in one of Hector's oversized beaters or my pj's.

"Much better." Hazel smirked, clapping her hands and shit, to be dramatic as always. I flipped her the bird and sparked up the blunt I had just rolled. Smoking had been my go to, my escape from my reality. I smoked before doing anything or going anywhere. The baby growing inside me didn't didn't stop me from needing my medicine and termination had been heavily on my mind.

After the blunt went in rotation a few times, we put the blunt out and got into Hazel's car. All three of us were high as hell with low, red eyes and all. At first, I was conscious about certain people knowing about me smoking, but now, I could give two fucks about what somebody had to say about me.

"So where are we going?" I asked, wanting to mentally prepare myself for the festivities that were to come.

"We need fill-ins." She stated and glanced over to my hands. "And by the looks of it, you need yours done too."

"Ha ha, bitch. I guess you got jokes." I sarcastically laughed. I took in my nails and I had definitely been slacking. I'd never even gone around with chipped polish let alone four broken nails. I let the shit between me and Hector knock me off my square, but between being with Hazel and Harmony, they'll get my ass together real quick and have me in tip top shape.

When we pulled into So Fleeky Hair and Nails, you would think they were giving away free full sets and quickweaves. The parking lot was full to capacity, so we had to park across the street. I prepared myself to be in here all damn day. They were always booked, but they always found a way to squeeze us in.

I took my seat next to Hazel in the waiting area of the salon. The waiting room was so huge, it was a salon in itself. Once they were called to the back, that left me alone, so I busied myself with my phone that I barely used. I used this free time to do some online shopping. I politely used Hector's black card to fund all my expenses. Two girls came and sat on the opposite side of me, gossiping like it wasn't no tomorrow. I silently cursed them out because I hated being around loud mouthed, ghetto bitches.

Forty thousand dollars later, their conversation had peaked my interests. They now had my full attention.

"And you really did that dumb shit?" The girl with the fucked up, bright ass red frontal asked, looking like someone's long lost transgender gorilla.

"Yes, girl. I never knew bitches could be so desperate though. He had to lug his heavy ass in that car. When he told me his cousin was scandalous, I didn't think she would go as far as drugging her baby daddy to get her pregnant again."

"Damn. This sound like some Lifetime movie shit. So bitches is really that pressed?" She shook her head with her face frowned up. I'm sure my face matched hers, because I always wore my feelings on my face. If you wanted to know how I felt, all you had to do was look at me. It was always written on my face.

I continued listening in on their conversation, with my mind racing a mile a minute. They didn't even know they had just cost someone their life. I wanted to clarify my speculations without coming off as crazy. When they were called to the back, my mind was in overdrive, trying to come up with ways to approach the conversation. Shortly after they went to the back, my nail tech called for me to come to the back as well.

After I had my coffin ombre nails, with my pink and white pedicure, all three of us walked to the car. I spotted both girls in the chair while walking past and they looked to be almost finished. We walked to the car and I told Hazel and Harmony the plan, and of course they was down, like I thought they would be.

As we sat and waited in the car, I sparked up another blunt to calm my mood and pass time. When I saw them coming out the door, looking halfway decent, I was just finishing off the blunt. I jumped out the car and jogged up to them with my hands planted at my side.

"Aye, lemme holla at you for a minute." I said as cool as I could.

"Do I know you?" The girl with the bright weave smartly asked with too much movement in her neck for my liking. It was always the ugly bitches, mad at the world with fucked up attitudes. Now why did she have to do all that when I tried to be chill. Well, at least I did try.

I let out an angry laugh and whipped out my 9mm, before they could process what was going on. "Bitch, you tried it. Don't ever try to get grim with me again. Now you." I turned to the girl with the short pixie cut. "Who is the bitch that drugged her baby daddy? What's her name?" I continued with a mean mug on my face to let her know, I meant business. It was nothing for me to let off shots to her skull. I guess you could say, I get it from my husband.

"Uh-uh-" Her eyes kept looking from me to my gun that was aimed at her. I get that she was scared and all but she now was wasting my time with the dramatics.

"I don't have all damn day. Speak the fuck up." I gritted through clenched teeth, tightening my grip on the trigger. I didn't know this bitch from Adam and Eve, so I didn't know if she had the balls to jump stupid or not, but I always had the upper hand, always.

"Lisa, the bitch name is Lisa!" She yelled and her simple ass must have forgot I was the one holding the fucking gun.

"Watch your muthafucking tone when you talking to me." I cracked her and her ugly ass friend in the head with the butt of my gun and jogged back to where Hazel's car was parked.

Before my feet were all the way in the car, Hazel was speeding off like the gutta bitch she is deep inside, underneath that naive exterior.

"Okay then, Bonnie." Harmony joked as we sped down the one way street, going the wrong way. Hazel's non-driving ass paid no mind to the traffic rules. She had made up her own damn rules when it came to driving.

"Yes, bitch. Now, it's time to get my Clyde back, so we can handle this bitch and her cousin accordingly." I smirked, thinking about how much I missed my man. I was glad and relieved he hadn't betrayed me like that.

The whole ride back to my house, I had a smile plastered on my face. Knowing that I was about to end this bitch's life had my pussy wet. I thought back to the first time I caught a body and that shit didn't phase me at all. Some Ohio cats came to my hometown gunning for my husband, because he had everything they wanted and he was stealing their clientele, so they threw a temper tantrums, trying to ruin everything my husband had built. I remember telling his ass, life ain't fair before I let off the whole clip in his body. I tried to warn people. Yeah, I may be cute and little, but don't forget I always have that strap on me. I can be a soccer mom and the grim reaper at the same damn time.

Hector González

~

When my wife called, telling me she wanted to talk, I came running. Not having her in the way I wanted and needed, had fucked up my attitude and my shit was already fucked up to begin with. I probably had my whole team gunning for me, because I wasn't letting shit slide. I just wasn't the same without my rib, my other half.

"Wassup." She greeted me at the door with her hands on her hip and a smirk on her perfectly shaped glossy lips.

I ran my tongue across my lips, as I studied my wife from head to toe. It had been a minute, but her body was just how I remembered. I studied her eyes, then the way her small perky breasts sat up in the tank she was wearing, with no bra. Then they traveled down to the way her fat pussy was on display in the leggings she was wearing, with no panties. She was good for walking around commando damn near about to get her head knocked off her fucking shoulders. "What's up." I finally said, walking into our house that was immaculate, but that was no surprise.

"Why didn't you tell me about the shit that happened with Lisa?" She asked, with a straight face, catching me off guard.

"Because I couldn't prove it." I said, shrugging my shoulders. I was half way telling the truth.

"No, you just didn't want nobody to know somebody caught you slipping." She said as if she was in my head. I expected nothing less from her. She knew me like the back of her hand and vice versa.

"Yeah, you right." I laughed it off. I didn't know what to say so we stood in the foyer in silence with our eyes trained on each other.

"I'm killing her." She stated calmly, like she just didn't admit to planning a murder without breaking our stare.

"Good luck with that shit. Her ass is M.I.A." I sighed, rubbing my temple. Money talked, so I was flabbergasted that no one had spoke up. It was really pissing me off. All I could do was hope my daughter was safe with her psycho ass Mama.

"Baby, she can't always be in hiding." She winked, walking off towards the kitchen. My eyes were glued to her ass that was sitting up nicely, thanks to me, for putting in major work all these years. "Are you hungry?" She asked, moving swiftly around the kitchen.

"I'm always hungry. Don't act brand new." I chuckled, turning on the TV. I was basking in this moment, I was content with just being in her presence.

Moments later, she came and sat a plate of ribs, macaroni and cheese, baked beans, and cornbread with a tall glass of kool-aid on the glass table. I ate my food quickly and sat back and watched Syan as she watched the chick flick that was playing on the Hallmark Channel.

"I missed you daddy." Syan whispered against my ear as she positioned herself so that she was straddling my lap. On cue, my third leg sprung to life. I hadn't gotten my dick wet in months, so he was long overdue.

"I missed you too." I kissed her soft lips and she opened her mouth just a little so I could insert my tongue. Our tongues did the tango as the sexual tension between us intensifies. I wanted, hell, I needed her in the worst way.

I knew shit was about to get real when her hands found my belt, trying to release little man. She raised her body up so she could pull my pants along with my boxers down. She pulled off my shirt and I snatched hers off, exposing her pretty titties. She pulled down her leggings and hopped back on the dick.

"Fuck." I grunted, her pussy was hella tight and wet as hell. It had gone too long, since I was in them guts.

As she bounced up and down, I grabbed hold of her left nipple with my mouth. I used my tongue to trace circles around her hard nipples, making sure to flick my tongue over it multiple times.

"Mmmm baby. You feel sooo good." She moaned as she dropped her head back and I switched to her right nipple.

"Damn baby. You showing out for daddy's dick." I whispered against her ear. She was pulling out tricks from years ago. I could feel myself about to bust and I wasn't no minute man.

Her pace quickened, pussy wetter, muscles tighter, sending me to the edge. I couldn't stop it if I wanted to.

I grabbed her up and threw her body over the couch. "Spread them legs." I demanded, slapping her ass in the process. I rubbed my dick along her pussy, teasing her for a minute then I plunged inside, hitting places that hadn't been touched for some time. I had a point to prove, because busting prematurely wasn't in my blood.

I gave her nothing short of hard dick, trying my best to knock the lining out that pussy. "Daddy, I'm about to cum." She cried out, barely above a whisper.

I kept giving her deep strokes, continuously hitting her spot and it wasn't long before she was squirting all over my dick. Three pumps later, I was releasing my kids in her. Damn, I needed to bust that nut.

"Where's my son?" I asked as we washed each other's bodies in the shower.

"He's spending the night with Hazel." She said, dipping her head under the water. I watched her intently. It was something about looking at my baby while she was dripping wet. I could look at her ass all day. I was a creep when it came to my wife, and I didn't give a fuck what nobody had to say about it.

After our shower, we laid right in the bed butt ass naked. It felt good to be home. The hotel I was at was one of the best, it just couldn't compare to being home. Syan was positioned with her head lying on my chest, her favorite way to sleep. I had my queen back, so I had no worries.

"I'm pregnant." Syan broke the silence. A huge grin spread across my face, because that was the best news I had gotten in a while.

"I know. Yo pussy was extra wet and tight." I chuckled, I knew her body like I knew my own.

"Don't say that like my shit not already wet and tight." She mushed my head and we both laughed. I went to sleep, feeling like a boss with a huge smile on my face.

Chapter Twenty-Four

~

Hazel Parks

"Get up. I know you not sleep." Xá sighed, raising his voice, because I had been playing possum for the past fifteen minutes.

"Okayyy." I whined, once he started tickling my feet, with his childish ass.

He was more excited about it being my birthday than I was. My birthday never excited me. If anything, I dreaded it being my birthday. Violet, my foster mom made sure of that. Living with her, had always been hell but on my birthday, it was fifty times worse. Like, how is that even possible?

On my ninth birthday, mother nature showed her ass. Not only was my flow heavy, I had cramps similar to labor pain. I remember going through ten pads in one day, my very first day of my cycle. That wasn't even the worst part. The fact that she made me wear all ten of my used pads on my face was. If her plan was to hurt, humiliate, and embarrass me, it worked and she did a damn good job at it. She always did. She even went as far as taking pictures and used them as blackmail to get complete compliance from me. I had to have that break out from all that bacteria on my face for a whole month.

So when I said that I hated her ass with every atom in my being, I'm not lying. I meant that from the deepest part of my heart.

I got out the bed and stretched. Last night was one of the nights where I'd had the best sleep. Xá ate my pussy until I tapped out. The last thing I remembered before I closed my eyes was Xá using his mouth like a vacuum as he slurped every drop of my orgasm. If heaven felt better than that, I wanted front row seats there.

"Hurry up." He said, slapping me on the ass. I lost track of how many times he's told me to shower and get my stuff together, because supposedly he had a lot in store for me.

After I showered, I put on my Gucci jogging suit with the matching sneakers. As I was pulling my curly hair into a bun, Xá walked in wearing a Gucci jogging suit, similar to mine, looking like a whole snack. He was smart for showering and dressing in the guest room, because had he been in there with me, all his plans would have been canceled.

Ever since he got a taste of this magical pussy, he stayed on my ass and when he wasn't on me, I was on him, practically begging for the dick. That's exactly why my hot tail ass needed some sort of birth control. Although, my doctor said what he said, I needed to be one thousand percent sure.

"Jock." I teased as I stood up from my vanity chair to peck his lips. Of course a peck wasn't good enough for him, so he dipped his head back to my level and forced his tongue, which I automatically latched onto.

"Great minds think alike." He smirked, placing a kiss on my forehead.

I didn't even ask where we were going, I just sat back and enjoyed the ride. The first stop was Kuzzo's, where we stopped and ate breakfast. After we left there, we went to Somerset. Xá damn near emptied the entire mall from both the basic, poor side and the rich folk side.

"Where to now?" I quizzed, as he hopped on the expressway. I was enjoying our little outing, but at the same time, I wanted to sit back and chill at the crib .

"You'll see." He chuckled, and by the look on his face, I already knew I should just let it go and sit back and relax.

I had a confused expression plastered on my face when we pulled up to Syan's house. It looked like she had a full house. There was big ass vans that could have been mistaken for buses parked in her driveway, along with a lot of other unfamiliar vehicles.

"Babe, what's-." Before I could get my full question out, Xá had his finger over my lips, shushing me.

"Don't start playing 21 damn questions. Just go with the flow." He stated sternly before he pecked my lips. This nigga knew he was a trip. He always said some slick shit, then called himself sealing it with a kiss.

When we walked into Syan's house, my mouth was damn near touching the floor. Her entire living and dining room was set up like a salon. There was pedicure chairs, nail stools, mirrors all over, massage tables, you name it. Not to mention all the unfamiliar faces that were scattered over Syan and Hector's home.

Before I could open my mouth to ask what was going on, Xá had already started talking. "You been on this bullshit about not wanting to go anywhere, so I called in a few favors and brought the salon to you." He smiled, and I cursed myself for not meeting him sooner. I was falling deeply in love with him and I had no control over it. My mind was telling me not to rush into a relationship when I literally just ended one with my high school sweetheart. On the other hand, my heart was telling me to go for the kill and fall head over heels for him.

"Thanks bae. You didn't have to do all this," I said, holding back the tears, as I passionately kissed his lips, tonguing him down for everyone to see.

"I know I didn't, but I wanted to. Do you not listen when I tell you I'll do anything to keep you happy and smiling? I love you, so stop demoting yourself of what you deserve and let me spoil you." He said as we stood close together with his hands planted at my hips. The tears that were once held, came running down without my permission.

"I love you too." I was able to say through sniffles.

"Happy Birthday, cry baby ass." Syan appeared, pulling me into a well needed hug. I needed to get my emotions under control.

"Thanks sis, and you on my hit list bitch. Y'all some sneaky asses." I laughed, watching Hector as he opened the door to let Harmony and Hunter in,

"Happy Birthday twin!" I ran and jumped on her. I was excited to be celebrating our birthdays together for the first time.

"Happy Birthday to you too." She sung, squeezing my body tightly. "What's all this?" She asked, looking from me to Hunter.

"Ask your man girl." I playfully shoved him and rolled my eyes. They were so damn cute together. How we pulled best friends without even knowing each other still amazes me.

He explained to her what him and Xá put together and her facial expression matched mine when the news was broken to me. We didn't have time to talk and gossip because all the guys were here and in our asses, because apparently we were on a time frame.

I couldn't stop looking at myself in the mirror after my full makeover. My face was beat to the gawds. Because I was turning the big 3-0, I decided to try something new, so I added cinnamon and blonde highlights to my hair. I loved my new look. It was no doubt in my mind that Harmony and I weren't the baddest twins in the world. Yes, I was that damn confident with a dab of conceited, now.

Harmony Woods

~

"You know it's rude to stare." I said to Hunter who was paying more attention to me than the road. I damn sure wasn't trying to die on my thirtieth birthday on the account of his stalkerish ass.

"Baby, it ain't shit nobody can do to stop me from looking at my sexy ass woman. Not even you." He smirked, never taking his eyes off me. He held the stare too many seconds over his limit considering he was operating a motor vehicle on the freeway.

"Well if you keep driving like this, you won't be looking at no damn body." I shot back, preparing myself for his smart ass comment, but instead he only offered a laugh.

We were on our way to my house so I could pick up a few things. He offered to buy me whatever I needed every time I left his house to get stuff from mine, but I declined every time. I just thought that was silly when I already had the items that I needed at home. I grew up in a poor family, so I knew what it was like to not have shit. Quite frankly, I'm still poor and don't have shit, but I'm making the most of it.

He pulled next to my assigned parking space in my apartment complex, and I could feel my heart beating outside my chest. This wasn't happening to me? Or was it? Betsy, my hoopty was no longer there. Instead, there was my newfound favorite car, a Porsche Macan Turbo. It was royal blue, my favorite color with a big silver bow smack dab in the center of the car, or should I say truck.

I opened my mouth to ask the million dollar question, but no words came out. I looked at Hunter who was staring at me. Instead of him speaking, he simply nodded his head and handed me a set of keys that were custom made in diamonds. I couldn't help the tears that slid down my face if I wanted to. No one had ever treated me better than him and I couldn't thank God enough for sending him my way.

I jumped out his car and went to admire my new truck. I had never seen a truck or car so beautiful. I climbed into the truck and I didn't know what looked better, the exterior or interior. Everything in the inside was rose gold and it even had a sparkle to it, outside of its natural shine. There was an H with a crown tipped on the upper left corner of the H, engraved on every headrest, the dashboard, and even the gear shift.

"Come here bae." I waved him over, because he was still sitting in his car, either recording or taking pictures. His motto is, you can't relive the same thing twice so capture it and you can at least go back and reflect on it. I loved his thinking process and I loved his mom even more for raising a man like him.

"You like it?" He asked with an uneasy look on his face, as if I was going to say no. I've never had room to be picky, so I wasn't going to start now.

When he got in close reach, I hopped out my truck and pushed him in, letting the seat roll back as far as it could go. I quickly jumped in his lap and closed the door. I kissed his lips hungrily, exploring his mouth with my tongue. I pulled his jogging pants and boxers down while I pulled his bottom lip between my teeth, sucking lightly.

After I pulled my leggings and thong off, I hopped on his dick, easing down slowly. I bounced my ass up and down, winding my hips in a circular motion to the beat that played the background from the radio.

"Damn girl." He grunted, holding my hips in place as he thrusted his body into mine. I leaned forward, placing kisses on his neck. I sucked here and there, leaving traces of my love.

"Mmm, Hunterr." I moaned as he pumped harder, making me feel his length in my stomach. Every time he was inside my walls, he fucked me like he had a point to prove, a mission to accomplish, and a goal to reach.

"You gone come with daddy?" He whispered close to my ear, licking it in the process. Taking my right nipple in his mouth and pinching the other , he turned me on even more.

"Yes, baby. Yess!!" I shouted as I took back control, maintaining a steady speed, riding the wave to an orgasm I'll never forget.

"Fuck." We both said in unison as we came simultaneously. We were both sweating and breathing hard, with our chests steadily heaving up and down.

After I put my clothes back on, I went in the house and quickly gathered all my things and followed Hunter home. I kept a smile on my face the duration of the ride. When we got to his house, he showered and proceeded to get ready.

I had no clue to where we were going and all I knew was I needed to dress my best and look like money. Those were his words, not mine. I stepped into my gown for the evening which was a royal blue sequin dress. I paired it with black heels and I had diamonds dancing on my ears, neck, and wrist. My hair was curled and pinned to the side. I dabbed on the lipstick I had on earlier on my full lips. I was thankful that the make up stylist had given me a little to take home to re-apply. Hunter was wearing more of it on his lips than I was.

"Bad bitch alert. Bad bitch alert." Syan said, mocking Red Cafe in "She a Bad One" as I stepped out the whip in front of Toxic Temptation.

"Ayeee!" I yelled, twerking my ass on the red carpet, putting on a little show for the people waiting outside.

Hazel and Xá pulled up next. She stepped out, looking like a pure goddess. Never, had we dressed alike, so she was matching me in the same exact dress, just a different color. Her dress was purple and all the accessories she had on were gold diamonds.

All three couples; me and Hunter, Hazel and Xá, and Syan and Hector walked in like we owned the shit. We were the type of couples that onlookers swore were relationship goals.

"SURPRISE!" Everyone who was already inside, screamed to us and I was indeed surprised. I was just expecting us to be going out and hanging at the club, but the entire top level of the club was rented just for us. Everything was decorated in blue and purple, our favorite colors. There were pictures of us decorated all over. There was a picture booth, a full free bar and food. It was everything and more.

"Thanks baby. I love you!" I beamed as I clung to his body and held him tightly. This was the first time I expressed my love for him out loud, and I was happy I did.

"I love you too baby." He tugged at my bottom lip with his teeth and stuck his tongue in my mouth.

"Let's get this shit cracking!" Hazel yelled with a bottle of Ace of Spades in one hand and a fat ass wood in the other. Tonight was going to be a great night, I could feel it.

Xá Black

~

Sasha did her thang and had transformed the V.I.P floor dope as hell. She never ceased to amaze me. I honestly was just happy to see that perfect, bright smile on Hazel's face. Her smile never failed at making any room light up.

"Thanks bae, for everything you did. I thank God for you everyday." She smiled, kissing my lips. I felt a tear hit my face.

"You get what you deserve. Thank you for being you and stop that crying shit." I laughed, pinching her cheeks.

"Whatever nigga." She laughed, dapping her face lightly with the handkerchief I had just given her, before punching me in the arm.

When Bad and Boujee came blaring through the speakers, all the ladies hit the dance floor damn near breaking their backs with all that twerking and shit. I lost count of how many times I wanted to snatch

Hazel's ass off the floor. Seeing her move her body how she moved on my dick had me ready to bust a nut all up and through those walls.

Me and the fellas were going to let them have this one and enjoy themselves. About fifteen minutes later, we had quickly changed our minds. The more drinks they sipped on, the looser they got and neither of us wanted to spend the night in jail, especially when we could be laid up in great pussy instead. Syan wasn't drinking and I found that to be strange considering she's always the life of the party and the turn up Queen.

Before the night ended, I had something up my sleeve. It was time. I stood and walked towards the DJ for the night. We exchanged a few words before he handed over the MIC. I had never been nervous before, talking in front of a crowd, but for some reason, my palms were sweaty and itchy, and I could see my heart beating outside my shirt.

"Hey everybody. How y'all doing tonight?" I started and they let out sounds, responding to my question. "Can I get Ms.Hazel Parks to the stage please?" Our eyes connected while she hesitantly got up from the booth she was sitting at. The closer she got to me, the faster my heart seemed to race.

"Yes bae?" She said shyly, staring into my eyes. Under the spotlight, her hazel eyes sparkled just like my diamond Rolex shined.

"Hazel, you've been my rock since we've met. God has a thing with timing and you came to me at the perfect time. Today, has been all about you, but that's nothing new because whenever you're in my presence, it's about you and only you. The only thing I want to know from you is, can I make this a forever thing? Can every day be about you and only you for the rest of our lives? Not only do I want you in my life, I need you in my life, like I need air to breathe. I mentioned time earlier and today is the perfect time for me to ask if you could give me the ultimate pleasure of becoming your husband?" I dropped to one knee and pulled out the ring that cost more than my home and car together. I didn't mind, because I would spend everything I had on my baby. She's priceless.

She nodded her head up and down as she held both hands up to her wet, tear stained face. I slid the big ass rock on her finger and tongued her down for everyone to see. Today was the happiest day of my life, so I wondered how my wedding day would feel. I had officially turned in my player's card, but when you have a woman as good as Hazel in your corner, that's not hard to do. Ain't no woman worth me losing my Queen, so why waste time? I had to stake my claim and mark my territory real quick.

"I'm kicking your ass when we get home. This is the second time you've made me cry on my birthday." She pouted, pretending like she was really mad, but I could see the smile forcing its' way through.

"As long as you kicking my ass while you riding this dick, I don't mind." I whispered in her ear as I squoze her ass and kissed her neck.

Her mouth hung open but instead of giving her the reaction she expected, I shoved my tongue in her mouth, allowing my tongue to dominate her mouth. People always say close your mouth before something flies init. In this case, it was my tongue.

As we wrapped the night up, we said our goodbyes and collected the birthday gifts that were given to her. The club was still lit, but we all had pussy to dive into so we decided to call it a night.

"Aye Hazel, let me holla at you for a minute." A nigga grabbed Hazel by the arm and I got angry immediately. No nigga was allowed to put their hands on her. I didn't care if you meant harm or not. I didn't play about mines.

"Ethan, I don't have shit to say to you." She gave him the ugliest look before she continued walking. Obviously, he didn't get the hint, because he grabbed hold of her again. I never cared for him cuz that was my sister's business, but now things had changed. Hazel was my business.

"Look nigga, I let you slide the first time. Move around muthafucka." I gritted through clenched teeth, hoping he got the message because I didn't want to have to show my ass in my boy's club.

"My nigga, chill. You too hype. You not the only one who got a taste of that pussy." He smiled, as if what he said wasn't going to piss me off.

I wasn't with repeating myself. I tried to warn his ass, but he asked for it. I punched him in the eye that had blood splatter everywhere then I came back with two more jabs, one to his other eye and the other to his mouth since the nigga had problems closing that muthafucka.

By the time security and the guys pulled me off him, he had blood leaking from every hole on his face. I was far from being in the streets, but the way these hands operated, you would think otherwise. All the girls, including my sister Brielle were off to the side watching with wide eyes. I rarely let this side come out, but when it did, it was the furthest thing from pretty.

"This shit ain't over." He huffed as he picked himself off the floor.

"You really think you're in the position to be making threats." I laughed before I grabbed Hazel's hand and walked out the door, like nothing even happened. Only God put fear in my heart. As far as these niggas, they bleed red just like I do.

Ethan Rivera

~

Seeing Hazel move on to the next nigga, like what we had didn't mean shit, had me hot as hell. Not only was she with another nigga, they were planning on getting married. Yeah, I should have treated her right and with respect when I had her, but that was in the past.

The fact that her nigga beat my ass in front of damn near all of Detroit, had me seeing red. I was coming for his ass if that was the last thing I did. Hazel was with me through it all. She was the definition of a ride or die so this whole situation had me pissed. She was out of her mind, if she thought she could move on and avoid me like the plague. If I couldn't have her, nobody would.

"I told you to beware my brother." Brielle said with a smile on her face. I wanted to slap the shit out of her so badly.

"Get the fuck out my face." I snapped, walking in the opposite direction, so I wouldn't snap her fucking neck.

"I ain't worried about shit." She winked before walking out the door with her nigga towing behind her. Between the Black siblings and Hazel, I didn't know who had me fucked up more.

I sped to Providence Emergency and judging by the way that I felt, I knew I was pretty fucked up. I made it there in less than ten minutes, ready to get checked out and back out the door. I hated the fucking hospitals.

"Oh my. Follow me." Who I assumed was a nurse approached me. I hadn't even made it to the front desk to check in before she was rushing to me. Damn, I must've been worse than I thought. I didn't even bother to look in the mirror. "Car accident?" She raised her brows as she looked at me again before taking me into one of the triage rooms.

I nodded my head, yes, lying was easier. I damn sure wasn't about to tell her how I got my ass handed to me over a bitch that was no longer mine. It just so happened that the hospital bed that I was instructed to sit on, had a mirror directly in front of me. My face was covered in blood. Both my eyes were almost swollen shut.

"Just sit tight and the doctor will be right in to examine you." She gave a warm smile, similar to the one my mom forced to try to reassure me that things would be fine after pops beat her ass.

My mama loved my pops to death. No matter how bad he hurt her, she'd always forgive him and accept him back like nothing even happened and I hated that shit. It didn't matter how many black eyes and busted lips she got, it seemed like she loved to sport that shit.

She never wanted me to interfere with their business and I respected her wishes. Well, I tried to anyway. The last straw was when he beat her so bad to the point she was in a coma for two weeks. When she woke up, she couldn't eat nor talk. She ate through a feeding tube for a month.

I waited until she was out to handle him once and for all. The third day of her being home, I sent him to his maker with twenty shots to the head. I had to make sure he wouldn't be able to survive. I thought I would feel some type of regret for killing my own father, but I felt nothing. I couldn't. He only got what he deserved.

If I could kill my own flesh and blood with no hesitation, I had no problem killing Hazel's so called nigga. He had a bullet with his name on it. Mark my words.

Chapter Twenty-Five

~

Brielle Black

"Mommy, mommy. Can we go there?" Bailey jumped up and down, pointing to the TV that was playing a Chuck E. Cheese commercial.

"Yes baby." I agreed to her, because honestly I didn't feel like arguing her ass down, if I had said no to her spoiled ass.

Christian gave me that look like, I told you so. Last night, we were having a petty argument about who spoils her more. He wins that, without a doubt. I'm more of the bad guy than him, so when she doesn't get her way with me, she goes crying to him and he tells her ass yes.

"When is Jaden coming home?" Christian asked, taking a sip from his morning protein shake.

"He should be here within an hour or so." I said, checking the time on my phone. It had been a couple weeks since my brother whooped Ethan's ass, but I knew he wasn't crazy enough to do something to harm our son, so I let him take Ethan for his break from school.

We all just chilled as we waited for Jaden. Christian played Call of Duty on the PS4 while me and Bailey were glued to our iPads. She was watching YouTube videos while I played Cooking Fever. When the doorbell rang, I blew out a breath, because I had to pause my game to get the door.

When I swung the door open, I was met with a tall, slender woman instead of my son. "Can I help you?" I asked with a raised brow.

"Where's Christian?' She asked, and what caught me off guard was the fact that she had an attitude.

"And who are you?" I folded my arms over my breast, rolling my neck in the process. She had another fucking thing coming if she was asking about my man with a fucked up attitude.

"Mommy, who's that at the door?" Bailey came behind me, peeking her little head around the door.

"Aw, hell naw. Where the fuck is Christian, my baby daddy? I'll be damned if she calling another bitch mommy." Ole girl tried to barge in but I pushed her ass back with the, "try again bitch" ,look on my face.

"Christian, come here, before I beat this bitch ass. Bailey, go finish playing your game baby."

"Why are you here?!" Christian yelled, making me jump.

"That's my fucking daughter Christian. What do you mean?" She snapped, giving my man too much attitude for my liking. I hadn't planned on beating ass today, but that doesn't mean I won't. The only reason I haven't went upside her head was the baby that was growing in me. But at the end of the day, the only one who knew about my pregnancy was me.

"Again, why the fuck are you here? I told you when you decided to leave her, you won't get the chance to pop up whenever the fuck you feel like it. You left her for that nigga, so stay wherever the fuck that is. She's my daughter. You won't ever have the privilege of claiming my damn baby."

"Christian please. I made a mistake. You can't keep my baby away from me." She had tears running down her face. I almost felt her, but I had to look at the bigger picture. It wasn't fair to Bailey and the pain she had for not having a mommy.

"Those court papers that say full custody, says I can. Get the fuck off my doorstep. She don't need you. You can keep that fake love and those crocodile tears." He slammed the door with all his might, damn near breaking it off the hinges.

"Baby, you okay?" I wrapped my arms around his waist. I had never seen him this upset, so I was feeling some type of way that a nothing ass bitch had my man mad at the world.

"Yeah bae. I'm good." He pecked my lips. That was the first lie he had ever told me.

Christian Byrd

~

The day Brittany left Bailey behind, I cried. I cried for my daughter, because I knew that one day she would want to talk about the mom she didn't have, and that I wouldn't have an answer for her. A child needs their mom in their life, more than their dad and that's the truth. Dads dip out on their children everyday but a mom, you would think since they birthed them, they would have that unconditional love. Not Brittany. She saw dollar signs and went on. For the first year of Bailey's life, I sent Brittany a picture everyday, because I thought her seeing our daughter grow would make her change her mind and she didn't respond to any of the 365 pictures. I wanted to do everything in my power to avoid hurt coming my child's way.

The fact that she showed up on my doorstep after four years, had me seeing red like a muthafucka. My gut feeling was telling me either Christina or Crystal told her where I laid my head and they know more than anybody, their brother don't play that shit.

"Baby, where are you going?" Brielle fussed, with her hands planted on her hips.

"I have some business to handle." I stated as I put my boots and hoodie on. Stopping by Christina's apartment was the first on my list.

"Behave." I could tell by the look on her face, she was worried about me. Her sensitive ass was on the verge of crying.

"Come here." She slowly walked over to me with her head hung down and a small pout on her face. I lifted her chin up and tongued her down. "You have nothing to worry about." I smacked her ass and left out the house. Any second longer, I would have been fucking her sexy ass all day.

***

"Well, isn't this a surprise." Christina teared.

"You seen Brittany?" I asked, cutting right to the chase. Christina was easy to read and that's why she was my first stop.

"And how would I, Christian? I haven't been to London." She sarcastically stated, while rolling her big, doe eyes.

"Interesting." I left out her front door and went next door to Crystal's house. I knocked a couple times before she came to the door, opening the door just enough to peek her head through.

"Christian...um, what are you doing here?"

"I can't come check on my little sister?" I put my hand over my chest, to pretend like I was really hurt.

"Um, yeah sure." She said but never moved.

"So you not gonna let me in? That's fucked up." I chuckled lightly. I knew Crystal was the reason Brittany showed up on my doorstep, the moment she opened the door.

"Umm."

"Who's at the door?" Speaking of the Devil, she made it so much easier.

"Let me holla at you for a second." I grilled, staring a hole through Brittany.

I had a few things to get off my chest. I would deal with Crystal's sneaky, unloyal ass later.

"Christian, I-" Before she even got to saying some shit I knew I wasn't gonna like, I cut her off.

"You're so fucking out of line. After four years of not being a mother, now you want to show up? Where the fuck were you when she was asking me if she could call my girl mommy? You could have had that opportunity, but you chose that preppy ass white nigga, remember? You made your bed now lay in it. Don't bring your ass around me, my girl, and our daughter again. This is your first and last warning. Try it if you want to!" I warned her. A baby wasn't a damn toy to be played with and picked up whenever she wanted.

"You didn't have to do that girl like that." Crystal fussed, after I sent Brittany pathetic ass on her way.

"And why in the fuck not?" I raised my eyebrows, ready to hear her ignorant response.

This was my punishment for fucking with my little sister's best friend. They were as thick as thieves and I regretted fucking her raw on some dumb, drunk shit. I didn't regret having Bailey, but I wish I could change who her biological mother was.

"Let her be apart of her daughter's life."

"Crystal do you hear what you saying? That might be your best friend and all, but she left her one week old baby for a new life. You're so damn stupid sometimes, man. You need to grow the fuck up. I'm out."

My sister acted so damn stupid at times. Maybe it was our age difference. She was twenty-four and dumb as hell. Common sense flew right over her damn head.

I sparked up a blunt in my car to calm my mood. I had a feeling shit was going to get ugly and I was ready for it.

Brigail Jenkins

~

"Thank you for all your help." I said, handing the guy a hundred and forty dollar tip for helping me move my things into my new home.

I thought long and hard about my marriage, and too much damage was done. I loved him, but it wasn't healthy. I glanced at the clock and figured I should show my face at the church one more time. I made sure to put on my Sunday's best.

When I walked into the church, all eyes were on me as I expected. I hadn't showed my face in church in months. My stomach stuck out more than my ass and I couldn't see my own feet. A lot had changed. Me and my body. As I walked down the aisle, towards the front row where I normally took my seat, Maya gave me the death stare and it took everything in me not to shoot her the bird in front of the entire congregation.

"Well, hello Jordan." I kissed his cheek and winked at Maya who was seated next to her husband, diagonally from us.

He gave me a nasty look, ignoring me in the process. He knew me, so he knew that I only came for one thing: to stir some shit up. But he knew the consequences of his behaviors when he decided to fuck me over.

"Anyone have any testimonies to share today?" Reverend Johnson said, and that was my cue.

I raised my hand and rose to my feet and grabbed the mic from his hand. Let the games begin, I thought to myself with a smile on my face.

"I just want to thank God for another day. He blessed me with my son that I'm carrying and the knowledge of knowing who the people are that mean me harm. With that being said, I would like to announce me and my husband's divorce. Not only did he commit adultery, he created two bastard children from the one and only sister Maya Clark. I'm sorry to be the bearer of bad news Deacon Clark, but those are not your little girls, they're my husband's. And another thing, the baby I'm carrying isn't my husbands, it's Reverend Johnson's son. Have a blessed day." I finished, dropping the mic. Several weights had been lifted off my shoulders.

All that could be heard and seen were the people gasping and covering their mouths. I pulled the big manilla envelope with the divorce papers. I waltzed out the church with confidence and heavy admiration.

I couldn't believe they had been sneaking around five fucking years and that's at minimum. It was only right that I embarrassed them, how they've been doing me. Spilling the tea on everyone, had me on cloud nine. I was on a special kind of high, knowing I hurt their ego. Yeah, that may have been petty, but they didn't care about my feelings. Sorry that I'm not sorry.

"You stupid bitch!" Maya screamed, charging me from behind. Typical scary bitch move.

I couldn't prepare myself if I wanted to. The hard impact at the back of my head had caused me to stumble forward. She kept the blows coming, hitting me all over my body. After I collapsed to the ground, I laid in the fetal position and covered my stomach as much as I could. I felt a warm liquid flow down my legs and I knew God was punishing me for my behavior.

"Stop! I'm pregnant." I managed to say as tears streamed down my face. I prayed for my baby's safety. If I would've known that would be the outcome of this visit, I would've stayed my ass at home in the apartment. I hadn't even had a full forty-eight hours.

"You made that very clear already." She snapped, looking at me with hatred in her eyes. She started walking away, but doubled back and she hawked up all the saliva her body produced, spitting it out all over my face.

God had a funny sense of humor. Had I not been carrying my son, who was probably coming any minute now, I would have beat the brakes off that stupid bitch. I couldn't drop this load fast enough cause Maya Clark has an ass whooping with her full, legal name written all over it.

***

Labor kicked my ass for sixteen hours. Because I was losing blood from the injuries I received from the fight, I couldn't get an epidural and the other medications they tried to give instead, didn't do shit. Really, I took it just for the hell of it. That's how it seemed anyway.

Although, the pain was horrible, and I never wanted to do it again, seeing Blake for the first time made it well worth it. He was perfect in every way possible. He was the perfect combination of me and Damon, it was almost scary.

"Aww. He's so handsome." Hazel cooed, admiring my son as she held him in her ams. Her and Xá were the first people besides myself and the hospital staff to see him.

"It's your turn now." I joked with her, catching the way she tensed up. She did that whenever anyone mentioned her and my brother having children.

"Girl bye." She waved me off and started communicating with Blake in her take on baby language.

"All I do is shoot shots. I bet we need to get tests now." Xá laughed, placing a kiss on Hazel's cheek. I was surprised he even semi responded to what I said. He had barely said anything to me after I told him I wouldn't say how I got bruised up. I didn't need him handling shit for me. I had this.

"Birth control, here I come." She laughed and Xá's facial expression had changed more serious. He wanted to be somebody's damn daddy so bad.

They reminded me of how me and Jordan's relationship was in the beginning. It's funny how the tables turn when you don't ever expect them to. I wish it was something we could do to fix things before it got out of control. Now, it was too late.

After all my family visited with me and my son, I called Damon once they were all gone. It wouldn't hurt for him to see our creation. I never knew a love so powerful and true until I looked into the eyes of Blake Black. As long as I had him, I didn't need a man. He would forever be my king.

Chapter Twenty-Six

~

Harmony Woods

I had officially moved into Hunter's apartment. The transition was smooth and I loved every second of it. When I woke, Hunter was no longer in the bed with me. When I heard the shower turn on, I climbed out of bed and joined my man.

"Good morning babe." I sung as I stepped behind him, placing kisses on the back of his neck.

"Good morning beautiful." He turned to face me, and I was met with his dick pressing at my stomach.

I kissed his lips, intertwining my tongue in his that tasted like mouthwash. I placed my left leg on the side of the tub and he knew what time it was. He took his thumb and played with my pearl, while I sucked on his bottom lip and massaged his balls at the same time.

"Oooh baby." I cried as he fucked me with his middle and index finger, while still applying pressure to my sensitive, pulsating clit. I could feel my nut coming sooner than expected. My baby was putting in major work.

"You like this?" He whispered against my skin as he moved his fingers faster and faster in my sopping wet pussy. His cool minty breath cooling my neck.

"Yesss daddy!" He flicked his thumb over my clit in circular motions and fondled my erect nipples with his free hand.

He dropped to his knees and latched on to my clit like a baby latching on their mom's breast with his long tongue, making swirls of his love. I felt my orgasm fastly approaching as he munched and feasted on my clit and inserted the same two fingers in at a faster pace.

"Hunterrr..I'm cumming. Shitt!" I panted as a shock wave entered my body while he slurped up everything my body had to offer. He never leaves a drop.

"Keep that leg up and put an arch in that back." He ordered while my juices continued to flow freely.

I arched my back, following his command. He guided his thick dick inside me and he planted his hands on my hips, precisely thrusting himself into me, continuously hitting my g-spot. Our body became one as I threw my ass back every pump. Our mind, body, and soul was in sink with one another as we made love in the shower.

"Baby, I can't take no moreeee." I whined as he continued to murder my pussy. My eyes rolled to the back of my head as another orgasm came.

"Fuck." He growled, pumping two times more before he let his load off inside me.

After he washed over my body gently and thoroughly, he carried me into the bedroom. All I could do was lay there while he moisturized my body from head to toe. My body was all discombobulated. I needed to get up, because I had a lunch date with Hazel. I slowly got up from bed and found an outfit to wear.

As I walked to my car, I could hear my phone ringing inside my purse. Without having to look, I knew it was Hazel.

"Hey sis." I said, putting my car into reverse to back out the driveway.

"Don't hey sis me. Where you at, heffa?" She snapped, which I already knew she was going to do.

"I'm about to get gas, then I'll be on my way. Blame your brother." I joked, making light of the situation.

"See you in a minute." She ended the call as I pulled into the Speedway off Jefferson Ave.

As I was getting out the truck, a car sped to the other side of the pump like a maniac. "Damn." I cursed under my breath.

"Well, well, well." I turned around to see Ivory, who wasn't looking too well. She looked extremely skinny and strung out from some deadly drug. It didn't look good on her at all.

The only thing I offered her was a blank stare. My life seemed to be going smoothly, so I was avoiding all bullshit. I continued walking into the gas station and I was supposed to be in and out, but my greedy ass just had to load up on snacks while I was in there. I believe I had the worse case of munchies there was so, I had to stay loaded with goodies. I was annoyed when I came out and Ivory was still standing there as if she was lost or stuck on fucking stupid. I shook my head and proceeded to pump my gas.

"What nigga dick you sucking that got you a whip like this?" She laughed, and it took everything in me not to punch her in the trachea, but like I said, I was avoiding all negativity. I was too old to be playing games with these childish ass bitches.

"Not the type of niggas you fuck with, judging by the looks of things. Take care of yourself, honey." I smirked as I hopped in the car. I was feeling like Cardi, why would I hop in some beef, when I could just hop in the porsche?

I pushed another one of Hazel's calls to voicemail, as I approached the light. As I was trying to brake, my car wouldn't slow down or stop. Everything happened so fast. My mind went blank as my car continued through the red light. By the time I saw the semi truck coming for the passenger's side of my car, it was too late...

Ivory Peterson

~

I sat off to the side, watching everything unfold. I knew she wouldn't make it far. I took the time she spent in the gas station to cut her brake line. Me and my cousin Rayneka stayed cutting bitch's brake lines. We had so much practice, because our niggas stayed fucking around. We had gotten so good, I could cut the brake line in any car, truck, or van in less than two minutes.

When I seen her car get smacked by that big ass semi truck, I smiled, For some reason, I just couldn't stand that bitch. She was always doing so bad and to see her doing better than me, had me wanting to end her life.

My life had gone down hill in such a short period of time. It's almost like I switched lives with Harmony. The day my life started crumbling down was the day that my dad left us after he found my mom cheated. He cut me off too because as he says, I'm just as guilty, because I knew about her infidelity. He cleaned out both our bank accounts, so I had to get a job, something I never had to do because I always spent my dad's money.

That job turned my life from bad to worse. I started working as a bartender at Ace of Spades, and eventually, I became a stripper to make more money. Stripping was cool and I made good money, but the day I let Kendrick and his big, baller friends run a train on me was when shit got real.

Not only was there a video of that night circling around social media, my doctor confirmed I had HIV. My time was limited on this earth and I felt like everyone should feel like I did, miserable. All because of my money hungry ass, my life was ruined. It was all my fault, but someone else had to take the blame.

"Ms.Peterson, thanks for coming in today. I'm no–"

"Just get to the point doc. You only called me in this damn place to tell me some shit that I know I don't want to hear, so please just get to the point." I scoffed, I really wasn't trying to be rude, but my life was already on borrowed time.

"Because you haven't been getting treatment for your disease, you have what's called CIN, which is the growth of abnormal precancerous cells. And because you haven't been treated for that either, it has progressed to invasive cervical cancer. It needs to be removed, but I don't know if your body is able to handle it and undergo a surgery."

"So this is a damned if I do, damned if I don't type of situation?"

"I'm afraid so." She replied, giving me a sympathetic look.

I hated sympathy. I didn't need anyone feeling bad for me. I felt bad for myself enough. I guess karma had a way of fucking your life up. I had done plenty of people wrong and it had finally caught up with me.

"Thank you for everything." I rose to my feet, fetched my belongings, and headed for the hills. There was nothing more she could say or do.

Once I got home to my studio apartment, I took off my clothing and ran me a bath. I needed to feel numb to my pain so I pulled the Jack Daniels that I had in my bar out. When I was a little girl, I never thought my life would go down this road. People always told me how promising my future would be, but it turned out it wouldn't be promising after all. I took my phone out and dialed the only woman or person for that matter who I knew loved me, despite all my flaws.

"Hey sweet pea." My mommy's cheerful voice echoed throughout the bathroom walls.

"Hey Mama." I smiled, while wiping away the tears that were sliding down my face. "What are you doing?"

"I'm getting ready for my date tonight." She replied, and I could tell she was smiling so that made me smile as well.

"Have fun mommy. I was just calling to tell you how much I love you and I always will no matter what. I'm sorry for everything I've ever put you through. I know I haven't been the best daughter, but I've tried. It's just that nothing I do is ever good enough. But it don't even matter because it will all be over soon."

"Ivory, baby you're rambling. I love you too. Have you taken your meds? Where are you?" She rained question after question to me.

I rolled my eyes at her mentioning my meds. It seemed like people always wanted to diagnose me with something. It all started when I was a kid. I was eleven years old when I was diagnosed with bipolar disorder. All my life, I had been classified as something whether it was a mutt or a crazy sociopath. I was tired of it all. Everything came to an end at some point.

"No. I don't need them. I have to go mom. Remember everything I told you." I ended the call and laid my head against the cool tub.

I lit a cigarette, something I'd never done, and brought it to my full, chapped lips. I took a long pull, while reflecting on my life. There were some things I wish I could go back in time and change, but in the real world, it didn't work like that.

I brought the remaining contents of Jack Daniels to my lips and swallowed it in one gulp. My problems seemed to fade away as time passed, but it was time for life to stand still.

I sunk into the tub and let the water cover my entire body. No matter how bad I wanted to sit up for air, I didn't. It had always been my way or no way. If my time on this fucked up earth was ending, I wanted to be the one who decided when. So, it was goodbye forever and always.

Hazel Parks

~

I had been sitting at the table at P.F Changs, waiting for Harmony's grand entrance. I sent over ten messages, called twenty times, and left seven voicemails. Once I decided I had been there long enough, I left the establishment and climbed into my car.

I drove in the direction of her house, because she had me fucked up if she thought she was going to ignore me and lay under Hunter's ass all damn day. When I came up at my exit, there was a lot of chaos. There were police cars, ambulances, and fire trucks everywhere. I shook my head because it was always something.

After switching lanes and looking back again, I saw Harmony's car caught in all that mess. She was the only one in Detroit, riding around in a Porsche like hers, because it was custom made. My heart rate exceeded as I threw my car in park and jumped out the car. I ran towards the police, because I knew they would be the ones with answers.

"My sister...that's her car.. Where is she?" I asked frantically, as I ran my hands through my head. I had never been so scared in my life.

"She's still-" My eyes drifted and followed his. When I seen that the firemen were surrounding her car, I ran over, because that answered my question.

"Oh my God! Nooo! Please, get her out!" I cried, as I seen her bruised face. Her eyes were closed and she looked at peace.

"Ma'am, please step back. She still has a faint pulse and we don't want to send her into shock with your frantic behavior." The fire chief stated, as he motioned with his hands.

I nodded my head slowly and backed away. I took that time to call my Mama and all of our family. When they all got here, which was incredibly fast, we watched as they pulled her limp, unconscious body out the car.

"FUCK!!" Hunter yelled as he dropped to his knees. He had been going through it, and the unknown always seemed to have that effect. Not knowing what was happening and what was to come, always hurted. Always.

"Calm down, son. God has the last say in this." My mom assured him and at that moment, I felt a wave of hope flow through my body.

We all got into our cars and followed the ambulance to the hospital. It seemed like we were waiting around for someone to talk to us and give us an update for days. I had been pacing the floor for the longest time, until Xá pulled me into his lap and I rested my head on his shoulder. My other half was laying on a cold table by herself, all alone. I didn't know how to feel about that, so my body was going through every emotion. I thought about the very first time I saw her face. The circumstances were unfortunate, but I was grateful because maybe that was my only chance to meet her.

"Family of Harmony Woods." I looked up to see two doctors, and they were whispering amongst themselves. They both held clipboards in their hands.

We all stood to our feet, and slowly, walked towards them. Everything seemed to be going in slow motion. The idea of losing the person who understood me most and loved me unconditionally, broke my heart,

"What's going on with my sister?" I spoke up, looking right into the eyes of the male doctor. He looked like he would have the most to say.

"Harmony faced a lot of bruising. Her right leg is broken in two places. Her ribs are crushed, but that's not why I'm concerned. The impact caused her kidney to fail severely and only five percent is functioning.

"So what does that mean?" I asked with tears streaming down my face. Was he really telling me my sister was dying?

"She needs a kidney. We can put her on the donor list, but she may not have that long."

"I'll give her mine. Test me, so we can get started." I quickly stated. She could have anything in my body if it meant she would survive.

"Okay, we will set that up. In the meantime, we can allow four people at a time to visit her. She is stable, but she is sedated." I nodded my head to let them know I understood, because at that exact moment, I had no more words.

Flashbacks from our first memory to our last invaded my mind as me, my mom, Hunter, and Syan followed closely behind the doctors, who lead the way to her room. I only wanted to meet with her to finalize wedding plans. I didn't expect this to be the result of a simple lunch meeting.

"Hey beautiful. Please let this be the last time you scare me like this. I love you too much." I placed a kiss on her cheek and forehead as I ran my fingers through her thick tresses.

After me, my mom, and Syan said what we needed to say, we left Hunter alone with her. I knew he at least needed that.

"Baby, you okay?" Xá pulled me into a hug and I embraced him tightly as I cried in his arms. I needed my sister to pull through. I couldn't have her snatched away from me just like that. We had so many plans to carry out and dreams to follow.

"Ms. Parks." The doctor approached me, and I pulled away from Xá and wiped my eyes. "Are you ready to get tested?" I nodded my head, yes, and followed behind him like a lost freshman.

I sat and waited on the results while bouncing my right leg uncontrollably and rocking my body. All the poking and prodding they did to me, only reminded me of how bad she needed this.

"Ms. Parks, I have the results and I'm sorry, but you're not a match. It's very rare for this to happen considering you're her twin, but because of the small changes that can happen in the womb, it can happen and in this case, it did. I'm so sorry. Is there anyone else we can test?"

Never have I ever felt so defeated in my life. Nothing ever went smoothly. Would I ever be able to do something right for once in my life? I pulled out the card that I kept in the very back of my wallet and dialed this number for the first time in my life.

"Thanks for coming." I gave a faint smile and he pulled me into a hug.

"Of course. I'm so sorry for everything." He whispered, and nothing needed to be explained.

This was the best thing he could have ever done for the both of us. After the results came back positive for a match, they set up everything that was necessary to continue the transplant process.

"Who would've thought." My Mama said as she wheeled herself on the other side of me.

"Tell me about it." I chuckled, rubbing my hand across my temple. It's crazy how things had a way of playing out.

I remember talking to my mom, and she was telling me that there was going to come a time when I forgave him. I always brushed it off, but it was time for me to be the bigger person. I knew, without a doubt, that no one was perfect, but it wasn't easy to forgive someone of something that tarnished your heart and soul. I knew what it felt like to be raped and because of it, I always used to wish death on myself. I wanted to die and that was my only wish as a child.

"You know her?" Hunter approached me, snatching me away from my thoughts. He showed me a picture of some high yellow chick with curly hair.

"Oh yeah, I know that bitch." I said, remembering the time Harmony pulled up her picture. After she told me all the shit that happened between them, I had to see a picture. Because it was on sight, I was fucking her up for even thinking about playing my sister.

"She cut her brake line." His jaws flexed as he spoke. I could imagine the rage and adrenaline going through his veins. "That's not even the worse part." He continued and I raised my eyebrow, confused as to what could get any worse.

"Just say it. I'm sick of the bullshit." This whole situation had me on ten and at this point, anybody's life could be ended on my watch.

"When I got to her house to handle the bitch, she was already dead. She committed suicide."

His quick disappearance from the hospital all made sense now. I shook my head because it was pathetic how hateful bitches could really be. I had to give it to her though, she was pretty smart. Because had I got to her, she was going to die a slow, painful death.

***

The surgery was a success and we had them put in the same room. We all sat around and waited for the anesthesia to wear off. We talked, reminisced, and joked around in the meantime. I lost track of how many times I laughed at these crazy folks that I called family. They all had a few loose screws, but I wouldn't trade them for nothing in the world. They were family.

"Did you get it?" I asked Hunter, and he nodded his head.

"Oh my! She opened her eyes!" My Mama screeched, and we all flocked at her side. She tried to open her mouth to talk, but we all shushed her and and informed her of the tube she had in her throat.

"You're so strong, baby girl. You get that from me." My mom smiled and grabbed hold of her hand.

Once I made eye contact with Hunter, he moved closer to Harmony, and I could see the way they were looking at each other. Anyone could look at them and see that they were madly in love with each other.

"Hey baby. I was praying so hard for you to wake up. I didn't realize how much I needed you in my life, baby. I prayed so hard, because I never got the chance to ask you if you wanted to be my wife. I had a dream about my Mama last night and she told me you were the one and that I'd be a fool not to marry you. Please baby, make me the happiest man on earth, right now." She nodded her head with tears streaming down her face and at that moment, I realized love was definitely in the air. Finally!

Chapter Twenty-Seven

~

Hector González
(Four months later)

"Good morning, bae." Syan smiled, right before her head disappeared between the sheets and she swallowed my dick whole, pregnant belly and all.

"Damn baby...you sucking that muthafucka." I grunted, as she continued to bob her head up and down my dick. She was determined to suck the skin off my shit. "Baby, I'm about to bust. Hold up." I pulled my dick out her mouth and got between her legs.

"Oh my God...Hectorrrr." She cried, as I pounded into her while holding up her right leg.

"Tell me how you want daddy to fuck you." I slowed down and then sped it back up, while gripping her breasts in my hands. When her little hand toyed with her clit, I knew our fucking was coming to an end. She knew that shit was a turn on for me, and her pussy being uncontrollably wet, always made me bust quicker.

"Oooh papí. Im cumminnnng." She whispered as her body shook, and my seeds emptied in her pussy. If she wasn't already pregnant, her ass would've definitely been expecting, after the load I had emptied. "Baby, you gotta stop fucking me so good. I'm going to keep getting pregnant." She sighed, as if that was a problem. I wanted to keep her ass pregnant every chance I got. I've always wanted a big family, so that was fine by me.

"I can't make any promises." I winked, while grabbing my things that I needed to shower.

"I would join you, but we would never leave this house." She laughed and I agreed.

After showering quickly and putting on my clothes, I pulled my hair into a man bun atop. Syan loved when I wore my hair that way, and I knew why. I was good looking as hell. I never lacked in that department, or any other one for that matter.

"I miss Jr." Syan whined, and I knew that in a matter of time, her ass would be crying. Her emotional state was the only con during her pregnancy. She was crazy enough, without a baby growing inside her.

"Me too, but we got shit to handle baby. You know he's good." I pecked her lips. Jr. was in India, so he could spend time with his family there and also, because we had shit to handle. We had finally located Lisa, and it was time to put our plan in action.

"You're right. Let me get back in character." She chuckled, before pulling herself together.

After she showered and got herself dressed, we went to breakfast to discuss business. Marrying Syan was the best decision I could have ever made. She was the true definition of a ride or die. She was going to rock with me until the wheels fell off, and that was a fact.

"So here's the floor plan of the house. Here is where we should come in, and there is where the men should be stationed." Syan stated as she marked the key locations on the blueprint. No matter where we were, seeing Syan boss up always made my dick brick hard. It was something about the savage in her.

"I agree. You sure you don't want to be apart of the team and show the guys some pointers?" I joked, but at the same time, I was semi-serious.

Syan took it upon herself to do a background of Lisa's history, and that's how she was able to find her. Her grandmother had a house out in Saline, Michigan that was empty and sure enough, she had been hiding out there with my daughter and some unknown nigga.

"I'm on your team, so that has to count for something." She smiled, and her face had a natural glow to it.

"More than you know."

After we had everything planned out, we left breakfast and continued our day, until it was time for us to meet back up again. She met up with the girls and after Harmony's full recovery, they were back at it. I headed in the direction of the warehouse to handle some business, until I made that little trip out in butt fuck city.

Syan González

~

This day was finally here and I had never been so excited to end someone's life, but it was a long time coming. She had disrespected and violated me to the highest power. Because she had tried me so many times over the last few years, she had to be eliminated. She brought this upon herself. She's the weakest link.

"Babe, you ready?" I asked him, as I stood in front of the full length mirror, smoothing out my bullet proof vest over my small. but noticeable baby bump. I was very confident in me and my husband's capabilities, so I feared nothing or no one. We would be fine, and so would our unborn child.

"Yeah." He pecked my lips and picked up my toolbox with the things I would need for tonight's festivities. He then took it to the car.

On the ride to west hell, I thought all positive thoughts. My mood for the entire day, had been good vibes only. It was dangerous and risky to be in the center of violence while carrying a child, but the world would be a better place without Lisa's crazy, delusional ass in it.

"Are you ready to do this?" Hector asked, rubbing his hand across my thigh.

I nodded my head, yes, while putting my game face on. No errors needed to be made. Everything had to be precise, every little step.

As we jogged to where the house was, very discreetly, he whispered into my ear. "Stay here while I go in through the back. After I check out everything, I'll let you in from the side door. You don't make a move until I say so. Watch yourself. Don't be scared to empty that clip if needed." He held my face in his hands and placed a soft kiss to my lips.

"Bae, you should know me better than that. My trigger finger stay itchin'." I giggled lightly, before he disappeared in the darkness.

I kept my eyes and ears focused on the outside world, while my husband handled the inside. I watched every movement and listened to every sound. I couldn't afford any fuck ups. I had too much to lose. We had too much to lose.

I remembered the first time we ever did some Bonnie and Clyde shit like this. We had grown so much since then, but I would do everything over the same way, because I cherish every moment I had with him. I'll ride for him and I'll die for him, without question.

"Pssst." I heard a light whisper and my head snapped back in that direction, and Hector motioned for me to come in.

"Where is she? How many people?" I whispered, as I followed him through the big, mani mansion.

"There were five." He chuckled, and I knew what that meant. I just wished I would have been apart of the action, but I understood why I wasn't. "And Gabby?" I asked with a raised eyebrow.

"She's sound asleep in the master bedroom, so we need to move quickly before she wakes." I nodded my head, because there was no way she could witness what we were getting ready to do.

He lead me to the basement, and I smiled when I saw her tied up to an old bed. Over the years, she had caused so much bullshit to my families' lives, and it stopped now. Happy wasn't even the word.

"Well hello Lisa." I walked closer to her, and I could tell she was scared and and she had every right to be.

"Please nooo!" You can't kill me. I'm pregnant!" She cried, while pleading with her eyes to me and Hector.

"You won't be for long. That's why I'm here. Baby, set up my equipment." I was far from heartless, so of course, I wasn't going to let the baby die. I would deliver her baby first, then send her to meet her maker.

After Hector helped me set everything up, we were ready to get shit started. I had injected a medication in her IV to speed up the process. I just wanted to get this shit over with and get back to my son. I still had friends at the hospital who were able to give me the shit I needed.

"You know what this means right?" Hector asked me, and I knew this conversation was coming. I wouldn't be here now, delivering this baby, if I didn't know I would have to take over and mother this child.

"Of course, I know Hector." I cleared my throat. We had come too far. It was happening, whether I was ready or not.

Some odd hours later, I had delivered a baby and sent two bullets to Lisa's skull seconds apart. Those two events had changed my life forever. Forever was the only thing that scared me. Every day of my life, I would have to love these two children, even though I hated their mother and killed her. Forever, I'd have to pretend and take on the role as their mother. Well, until death.

Chapter Twenty- Eight

~

Xá Black

It's crazy how I'd been looking forward to this day. I've imagined this day all week, but I didn't know it would feel like this. I was beyond nervous. I didn't have cold feet. I was just nervous, because I wanted today to be perfect. Hazel deserved this moment. Her face lit up every time the wedding was brought up in any conversation, and that's why I stressed everyday for her to not spare any expense. Whatever she wanted, I wanted. This was her day, and at the end of it, I wanted to see that beautiful breathtaking smile and sparkling Hazel eyes.

"Talk to me." My mom put her hand on my shoulder, squeezing lightly. while using her other hand to put a plate full of breakfast foods in front of me.

"Thanks Ma." I looked up at her, and smiled. She had been my rock since day one, and I was glad I had her to experience this moment with.

"So what's on your mind, son?" I swear this lady knew me better than I knew myself. She paid close attention to all her children and that's why she could never fail as a mother.

"I need everything to be perfect. For once in Hazel's life, things were getting better, and I want it to stay that way." I stated as I looked into her eyes.

"You remind me so much of your father. I'm glad that you have a lot of his ways. Don't get me wrong, every trait you have from him, isn't good, but you're perfect to me. You're going to be a great husband. You're your father's son." She sighed, while she quickly wiped the tears that reluctantly fell.

"I miss him too you know. We all do. He would have loved Hazel and been proud of me."

"Yes, he would've." She agreed while leaving the kitchen, and me, to my thoughts.

I pushed everything to the back of my mind, as I saw Hazel's name flash across the screen of my ringing phone.

"Baby, I miss you. Why did we even agree to this?" She whined, and I could tell she was pouting those pretty ass lips.

"I miss you too, and because we both want everything to be perfect. It'll all be worth it in the end when you're walking down that aisle to become my wife."

We had let our sisters convince us into staying away from each other for two days. It was hard as hell, because when we weren't working, we always wanted to be laid up under each other. I rarely got sick of being around her but when I did, it only lasted a couple hours.

"Yeah, you're right. 12 o'clock can't come fast enough." She sighed, and I could see her rolling her pretty eyes like she always did.

"I know, bae. And just so you know, I'm wearing out that sexy ass body tonight, so get ready." I smirked, thinking of all the ways I was gone beat that pussy up.

"I'm already ready daddy, but I have to finish getting glamorous, so I'll see you later. I love you baby." She made kissy sounds through the phone, and so did I before we ended the call.

After I finished eating, I showered and dressed myself, so I could get my hair and facial hair in tact. Me and Hunter decided to go together, since we both needed to go anyway.

"What's up bro?" Hunter dapped me up after we got out our cars. "Can't believe yo ass finally about to tie the knot." He cheesed extra hard, like he had told the funniest joke ever.

"Nigga you're right behind me. I give you six months and we'll be reliving this shit again." I chuckled, because he knew better than that. Harmony was not about to play with his ass. She wasn't going to be a fiancee three and four years, waiting for it to be official. He had two years at the most. Me personally, I didn't believe in all that waiting around bullshit either.

"Yeah, I know. So how does it feel?" He asked, while we both took our seats in the barber chairs.

"It feels good, especially because I have Hazel all too myself for the rest of our lives." I smiled, and I thought about the kids we would have and how perfect they would be.

"She won't be all yours considering Syan and Harmony's crazy asses, but I get the point." He joked, and I laughed because there was a lot of truth to what he said. They would literally kill my ass, before they let me keep her hostage.

After we left the barbershop, we grabbed our tuxes and we went our separate ways. He had business to handle before the wedding, and so did I. I had to visit pops and talk to him for a little while. Although he wasn't here with me physically, spiritually and mentally he was.

Hazel Parks

~

Today was the day. The day that I would change my last name and become someone's wife. After all the shit I've been through with Ethan, I didn't think I deserved to be a wife, or that someone even wanted me to be their wife. That all changed when Xá became apart of my life.

As I looked at the reflection of myself in the mirror, I fell in love all over again. I had fell out of love with myself somewhere down the line while I was with Ethan, but now, I had a love and respect for myself that was so powerful and I had Xá to thank for that. There's been plenty of times when he's told me that I had to love myself first, before I could love anyone else. It took me some time to realize that, but the best thing about it is, I knew now. I knew that self came first.

"Are you ready?" My mom asked, as we sat in the dressing room of the church that I was getting married at.

"I'm as ready as I'll ever be." I smiled, and before I knew it, I had tears falling. No matter how many lectures I gave myself this morning, the tears still fell. "Mama, this is truly the happiest I've ever been in my life. He brought out a side of me that I never knew existed. With him, I am complete and I can't wait until I'm pronounced as his wife." I continued as I dabbed my wet face, dry.

"I'm so happy for you baby. You deserve this. Seeing my two babies happy and in love is the best feeling in the world. I love you Hazel and I'll always want the best for you."

"Mama, I hate to say this, but you have to get out. As long as I keep talking to you, my makeup is going to continue to slide down my face. Harmony, please tell Brielle to come help me." My Mama always seemed to tug on my heart strings and thatshit never failed.

"Hazel boo, this is my last time fixing it for you. Get it together, or at least wait for my brother to see how beautiful you are." She sassed, as she put a little more foundation to the areas that faded away.

"I'm sorry sis. I promise I'll get it together." I said, and I didn't know if that was a lie or not, but I would at least try.

"It's time." Harmony smiled, as she held my dress up so that I could step inside it. Syan zipped the back, and Brigail handed me my white and gold bouquet of flowers.

"You look breathtaking." Syan cried, and I knew it was coming. Her emotional, pregnant ass was so damn hormonal.

"Thank you." I hugged her, and placed a kiss on her cheek.

As the doors opened up for me to begin my walk down the aisle, I was taken aback at how beautiful the venue was set up. Sasha had outdone herself, once again. Everything was decorated in white and gold. There were doves in cages, hanging from the ceilings. There were gold, glitter covered bows on every row of chairs. The bridesmaids and groomsmen looked stunning in their white and gold attire. And then there was Xá, and he was more sexier from the last time I laid eyes on him. When our eyes connected, I felt butterflies at the pit of my stomach. He always had that effect on me, but this time, it was different, it was more special.

"Let's do this, baby girl." My dad took my hand in his and we walked down, and it felt like time stood still as I looked into Xá's eyes the whole time. Nothing or nobody else mattered in this moment, only him.

The pastor said a few prayers and told a few jokes. He was very cool and outgoing. He wasn't one of those holier than thou pastors, and that was my first impression of him, so that said a lot.

"It's now time to exchange the vows that these two, lovely people before me created. Since you're the man, the head, you go first." He said, as he patted Xá on the shoulder.

"From the first day I saw you, I knew that I was going to make you my wife, sweaty and all." He paused to laugh, and so was everyone in attendance, including me. "God sent me to be your healer, your protector, your provider, your KING. There won't be a day that goes by that I stop loving you. You are my everything. I will always put you first." He finished as the tears cascaded down both our faces. It was now my turn and I didn't even know if my heart would let my words come out.

"I'm glad that God brought you into my life when he did. I didn't know if I could ever love again after everything I've been through, but here we are now. You opened up my heart and stole the key. With you, I feel whole, full, and alive. My love for you will never go away. You are my breath, my every heartbeat." I was stuck looking into his eyes, capturing this beautiful moment. I was in a trance.

That moment only lasted briefly as I saw my almost husband and father of our unborn child, take his last breath. When I saw the bullet fly between his eyes, my heart stopped. I looked towards the screaming guests and there was Ethan, holding the gun. I let out a gut wrenching scream, before everything went black.

Brenda Black

~

Panic was everywhere. It all happened so fast, but too many bad things happened when you panic or fold under pressure. I had to be the one who kept it together, besides I had the most to lose. My only son, my baby, had a gunshot wound to the head and my daughter was laid beside him comatose.

My mind and heart was racing faster than I could process, but I couldn't lose my baby. I couldn't. We weren't far from Receiving Hospital and I could get there in five minutes, which meant it would take the ambulance at least fifteen to get here. We couldn't wait.

"Help me get him to the car." I yelled, and Hunter rushed by my side along with the other groomsmen.

They carefully brought him out to my truck that I had backed up against the door. I had bystanders gawking, but now wasn't the time.

"Hunter, get Hazel and bring her to the hospital. You better be right behind me with my damn daughter!"

I sped all the way there and it only took me four minutes. I parked my car in front of Emergency, and I jumped out the truck. I ran inside, frantically screaming for help.

"Please, someone help! My son's been shot in the head!"

About ten people came running to help and after they put him on a stretcher, I looked at him and it brought back memories of my husband's death.

I remember that day like it was yesterday. I had just gotten out the shower and I felt uneasy about something. I felt something bad was about to happen, but I shook it off because my head was in the clouds. We were getting ready to celebrate our twentieth anniversary and everything was a surprise. I had the most beautiful gown on and my hair was laid. My husband had took his time to plan the perfect night that he'd been planning for months, as if I didn't know.

I had long ago heard him come into the house, but I proceeded to get ready, because I wanted to be on time for once in my life. I seen how excited he was about planning everything, so I wanted it to be perfect.

"Baby, I'm all ready." I announced as I walked down the staircase, heels clicking along the way, but it wasn't him I was met with. Instead, it was John, his right hand man. "Where's Zeek? He better not be still working." I fussed, and the look he gave me, I knew something was wrong.

"BB, the Johnson brothers are back. We didn't know until it was too late. He's gone. I'm so sorry." John said, while he rubbed his temples.

"No, no, noooo! John, please tell me this is a joke. This can't be real. Where is he, seriously? I can't live without him. Pleaseee John!" I cried as I hit the floor, because my knees had given up on me.

At that moment, I was pissed at my husband for doing that to me, our children, our family. He had broken that same promise for years, but just when I finally thought he was done for good, he's dead. I thought he was done 'working' and he had been doing so good with hiding it, but I just had to find out through his death, that he was in fact still doing the same thing he promised me he wouldn't. He was back in his assasination business, as he called it, and it had finally caught up with him. I just wish I would've left with him. At least that way, we would still be together.

"Mama, what's going on with Xá?" Brielle asked, and I snapped back into reality. I wiped the tears from my face, because I couldn't let them see me down. I had to be strong. I had to keep it together.

"He's in surgery baby. I don't know anything yet. How's Hazel?" I asked, because just that quick, I had wrapped up in my thoughts and I had forgotten about her.

"She's awake, but she's not doing good. She won't let the nurses do their job. She's trying to snatch her IV out to see about Xá.

I ran my hand over my temple and I was truly overwhelmed. This day was supposed to be special and perfect, but that quickly changed into a nightmare, just like my anniversary, eight years ago.

"Let me check on her." I stood from the chair I was sitting in, and I rode the elevator down to the third floor. When I walked into her room, Harmony and Syan were scattered across the room and Hazel appeared to be sleeping.

"They had to sedate her, because she was losing it." Harmony stated lowly with her head hung down.

I nodded my head and proceeded closer to the bed, until I got by her side. I brought my head down and started to whisper things I knew she needed to hear. Although she couldn't respond at the moment, I knew she could hear me.

"Mama, he has to be okay right?" Brielle asked, and I buried her head into my chest like I used to when she was a child. I ran my fingers through her scalp and for the first time, I didn't know what to tell my daughter. I was scared too.

"Family of Xá Black." Everyone stood and that included all who was in the lobby. Pretty much everyone who was at the wedding, was here at the hospital. I looked around and I knew I wasn't the only one nervous of what they were about to say. Nothing prepared me for what they had to say. A lone tear escaped my eye as he continued to talk, but I had long ago stopped listening.

Ethan Rivera

~

I felt so much adrenaline going through my veins as I weaved in and out of traffic to get far away. I didn't know what my next move was. All I knew was I had to get the hell out of dodge.

I tried to let her go, but I couldn't. I stalked all her social media accounts with fake accounts that I created, and all she talked about was the wedding. I wanted her to be happy with me, not another nigga. The thought of him touching her in places that only I should've had access to made my skin crawl and my blood boil.

I found myself pulling into the cemetery that my dad was buried at. I hadn't been in so long, but I felt the urge. Although, he couldn't hear me, I felt the need to talk anyway.

"I'm more like you than I've cared to admit, but it's the truth. I hate you even more, because I vowed to never become you, but here I am." The tears came down my face and a rush of emotions hit me at once. I never opened up to anyone about how I really felt about my father and how he negatively affected my life.

"You're the reason why mom isn't the same. It's because of you that she can't look at me longer than two minutes, without seeing you. You broke her down to the point, she stopped loving herself. You had power over her and abused it." My vision was blurry as the tears continued to fall. I had no control, they needed to fall. As men, we're taught not to cry and that it wasn't okay, but bottling it in for so much time, is even worse. Those pent up feelings and aggression hit harder than any tornado, and erupted harder than any volcano. Feeling like that could be deadly. It was very life threatening to feel so much emotional pain.

As I wiped the tears from my eyes, I stood to my feet and a sharp pain hit my shoulder and brought me back down, to my knees. "Ahhh!!" I screamed in agony while I gripped my throbbing shoulder that was leaking so much blood. It was no secret that Karma had come to bite me in the ass. All my wrongs out weighed my good and I wish that wasn't the case but it's the truth.

"Who the fuck are you?" I harshly asked the guy who held the gun. It's crazy how this same guy who I've never met, determined my fate in this moment. Some unknown stranger decided whether I lived or died. It's funny how life goes. In life, even the impossible can happen.

He looked at me and through my soul with hate in his heart. I could feel the heat radiating from his body into mine as he stood over me. "This is for my son, Xá." He said, and it didn't dawn on me that he was in fact, Brielle's dad and my son's grandfather. He let off two shots that pierced my chest and I'd always thought that a gunshot wound to the chest, would kill you instantly, and in this moment, I wished it did. But of course, I felt it. I felt everything, the stinging and burning sensation throughout my entire body, and I even felt my heart stop beating and everything faded to black.

Chapter Twenty-Nine

~

Hazel Parks

I felt like my heart was going to explode as I walked to the room that Xá was in. He took up my whole heart, and I wasn't prepared to see him like that. Time stood still as I saw him lying in that hospital bed from the doorway. For some reason, I couldn't bring myself to walk in.

"Hazel." I heard my name being called, and I knew that voice from anywhere. Hearing their voice, I didn't know how to feel, how to breathe. At this moment, I didn't know anything.

I turned around to face her and she looked the same. Her hair was braided in one long braid going down the center of her head. That seemed to be the only way she ever styled her hair. Too much hadn't changed. Only the few strands of gray hair and the few wrinkles on her forehead. "What do you want, Violet?" I uttered and it shocked me that I even responded. Over the years, I often thought of what I would say if I ever saw her face again. And here I was.

"I know you hate me Hazel, and you should. I don't blame you. I just thought you should know, you deserve the right to know. Ava is dying. She has leukemia." I didn't know what she expected me to say. Ava was a product of rape. Yes, she was my first born child, but still, I didn't know how to feel. I got pregnant at eleven years old. How was I supposed to feel?

"You know, my chances of carrying a baby full term are slim. I may not ever have a child of my own and you're telling me, that a child that shouldn't have been here in the first place, is dying and what, you expect me to care? You have your fucking nerve. I had those twins at twelve years old. I was a baby myself and you let your sick ass husband rape me. So if she dies, she just dies, because she wasn't supposed to be here in the first place. Get the hell out of my face, before I kill you with my bare fucking hands." I snapped on her ass and I felt good about it. Her and her husband took my youth and innocence away from me years ago, and there wasn't anything anyone could do, to bring it back. It was already gone.

I wiped away the tears that I should have never let fall, and proceeded to go into the room that Xá was in. When I walked in, his mom and sisters were all in the room.

"Can I have a moment alone with him please?" I whispered, and they all stood to their feet to leave the room and gave us some privacy.

I pulled a chair up to his bed and I took a seat. I examined his body. His eyes were closed and his head was bandaged up. There were machines hooked up to him to help him breathe.

"Babe, I love you so much, and I know you love me too, but there's some things that you should know. I may not be able to carry a child full term, because my body has been through so much over the years. I don't blame you if you don't want to marry me anymore. I understand completely if you do leave. You deserve to be a father, and I don't want to take that away from you." My voice cracked and I began to cry uncontrollably. I knew I didn't deserve to be happy. It never failed. Somehow, I was cursed, and it was time that I just came to grips with it.

"You know, I have twins. Twins that I didn't want. I delivered on the basement floor. Twins that I had at twelve years old. My life never gets better Xá, so again, I understand if you wouldn't want to marry someone like me. I'm bad news."

I felt his hand touch mine, and I thought it was just in my head, until I looked up and saw that he was looking at me and he had tears coming down his face too. I was happy and sad all at the same time. I was happy that he was up, but sad that this might be the end of our journey together. At least, I got the chance to meet someone as special as him.

I kissed his tears away and placed a kiss on his forehead then his cheeks before I went to get his family and the doctor.

"Don't ever scare me like this again, Xá. I mean it. I thought my world was over. " Brielle cried, as she walked closer to his bed.

"Thank you, God." Mama said and I could see the relief all over her face. No parent wanted to see their child that close to death. It was scary, it was unbearable. It was just too much.

"Mr.Black, you're a strong man. You're a fighter." The doctor started, and he had a genuine smile on his face. "We have never seen a case like this before. The metal plate in your head from your previous injury from the motorcycle accident years ago is the reason you're alive now. Count your blessings. I will have the nurse remove some of the tubes to give you some comfort. I'm glad you're with us." He gave us a sympathetic smile, before he walked out the room.

I looked up to towards heaven and thanked God for saving him and bringing him back, even if he wasn't coming back to me. He didn't deserve to die.

When the nurses came to take the tubes out his throat and the oxygen mask off his face, he tried to talk immediately, but he couldn't. After a couple of minutes of drinking cups of water, he was able to talk lowly.

"Call Minister Gray." He whispered and my heart and soul smiled, because I knew he truly loved me, flaws and all.

The ordained minister, who was marrying us, showed up in the hospital room fairly quick, but because Mama made the phone call, there was no telling what she said to get him there that fast. The hospital room began to fill out with our closest family and friends, so they could witness this unique but very special, beautiful moment.

Because we had already said our vows, he pronounced us husband and wife, and I felt a joy in my soul that couldn't be explained. Never had I ever knew a love so strong, so genuine and so unconditional. Our first kiss as a married couple sent butterflies throughout my entire body.

"Xá, there's nothing I won't do for you." I smiled, before kissing his lips once more.

"Congratulations, son." A male voice said, and we all turned around and looked behind us and here stood a taller, slim version of my husband. I looked from him to Xá in disbelief, cause this couldn't be him. He was dead.

Ezekial Black

~

Being in hiding all these years wasn't easy. It was hard being away from my family, missing so many memories, but I loved them so much more alive. Had I stayed around, we would have all been dead. I knew my absence broke my wife down in more ways than one, but I did it for them. Faking my death was for the best. I had been living in Germany for the past eight years, basically starting my life completely over.

"Zeek, tell me this is a dream?" My wife walked over to me and used her hand to touch all over my face. "Why did you do this to me?" She cried, and I knew she wanted to kick my ass.

"I know I owe you an explanation, but now is not the time. Right now, I just want to spend time with my family." I whispered into her ear, while rubbing the small of her back.

She nodded her head and she took me over to meet Hazel, my son's beautiful wife, and he picked the right one. I was good at reading people and I knew that, without a doubt, she had my son's best interest at heart.

We stayed up there talking, laughing, and catching up, until the hospital pretty much kicked us out, all but Hazel. They informed us that Xá would be getting out in a day or two, depending on a few factors, such as blood pressure and heart rate. My daughters had grown up to be beautiful women. So much had changed about them.

When we pulled up to our home, it still looked as I remembered from the outside. Walking inside, everything was different. She had changed the paint on all the walls, the furniture, appliances, everything was new and improved.

"You bet not ever pull a disappearing act again or I'll kill you myself." She winked, and blew out a kiss to me like the crazy woman she was.

"You just worry about getting out those clothes. I need to make sure everything's how I left it." I smirked as I stripped out my clothes. It had been way too long since I've been in them guts. She followed suit and took everything off. That's my girl.

Chapter Thirty

Syan Gonzalez
(Two years later)

"Zuri and Haylee get y'all bad asses off the top of that refrigerator right now!" I snapped at my girls who seemed to love getting their asses beat. They were pretty much twins, because they were only a couple months apart. To be exact, I had Haylee on me and Hector's anniversary.

"Mommy, they're just bad." Jr. said as he helped them down. He had his nerve, because he was just as bad if not, worse. I didn't know which child got their ass beat the most. They all stayed in shit, constantly.

"That's yo baby. Did you feed my son?" Hector asked, and I rolled my eyes, because he had set me up for the last time. Here I was, pregnant again, totaling five children. He had another thing coming if he thought anything else was coming out of this here vagina.

"I've eaten five times already. Trust me, your son isn't starving." I sarcastically stated, as I flipped him the bird. It was only noon and I had already ate enough for the entire day, but my baby boy was greedy as hell. It seemed like I was hungry every ten minutes, which meant I would be in the gym a week after I deliver to get my body back like it was, three children ago.

"Ma, what time is our hair appointment?" Gabriella asked, and I dreaded this time of the week. I thought my hair was a lot to handle. Hers was extremely thick and the fact that it came past her butt, made it even worse.

"Get your shoes on and then we'll be on our way." I said, as I managed to put my boots on without anyone's help, surprisingly. After I became eight months pregnant, there were a lot of things I needed help with.

My life was centered around being a wife and a mother to my five beautiful children; Gabriella, Hector Jr., Zuri, Haylee, and Zyair. Anything else, fit wherever it could. My hands were pretty much full and I loved every moment of it, but don't let the kids fool you, I'm still that bitch! Forever and always.

Brielle Black-Byrd

~

I was a married woman now. The day I became Mrs. Byrd, was the happiest moment of my life. I could honestly say, I was happily married. Christian brought out the best im me and I loved him so much for that. I had finally went back to school and I now had my bachelor's degree in Music. I had never thought to get a degree in music until Christian put that bug in my ear. I loved music and it was more rewarding to do something you loved as a career.

With Christian's business skills, and my knowledge, we were able to open up a music talent agency where we helped young music artists get themselves off the ground. We booked them shows, photo shoots, tours, etc.

"Mommy, can we get pizza?" Bailey's always hungry ass asked. If anything, her ass ate more and more the older she got.

"Ooooh pizza." My two year old son, Jr., said as he ran up to me and hugged my leg. I scooped him into my arms and placed kisses all over his face, while tickling him.

"Ma, I'm going to the Rec with Xá. See you later." Jaden kissed me on my cheek and went on his way.

Ever since my dad told us he killed Ethan, because he was the shooter at the wedding, he had been spending more and more time with Xá at the center. I knew he missed his dad, but I couldn't feel bad. Life's a bitch and he only reaped what he sowed.

"Babe, I'm taking the kids to get pizza and do a little shopping. We'll be back." I peeked my head in his office where he's been more and more lately, because he was in the process of opening another restaurant and a sports bar.

"Take my black card." He stated, never taking his eyes off his laptop. One thing for sure, he didn't have to tell me twice.

"Bailey, Chris. Come on so we can get pizza." I called out for them and we got into my new truck, then we were on our way.

My life was going extremely well. I loved my family. Business was good, my ass had gotten fatter. I had no complaints this way.

Brigail Black

~

"Damn daddy...please don't stop!" I moaned loudly, as Damon beat my pussy up. My hands and ankles were tied to the bed posts and he was showing his ass as he hit my spot every time.

"Let me know when that pussy is about to cum." He grunted as he fucked me harder while roughly playing with my nipples. I was turned on in the worst way. He knew exactly how I liked it. I liked to get fucked. You could miss me with the sensual slow love making shit. I wanted to feel that shit until it felt like I couldn't breathe.

With every stroke, it was faster and deeper than the last. I had lost count of how many times he has made my pussy squirt, with all the shit he pulled.

"Fuck, I'm cumminnn....Damonnn!" I cried, as a load of cum came from my body, leaving my body limp. With the nut I just busted, he bet not look at my ass for two days.

"You never answered me earlier." Damon blurted, as we laid in bed in silence, both tired from the intense fucking.

"Damon, let's just take it slow." I sighed, rubbing my temples.

He had been asking me to marry him for the past few weeks. Jordan had finally signed the divorce papers, so for two months, I had officially been a single woman. I felt like I had been tied down damn near my whole life, so this freedom had me in the clouds. I didn't have no commitment and no vows to uphold. I was free to do whatever with whomever. At thirty eight years old, I felt it was time for me to test the waters. I had only two sex partners my whole life, so it was time for me to explore, experience, and have fun.

My son was almost three, so he was out the way. I had plenty of baby sitters, so I planned on enjoying my life until I couldn't anymore.

"Well, I'm not about to keep fucking you, and I can't have you to myself." He said, like it was going to make me change my mind. If only he could get in my head, he would know that he's not the only one with good dick. Matter of fact, I had a dick appointment next weekend with some new meat. Like I said, it was time for me to live. You only get one life.

Harmony Woods

~

"Babe, what do you think about this color scheme?" I asked Hunter, who was all in his video game. He was no help as far as planning this wedding that was happening in less than four months.

"Did you ask Hazel?" He asked, and that was his response every time. If only he knew how much that really pissed me off.

"My sister isn't the one I'm marrying, Hunter. This whole thing will be canceled in a minute." I cussed, while rolling my eyes and talking with my hands.

"Yeah, I like it." He said, without looking up from the game. I'd had it with his ass. I stood from the couch and yanked every power supply that was plugged into the wall. "Just six more months." He mumbled under his breath and I didn't know if it was my hormones or the fact that he was really pissing me off, that made me want to slap fire out his ass.

I had something for his ass though. When we're laying in bed tonight, and his hands start to roam my body, I'm going to hit him with, 'Did you ask Xá?' and take my ass to bed.

My ringing phone distracted me from what I was going to say. I glanced at my phone and saw that it was Merci calling me. Since she started working with Xá and Hunter and going to school full time, we didn't have much time to spend together. She had her own car and apartment. She was doing very well and I was extremely proud.

We talked for a little bit, until it was time for her next class and time for me to get ready to go out with my parents and Hazel. We spent time with each other, at least once a month to bond with each other, since we were still kind new to this family thing.

Life had a way of working out, but I wouldn't change a thing, because I am who I am today because of everything life threw my way. After finding out that Ivory's sneaky ass was the cause of my accident, it showed me how much you really can't trust bitches. I kept my money tight and my circle even tighter cause one hating muthafucka could be the reason for your downfall. Because I am steering clear of all bullshit, if you're not family, you can get the fuck up out my face. Period!

Hazel Black

~

If you would have told me this would be my life three years ago, when I was that broken girl, I wouldn't have believed you. After a while, I didn't think I deserved happiness. I'd been through so much, but if I hadn't gone through those things, I wouldn't be as grateful and as humble as I am today. I hated that my life was that rough, but I could use my life to tell a story and help young girls and women who were going through what I'd already gone through. With every obstacle, there was a lesson to be learned.

I was pulling up to my women's empowerment class and today was the first day. I was excited and nervous at the same time. My husband convinced me to take all my negative thoughts and use it towards something positive, so here I was, holding my head high, ready to change peoples' lives.

"Welcome to my first 'Self Love' class. I'm Hazel Black. We can all go around and introduce ourselves. We're all here to learn and grow, so don't be scared to share with us. I'll go first. I've suffered from rape and abuse since I was ten years old. I was in a relationship that broke me down, until I no longer loved myself. I suffered from low self-esteem, but with time, positive friends, and God, I made it through and you will too. We're all here to help each other. Who wanna go next?" I asked, and there were a lot of volunteers, surprisingly.

I had a room full of women that were all going through things, but that's what life was about. Women needed to stick together instead of talking about the next without knowing their story. We spent the entire class with introductions and we did some exercises that only involved positive thinking.

When I left my first teaching class, a weight was lifted off my shoulders. I felt so good for helping other women get out of situations that I'd been in before. I headed straight home to my babies to cuddle and love on them. That's how I wanted every night to end.

"Little Xá and Amor, come here!" I yelled as I walked into our now five-bedroom, six-bathroom estate, feeling truly blessed.

"Mommy!!" They both screamed in unison, as they ran into my arms.

Life had a funny way of working out. My chances of delivering children were very slim however, I was granted with twins; one boy, one girl. Although, I had a terrible layout that resulted in me having a hysterectomy, at least I was able to fully enjoy motherhood. They were my entire world and I was so very thankful to have them in my life. I vowed to love them more than anyone ever loved me. They would never experience anything I went through and I put that on my life.

"I can't get no love." Xá walked up behind me, grabbing my ass like he always did. He placed kisses on my neck, before he turned me around, facing him, so he could kiss my lips. Before I knew it, we were tounging each other down. We could never leave it as a simple peck.

"Ewww." Amor fussed, as she covered her eyes. Little Xá, on the other hand, stared in amusement while he laughed. In that moment, I realized he was going to be a freak, just like his damn daddy.

I looked at my family and I knew I had to be the happiest woman in the world. My life turned around when I let go of that dead weight that held me back from my full potential.

Ladies, if you have a deadbeat nigga holding you back from being the great woman you are, let him go. If he's constantly feeding you *broken promises*, let him go. Of course, it's easier said than done, but you won't be the first and definitely not the last woman that goes through it. Love yourself first and let go of *broken promises!*

Thank you for reading! Stay on the lookout for Love Without Permission 2 to learn more about Renae and so much more. Also, please leave a review. That is very important to me as an author.

To stay tuned with myself and new releases follow me:
Facebook: Kachet Williamson (Kachet the Authoress) and like my author's page Kachet'
Instagram: authoress_kachet

For updates, contests, and giveaways join our Facebook reading group :Danielle Marcus Presents Reading room and text Dmp to 22828

www.ingramcontent.com/pod-product-compliance
Lightning Source LLC
Chambersburg PA
CBHW061248120726
48001CB00001B/202